WINTER'S COMPANION
A COMPLEMENT TO THE DAUGHTER OF WINTER SERIES

CORINA DOUGLAS

Burning Legacies Publishing

ALSO BY CORINA DOUGLAS

(* = releasing soon)

Publishing by *Burning Legacies Publishing Limited*

Cover design by *Maria at Artscandare*

ISBN: 978-1-99-115178-0 (ebook)

ISBN: 978-1-99-115179-7 (paperback)

TRIGGER WARNINGS

Before reading, please be aware there are a number of trigger warnings applicable to the five stories in this book. These triggers include the following:

- *Pagan rituals*
- *Infidelity*
- *Emotional and physical trauma*
- *Unsavoury dialogue*
- *Child trafficking, and*
- *Violence and gore*

In terms of spice levels, where there is romance between the two main characters, this fluctuates from fade-to-black to open door between all the stories.

If any of the above is not to your reading pleasure, please reconsider reading this book. Your mental health matters.

WELCOME TO A WORLD OF FAIRYTALES, FOLKLORE, AND CELTIC MYTHOLOGY!

Winter's Companion is a complement to the author's *Daughter of Winter* series, which is a seven-book, slow burn, dark fantasy romance series based on pagan Scottish, Irish, and Welsh folklore, where you'll meet Celtic deities, druids, the Tuatha Dé Danann, selkies, dwarves, & many other mythical creatures. You'll also learn about the myths and legends in the folklore.

On reading *Daughter of Winter*, the reader comes to know a large breadth of characters, and *Winter's Companion* delves further into some of the relationships explored in the series by offering five individual stories on the following characters:

Gage in *Rising from the Ashes*
Morrígan in *Morrígan: Wings of War*
Cernunnos in *Cernunnos & the Winged Changeling*
Dagda in *Dagda: A New Dawn*
Cailleach in *Winter Solstice*

This book (and these five individual stories) can be read as standalones, however, they are best read and understood after the third book in the series, *Winter's Shield*. Should you choose to embark on this journey now, never fear, you'll just have to come back and explore these stories again after you have finished reading the main series :)

I truly hope you enjoy this complement to the Daughter of Winter series.

See you on the Other side,

Corina x

PRONUNCIATION GUIDE

Just like there are numerous versions of the Celtic myths themselves, there are various ways to pronounce the names below depending on which dialect you choose to follow (Scottish, Irish, or Welsh). It is important to note that I have not stayed true to any one dialect in this pronunciation guide; rather, I have chosen the pronunciation that best reflects how I perceived the characters in my head. And as I am English speaking (with a New Zealand accent!), keep this in mind when reading my English phonetic below.

PEOPLE:

Arawn – aah-ron

Cailleach – car-lee-arch

Drust – drus-tt

Talorgan – tell-lore-gone

Tritus – try-tis

Cernunnos – kern-a-noss

Morrígan – more-a-gone

Dagda – darg-der

Brighid – bridge-it

Tuatha Dé Dannan — too-ah day dan-in

Nuada — nu-ah-dah

Boann - bow-in

Brighid – bridge-it

Brenna - bren-na

Cerridwen - kear-a-dwin

Eiros - Air-ross

Events:

Samhain - sow-win

Yule - you'll

PLACES:

Aviemore - a-vuh-maw

Cairngorms - keuhn-gawmz

CONTENTS

RISING FROM THE ASHES

RISING FROM THE ASHES

CORINA DOUGLAS

DEDICATION

To all those who search for the stars in the sky. Keep dreaming.

RISING FROM THE ASHES

"Why is my grandson in chains?"

Fergus, the leader of the Institute, turned his gaze to the door. "Reuben, thank you for coming on such short notice."

Grandfather ignored the pleasantries. "Why, Fergus? I understood the boy hasn't hurt anyone."

"Not yet, but he's burnt down Seraph's lab. He's volatile, and that means he's dangerous."

I jerked in my seat, the magical bindings on my wrists burning.

"Something to say to that, Gage?" Fergus inquired.

I glared at him. I just wanted to get out of here. Fortunately, having Reuben here would accelerate the process for I was his protégé, and he needed me.

"He is prophesied, Fergus." Grandfather's words were sharp. "We all need to support him."

A stony glare came over Fergus's face. "No, we don't. The law's clear. The Institute stands outside prophecy."

I'd heard the words many times before. The Masters gave it to me every time I stepped out of line. They disliked me intensely. However, their dislike had turned to fear after I'd burned down Seraph's lab. The truth was, they were right to feel it; I knew how little control I had.

Grandfather's brows snapped together. "That's rubbish! By not supporting him, you're taking a goddamned side! You're letting *him* win!"

Fergus stiffened. "I refuse to get into a debate about the prophecy. Until our laws change, our stance remains the same. The boy will continue to be treated like everyone else."

A muscle ticked in Grandfather's jaw. "Fine! That debate won't end anytime soon," he relented. "But I want to know why Gage was alone in the lab. Surely Seraph had mechanisms in place to prevent entry outside of hours? If you ask me, the blame should equally be laid on Seraph's shoulders, and it definitely doesn't warrant my grandson being suspended!"

Fergus opened his mouth to reply, but there was a knock at the door, and two people were ushered in.

My breath froze in my chest. I recognized them immediately.

The woman had fine lines marring her skin, but she was still beautiful and impeccably dressed. She'd taken the room in at a glance, her expression arranged to her advantage.

The man by her side was a few years older, his skin sunken and sallow, the spark dead in his eyes. I clenched my teeth, fully aware that he'd been beaten by his own demons.

The woman spoke first. "Gage! My baby, are you alright?"

It was as if the last eleven years had never been.

"Get out!" I snapped coldly.

The heat was gathering inside, the pressure building. I

felt perspiration break across my forehead as I fought to retain control, pushing the old memories away. This couldn't happen again, not here, not now.

Reuben sensed the change immediately, moving to stand beside me. One of his large hands dropped onto my shoulder, squeezing hard. "Danielle, Steven, there's no need for you to be here. Gage is my responsibility."

My father stiffened. "We were called in. We heard he's destroyed a building." His eyes were haunted as he added, "It's not the first time this has happened."

An inferno was building inside me, my father's words another trigger. Reuben squeezed my shoulder again, his fingers biting deep into the tissue. It hurt, but it pierced the veil of my emotions and shifted my focus to that one place.

Danielle laughed. "I'm surprised you remember, Steven!"

I bit my lip, fighting the urge to scream.

"Enough!" Reuben roared. "This is not about you!" He turned to Fergus. "Why are they even here? I'm Gage's first point of contact."

Fergus clasped his hands together in the folds of his robe. "Because Gage needs somewhere to stay. As a result of his actions, he will be leaving the Institute."

Danielle gasped. "He's being expelled?"

"No; rather a suspension. Gage shows promise to be one of the most powerful druids we've ever had; however, he battles with control. The first few years of study are the toughest, and we expect a tolerable level of accidents, but Gage is sixteen now, and he's still struggling. This must be remedied immediately. If he fails to attain control, we'll have no choice but to expel him."

A hushed silence fell over the room. Being expelled meant my magic would be revoked. It was inconceivable. My magic was an integral part of who I was. Without it, I wouldn't be whole, not after losing my brother.

"Gage will be taking a leave of absence from the Institute for three months," Fergus continued. "During this time, it's expected that he'll work on his control. I'll send a Master to assess him for suitability at the end of the tenure. If he shows improvement, he'll be accepted back in."

My stomach dropped. *If* I was accepted back in.

"This doesn't make any sense!" my father burst out. "Someone has to have complained. I don't remember a student being suspended for an accident!" I saw his fists clench with aggression. "It was Creag, wasn't it? He's been financially supporting the Institute for years. It's no secret he's wanted one over me since Danielle chose me instead of him!"

Fergus's face darkened. "I don't respond to influence, Steven. Druidic lore alone guides me."

The reprimand was firm, with enough conviction that my father turned away.

Danielle cleared her throat. "Unfortunately, I can't help. My mother requires my full attention."

Reuben's voice was mocking. "Still running with that story, Danielle?"

She flushed. "She's bedridden. I can't leave her side."

"So that's why you're here now?" Steven queried mildly.

Danielle sneered at him. "And I suppose you think you're capable of looking after Gage yourself then?"

It was happening again. I didn't need this. "Stop it! I'm not going with either of you!"

"That's right," Reuben interjected firmly. "Gage belongs with me. You two are incapable." He turned to Fergus, adding, "I'll ensure he gets all the support he needs."

"I agree," Fergus replied swiftly, palpable relief

peppering his tone. "Give me a half-hour, and he'll be ready for release."

THE RIDE HOME WAS QUIET. Reuben didn't try to fill the silence.

I sat there, numb from the encounter with my parents. I hadn't seen them since that fateful night. I hadn't meant to burn down Seraph's lab, just like I hadn't meant to burn down the family home.

In the quiet, that memory crowded in. I fought it, like so many times before; trying to push it into a dark corner of my mind and slam a lid on it. But it refused to be ignored. Seeing my parents again for the first time since that event was too much of a catalyst, and in the quiet of the car, the past broke through my barriers, and I relived the moment that irrevocably changed my life.

Father had come home early that night, one fish his only catch for the day.

"I'm sick to death of fish!" Mother cried.

He turned to her, a slight sway to his movements. "Come on, Dani," he cajoled. "It's only for tonight. My catch will be better tomorrow."

"The only thing guaranteed tomorrow is that any profit you make, you'll be drinking from a bottle!" She shook her head. "I'm sick of pretending to be happy with the lot you've given me!"

My insides twisted. She'd confirmed what I'd always

believed: she didn't want us. But it was Father's face that caught my attention, his expression taut.

"What are you saying, Dani?"

Mother's face blanched, but she held her ground. "I want out, Steven."

Father went still, a hard glint in his eyes that caused me to sink low in my chair. His voice was almost conversational. "It's funny you say that, Dani. A few of the boys mentioned they'd seen you around the docks recently, dressed all fine." His gaze pierced hers. "I know you Dani; I know you hate it down there. What was so important that you'd risk the smell and the filth?"

My heart pounded. I knew what she'd been doing. So did Logan.

We'd been playing a game, following a cat we'd glimpsed on the coastal hills behind the village. We'd watched it creep into town; the bones visible beneath its dirty, white fur. Skittish and feral, it would hiss and scamper away if we came close. It was a challenge a five-year-old couldn't resist.

We maintained our distance as we tracked it to the docks, knowing it sought a meal of the fish guts that permeated the air. We saw it slip into one of the warehouses.

"Come on; we can trap it!" I urged Logan.

"What if we get caught?" he whispered.

I reached out and gripped his hand. "No one will catch us," I said confidently.

We slunk into the building and crouched behind a pallet of drums, searching for the cat. It was the sounds that alerted us— grunting, moaning, then a rhythmic slapping. I froze, a finger to my lips as I cautiously peered around the pallet.

I saw two figures. One was Mother—unmistakable with her long, dark hair—her dress about her waist. She was entangled in a tight embrace with a tall, bearded man. He was wearing fancy black shoes, clean and shiny. There was only one family with shoes like that in our village.

A cold tendril of dread stirred in my stomach. I knew what she was doing was wrong. My first thought was to check if Logan had seen. He had. His distress triggered that tingle on the back of my neck that was becoming familiar. From early on, I'd known not to provoke it.

I jerked my thumb over my shoulder, indicating that we retreat.

Logan paused. "What about the cat?" he whispered, his face showing his reluctance.

"We'll find her tomorrow. I promise."

He looked at me, trusting that I'd keep my word. "Okay."

We scampered out of there as quickly as we could.

Now, as my father questioned my mother, that memory and the accompanying riot of emotions returned. I looked at Mother, intent on her answer to Father's question.

"Lies!" she cried. "You know I'm minding the boys during the day."

Father looked at us. Logan's head was bowed, but I looked him in the eye.

"Is that true, Gage?"

"She's lying," I said firmly. "I saw her with the Provost's son in a warehouse on the docks."

I heard Mother's sharp inhale.

Father's voice was deadly quiet. "What were they doing, son?"

"You know what a trouble-maker Gage is," Mother interjected desperately. "He's just saying that to cause trouble!" She pointed to Logan. "Not like his brother."

Father paused, his gaze turning to Logan. "Look at me, boy."

Logan reluctantly lifted his head.

"You two are inseparable. If your brother saw, I know you would have too. Is what Gage said true?"

Logan looked at me, and I saw the conflict in his gaze. His voice was small. "No."

In that moment, I lost everything.

I felt shocked at my brother's betrayal. Then came anger. Instead of a familiar simmer, it was a firestorm. The back of my neck felt like a thousand needles piercing my skin. I sensed I was on the verge of an eruption.

I desperately looked for an escape. That's when I saw the candle on the table. The flame was bright and pure. As I stared at it, the flame evolved, became a bird. No, not just any bird I realized, a bird of fire—a Phoenix.

Understanding hit me. The Phoenix was a bird of rebirth and fire cleansed, made everything anew.

I exhaled, and the flame burst into a shower of sparks that grew into a roaring inferno, greedily licking the roof of our small fishing hut. Logan screamed as Mother and Father cried out. But I stared at it, captured by its brilliance.

I didn't see the fear glinting in my brother's eyes, or Mother leave in a panicked rush. I didn't feel Father grab my shirt and drag me outside.

I was thrown to the ground next to Logan. Father dropped to his knees beside us, coughing uncontrollably. It was the cold night air that broke my trance. I jumped to my feet, wanting to return, but a hand on my arm stopped me.

"No, Gage!"

I turned to Logan, remembering his betrayal. "Don't touch me!"

Soot stood out in stark relief on his ashen face. "I was trying to save us," he whispered over Father's coughing. "If I told the truth, Father would attack the Provosts son! The Provost would make our lives a misery. It's better this way!"

I stared at him, emotions roiling. "No, it's not!" I cried, pointing at the burning hut. "We've lost everything! I did this Logan—and all because you made the wrong choice."

Twin holes of despair stared back at me, but he didn't have time to reply as the villagers came running.

Reuben arrived the next day. I'd known he was family the moment I laid eyes on him. He'd come to take me away. I was destined for other things, he said, and my place was with him.

Father didn't argue. "Take him," he returned, his voice devoid of emotion.

But Reuben was angry, and he left with a warning. "You should have been watching him, Steven. If you had, I could have prevented what happened." He glanced at Logan, who lingered a few feet away. "You have one son left, Steven. He needs you. If you don't lose the poison—and I don't just mean the drink— you'll lose him too."

Father's gaze traveled past Reuben to rest on my own. His eyes were bloodshot, his face expressionless. I didn't see regret there—I saw nothing, before he turned his back and walked away.

I blinked, resurfacing from the memory; the remembered pain a wound that never healed.

It was pitch black outside as I peered through the window. We were driving through the popular tourist town of Aviemore, almost home.

Reuben turned right, keeping the Cairngorm Mountains in our sights. Five minutes later, he took a hard left onto a graveled road. It became narrow and winding, the forest crowding the edge of the tarmac. A 'no-exit' sign flashed in the headlights, but we kept on going.

I hadn't traveled this road for six years, but I could still remember every stage of the journey. On point, Grandfather swung the wheel sharply to the left. I didn't flinch as we drove directly towards the lofty trees, passing through the mirage. At the same time, a familiar pressure squeezed my temples. The protection wards.

We drove around the last bend and there it was. *Mothacail*. The old Gaelic translated to 'Sentinel', and the castle was aptly named given the treasure inside.

I noted the lights were on in the eastern wing.

Reuben came to a stop in front of the steps leading up to the entrance and turned to me. I could just make out his face in the soft sheen of moonlight. "Welcome home, Gage."

They were the first words he'd uttered since we'd left the Institute.

"Thanks for coming to get me."

"There was no question that I wouldn't come."

"Sure, I understand—you need me."

The old man tensed, then ground out, "Nora's waiting." He wrenched the door open and marched up the steps.

Why did I say that?

I grabbed my duffle bag and followed him into the castle. As soon as I entered, I felt it. That familiar spark of power. The air fairly thrummed with it. The energy wasn't coming from the building itself, though. It was emanating from the person waiting inside the library.

As I walked down the long hall, memories of my second childhood surfaced. Reuben had broken me in here, taught me to nurture my magic rather than fight it. He'd been relentless, dragging me out of bed at the crack of dawn to run drills and build physical endurance. He'd tested all my weaknesses, eliminated all my tells.

"Magic requires endurance," he'd said. "And sometimes, we simply need pure strength. You must excel in both these areas, Gage. Nora's life depends on it."

During the five years I was here, he'd molded me into a weapon. Someone who could protect as well as kill. I'd relished the violence. More disquieting was the fact that I knew I needed it, almost to the point that I craved it. I often wondered if this was prophecy playing its part, or my innate urges. Regardless, these needs would only benefit the role I would one day play.

When I turned ten, I came of age to complete my Druidic training at the Institute. I hadn't been back since but walking down this hallway felt like it was yesterday.

The library door was ajar, and I could hear Reuben's deep timbre. They both looked up as I walked in.

Nora immediately came forward to clasp my hands. "Gage! It's lovely to have you back."

Nora commanded my respect. Which was good, because one day we'd be working together. The back of my neck prickled as her skin touched mine. "Thank you; I hope I'm not an inconvenience."

I'd forgotten how petite she was now, barely reaching my chin.

"Nonsense! We're family."

Family. Not a word I responded to. I gave her a cool smile and stepped back. "Will I be under house arrest these next few months?"

Her forehead furrowed. "No. Reuben will continue your studies here."

I raised a brow. "Fergus said I shouldn't resume training until I have control. I could hurt the old man."

The backhand blow took me by surprise.

"Shut your mouth!" Reuben grunted. "I'm still stronger than you are."

"Reuben," Nora said warningly, reaching out to grab his arm.

His frame tensed. "Leave it, Nora."

The words were gentle and his actions even more so as he removed her hand. I swallowed as recognition burned. The old man was in love with her.

I couldn't help aggravating him, lifting a hand to rub my cheek. "I should be flattered it took you eleven years to follow in my father's footsteps."

Reuben growled. "Fool! You've become weak and fallen back into old habits! Self-pity has no place in this game."

"No, but control does," I said firmly.

He stepped forward. We were nose to nose, and his words were soft. "I know why you lose control Gage; I've always known."

I jerked back. "You have no idea what you're talking about!"

"Oh? You think I'm not aware of the letter that came two weeks ago? You think your brother would know how to contact you at the Institute?"

My blood chilled as the fragments fell into place. "He sent it here."

"Yes," he affirmed softly. "He wanted to make contact with you."

For a moment, I found it hard to breathe. "Did you initiate that letter?"

Reuben's eyes glinted. "It doesn't matter who initiated the letter! What matters is that you need to resolve things between the two of you. Logan was shipped off to boarding school after the fire. He's been as alone as you have."

I couldn't believe it. The old man had betrayed me—gone behind my back and made contact with Logan. "You think you're my shrink now?"

"Bloody hell, calm down!"

I could feel Nora's gray gaze on mine, pinning me in my place more effectively than any restraint.

"You're a powerful Druid, Gage," Reuben continued. "I've no doubt you'll protect Nora well when the time comes, but if you don't resolve this hurt between you and your brother, you'll never succeed in fulfilling the prophecy. He's just as lost without you, just as incomplete. He needs you as much as you need him."

My stomach roiled. "You know nothing!"

"You know that's not true." His voice was quiet but firm, as if gentling a horse. "If anything, I know you too well. I also know you haven't read this." He pulled a sealed, white envelope out of his back pocket and waved it in the air—the letter Logan had sent to me.

"How did you get that?" I demanded.

He ignored me. "Why haven't you read it, Gage? What are you scared of?"

"ENOUGH!" I was panting from exertion as if I'd run a race. Reuben was too close.

"You're way off the mark, old man! I don't need him! What I need is control of my magic! If you don't help me with that, I'll never return to the Institute. I'll never finish my training. And you know what that means, don't you, old man? It means all this"—I gestured between the three of us—"will be for naught and Nora will die!"

Reuben's face darkened, and I saw the moment all rational thought fled. However, before he could respond, Nora interrupted.

"I think that's enough, Reuben. You've sown the seed."

He gritted his teeth, eyes on mine with a vengeance. I'd finally rattled him; made him feel what I felt. I forced myself to hide the emotional turmoil inside. The old man saw too much as it was.

Nora turned to face me. "Reuben's only got your best interests at heart, Gage. Do you understand?"

I stared at her, my body rigid, but she was demanding I acknowledge that. I jerked my head.

She gave me a cool smile. "Good. Now it's late, and you look tired. I've had your old room made up for you. Get some sleep as Reuben will be commencing your training at first light."

I inclined my head; studiously ignoring Reuben as I left the room.

A month passed in a tentative truce.

Reuben pushed me hard. I was on edge, my control tightly tethered. He watched me closely and saw too much that I couldn't hide.

I spent any free time I had retraining myself to become mindful. The ability to stay mindful was a true indication of druidic power. If you weren't present in the moment, you were unable to block out the distractions. Ultimately, you lost control and consequences could be fatal. Hence, the reason I was on suspension.

During those four weeks, Reuben didn't bring Logan up again. It should have put me at ease. It didn't. It felt as if time was in stasis. As if something was coming—something inevitable.

The feeling evaporated when I entered the dining hall that evening. I'd only taken a few steps into the room before I slammed to a halt.

The eyes that stared back were my own, but less jaded. The hair was dark like mine but clean-cut; the build similar, only leaner. He was unmistakable.

Logan.

Reuben stepped forward in the sudden silence. "I've invited Logan to come and stay with us for a few days."

My heart was racing to a sharp stucco, a myriad of emotions escalating inside. The word rasped from my throat. "Why?"

Logan's voice was quiet. "Because I wanted to see you."

"That's not what you said to me eleven years ago! Have you forgotten I burnt down our home?"

His brows pinched together, a dark slash on his pale face. "No, but that night was as much my fault as it was yours. I should have helped you."

I laughed harshly, and the sound had no mirth in it. "How? You're a Dormant; you have no magic!"

"That's not what I meant," Logan returned quietly. "I should have reached out to Reuben as soon as you started to show signs—done something at least! Instead, I did nothing."

"You were only five!"

Logan's expression was somber. "So were you, Gage."

Suddenly, I felt suffocated. I held my hands up. "I can't do this!"

Logan stepped forward. "Please, Gage—"

I did the only thing I could. I turned my back on him and walked away.

I DIDN'T SLEEP that night. I couldn't.

My sixth sense had become reattuned to him, as it was when we were kids. I could feel him with every breath, his presence a noose around my neck. We came from a line of powerful druids dating back more than a thousand years. Even though Logan was born a Dormant, he had a strong sixth sense. As a result, between my druidic powers and Logan's sixth sense, we had a formidable connection. I'd missed it.

I closed my eyes, seeking oblivion, but it just wouldn't come. He felt too close.

As the hours rolled by, I couldn't help testing our connection. I closed my eyes and searched. It appeared in my mind's eye like a gossamer thread. I reached out and touched it. As soon as my fingers connected with the line, I was flooded with a riot of emotions—turmoil, anger, frustration, and sadness.

Recognition hit. This was how he felt!

I snapped back, breaking the connection. *If I could feel him, he could feel me.* I didn't want that; I had too much to hide.

I wasn't the Gage he remembered from childhood. I was darker, stronger, and more powerful. I'd been trained to do things; unimaginable, horrible, desperate things to prepare myself for the future that lay ahead. A future that was filled only with danger.

I'd long ago learned that losing my brother was the best thing that could have happened. Having a connection to anyone—other than Nora and Reuben—would put them in jeopardy. Losing contact was the only way I could protect him.

When the first fingers of dawn pierced the sky, I was more than ready to start the day. As I bent down to lace up my running shoes, I tentatively tapped into our shared line. It was the second time I'd made contact with Logan. To my surprise, I felt him on the move, somewhere outside.

I frowned, leaning back. Then I heard a car door slam and the quiet hum of an engine starting. I froze, tapping into our connection again as the vehicle accelerated down the drive. The line was faint, becoming thinner with each passing second.

He was leaving.

The back of my throat burned, and I swallowed hard, acknowledging that his departure was my fault. He'd made himself vulnerable, first by sending me the letter, secondly by coming here. I'd denied him, refusing to make contact. He hadn't left—I'd turned him away.

The rift between us remained unhealed because I'd made it so.

Another three weeks passed in quick succession.

Reuben continued to push me ruthlessly. Every day he

found a reason to bring Logan into the conversation, relentlessly reminding me of my loss.

I awoke one morning, again barely having slept. I'd been afflicted by images of the fire, my mother locked tight in a clandestine embrace, and my father's threatening fists. But what lingered at the edge of my consciousness that morning was my brother's face the day Reuben had taken me away.

I shook my head, trying to erase his image as I pushed myself to my feet. Dawn had already touched the horizon, and Reuben would be waiting.

I left the castle, striding across the lawn to the edge of the forest. A figure detached itself from the shadows.

"You look terrible."

I shrugged nonchalantly, maintaining the façade. It was all I had. "How I look doesn't affect my abilities."

"On the surface," Reuben retorted sharply.

"I'm not sure what you mean," I replied in a bored tone.

Reuben placed his hands on his hips. "Stop denying it. Admit it; you're a mess without him. This is the last time I'll say it: make amends before you lose him forever!"

My fists clenched. I didn't want to discuss this again. Time would resolve the issue with Logan, for ignorance conveyed a lack of care. But Reuben was a different story. He wouldn't let me forget; wouldn't stop pushing.

I gritted my teeth. "Just leave it alone, old man!"

"Never."

Damn him!

I searched for the right words to turn him away. Nothing seemed appropriate. Finally, I did the only thing that would put space between us.

I ran.

I ran like I never had before, my feet pounding heavily into the forest floor. The trees closed around me, their tall limbs standing sentient. I twisted my head back, searching for Reuben but he hadn't followed.

Eventually, I collapsed at the edge of the scrub, the proud snow-covered peak of Ben Nevis glistening in the morning light. My chest burned with more than exhaustion. It hurt.

I groaned. Even though my body was exhausted, I hadn't outrun my internal demons. I knew then I never would.

So, face them, you coward!

I released a breath, admitting the old man was right—had always been right. Without Logan, I wasn't whole. Since the fire and our separation, I'd been missing a vital piece of myself. I'd denied it, knowing that keeping Logan at arm's length was the best way to protect him. The problem was, pushing him away left me vulnerable. So vulnerable that my control over my magic was eroding.

The pieces slipped vehemently into my mind, confirming what my heart already knew—I needed him more than I needed to keep him safe.

There was only one way forward. I had to see him and make amends. My heart squeezed as I made the promise. But fear would not hold me back, although I had everything to lose.

Facing your fear makes you stronger, I told myself as I pushed to my feet. The wan winter sun touched my face in a blaze of warmth as I faced unerringly toward home. I closed my eyes against the bright rays, and it was then that an image of a phoenix burned behind my eyelids. A bloodless smile touched my lips at the significance. *Facing your fear makes you stronger, but so does rising from the ashes.*

THE MORRÍGAN:
WINGS OF WAR

THE MORRIGAN:
WINGS OF WAR

CORINA DOUGLAS

THE MORRÍGAN: WINGS OF WAR

"**W**hat will you bring to the battle, Morrígan?"

Her lip curled. "What I always bring, m'lord: death."

The king of the Tuatha grimaced. "We understand your gifts, Morrígan. What we need to know is how you will achieve this? The Fomorians are not our average foe. This is the second time they will grace our shores and seek to take our land. King Indech is known for his prowess on not just the battlefield but in sorcery. How will you get close to him?"

"With my womanly graces."

King Lugh snorted, eying Morrígan's indecent black shift under her feathered ebony cloak. "And how would you do that in the midst of battle?"

Morrígan smiled coyly, aware that he was remembering his own time with her when he had ascended the throne. "I have my ways."

"Indeed," the king replied, his gaze skating over her taut nipples that were clearly outlined under her shift. He dragged his gaze to Dagda, who stood silently watching the exchange. "And I'm sure Dagda here will vouch for that."

Morrígan caught Dagda's movements as he adjusted his stance. Her mask remained in place as her heart skipped a beat. *Was he uncomfortable of her mating with Lugh?* Her role as Sovereign Goddess required her to lie with their chosen king. The act was the seal of her approval—an agreement to pass the mantle of leadership into his hands.

Dagda cleared his throat. "Her legendary prowess is not understated, my king. I am sure Morrígan could bewitch him, even in the middle of a bloodbath."

Her spine relaxed, and she let her smile become natural. "Legendary prowess? I am humbled, Dagda. I believe we may make a good match yet."

His lips lifted slightly. "We've had enough practice, Morrígan. I admit I am a slow learner when it comes to love."

Her heart stopped. *Love.* A word he'd never shared with her. A word he'd reserved only for his other...women. Women she'd wanted to kill—women she'd wanted to maim with a visual reminder to never, ever touch her husband again. But then, she'd known he was also to blame. The tryst between her husband and his women went both ways; he would have had to initiate or reciprocate, both of which made him a guilty party.

But this banter, this deference to her power—was he changing? Was he finally falling for her? Morrígan didn't dare consider the merits of this thought. Not now, not when death loomed at their door. She'd done her part; she'd passed on the warning, shared the future that she'd seen coming—that the Fomorians were coming back and this second war; it would cost them more than before.

King Lugh interrupted her musings. "I am glad to hear

of this recent development, Dagda, because I have an important task to ask of you both."

The king gave her his piercing gaze, a gaze from which Morrígan could not escape. As her king, he had her respect. A respect that she'd helped him to acquire, sealing his right to govern the Tuatha and their land. A respect that he proved to her right then with his next words that he still deserved.

"Morrígan, as you know, I am not one to leave things to chance. And even though you are a powerful sorceress, I know the Fomorians. These sea raiders are powerful—gods in their own right. Their powers rely on death and destruction; chaos is their name." His brow furrowed as he studied her face. "Their power, I grant, is similar to yours and your sisters', but I will not leave the balance of power down to chance or see countless numbers of our people lost if we do not justly prepare.

"This means *you* need to be more than you've ever been before. Thus, I would call upon your union with Dagda one more time. Your union was forged to protect our people—a shield against the coming darkness, and when your powers meld, the world trembles. To be successful, I need both of you to commit to this union with everything you have." He paused and cut his gaze between them as he added, "And if true feelings have now come into it, your power will be even greater than it has been before. So I ask you, for the lives of your people, will you agree to this union of power once more?"

Morrígan kept her features still as she turned to face her husband. She would not show vulnerability or how much she craved his touch once again.

Aware of her silence, Dagda cleared his throat and replied, "Yes, m'lord."

He came upon her by the River Unius—a river she'd created when her powers had matured. They hadn't agreed on where and when, just that they'd promised their king that their union would happen before the battle five days hence.

Morrígan had been trying to find a sense of calm amid the clamoring chaos in her mind. But thoughts of when he would visit had gnawed at her day and night. Three days it had been. *Surely, he would come soon?* Because he would know she wouldn't come to him, not after he'd denied her once before, and Morrígan would never put her pride or her emotions at risk again.

The water was icy cold as she walked into its frigid depths. It lapped against her naked skin with a shock that chased all other thoughts from her mind. Without pausing to allow the cold enough time to grasp hold of her blood, Morrígan dove into the river's depths, making sure to stay out of the main current. As her head broke the surface, she felt a change in the air and knew who had come.

Treading water, her head whipped to the side, and her eyes confirmed what her sixth sense had forewarned: Dagda was here.

His burnished brown hair glinted in the late afternoon sunlight, a shining beacon against the backdrop of the dense trees behind him. His clothing was simple and unadorned—boots and a tunic.

"Come out, Morrígan," Dagda called softly. "It is time."

He wanted to cement their union here? At a place she had created?

Morrígan denied herself the sliver of hope that confirmed he'd chosen this place to make her feel at ease—

to show her that he respected her. That hope had only been crushed in the past. She blinked, pushing the memory away, and reminded herself that she was not that vulnerable sap —she was the Morrígan! A woman of power. A sorcerer whom people feared. And a Sovereign Goddess who approved a king's right to rule.

She should be feeling confident. She should be feeling all-powerful. But she wasn't, and Morrígan didn't want to leave the protection of the river. Leaving its cold depths would expose not only her skin but also her heart, and his comment in the war council about love had stirred a hope she shouldn't have. A hope that she chided herself she shouldn't feel. After all, the words he'd shared could well have been a guise to cement her agreement to this sexual union.

"Morrígan," Dagda called again. "Come!"

This time, his words were forceful—no longer in a tone that would settle a frightened filly, but with a command that she found herself obeying. Her feet found the smooth stones of the riverbed, and she forced her limbs to move forward. The water sluiced off her skin as first her chest, and then her torso rose above the water. Her eyes did not leave Dagda's as she moved toward him.

The moment his eyes dropped to her chest, she felt a semblance of control return. Morrígan knew the power of her body, knew the power of a man's lust, and even gods were not exempt from a desire that moved the hands of time.

One more step and her woman's heart was exposed. Morrígan saw his eyes dip even further, arrowing to the black hair around her groin. She caught the infinitesimal change in his stance, the slight movement of his muscles as his body tensed. It was a tell of desire. This confirmation caused a flutter of hope to take flight in her chest because speech could be twisted, but the language of the body was a shining light of truth. It spoke clearer than any veiled words ever could.

Now feeling a measure of feminine power, Morrígan paused to peel her long dark hair off her back and wring the excess water from its depths. Dagda just watched her, unmoving, but his eyes did not lose their intensity. Deciding that she couldn't handle his taking the lead, Morrígan flicked her hair back over her shoulder and lifted a hand, curling her finger. "Your turn to come to me, husband."

His lips quirked. "Is this how it will be, wife? A battle of dominance in the marriage bed as it has always been outside of it?"

"That depends on you," she replied softly. *And how genuine your feelings are.*

Dagda spread his hands. "I am here, wife. That is answer enough." He paused then, his eyes shifting to the flowing current in the river as he added, "Besides, I tire of our relationship. I wish to explore what we could be—unified as one."

Morrígan stilled. "You had that chance before, husband. You denied me for another." *And another, and another.*

He nodded, his features twisting with remorse. "Yes, and I admit I was wrong."

His tone was genuine, but he was a master at veiling his true emotions. Morrígan took a step closer, moving her body in a languid sashay that showcased her assets. "Do tell, husband."

She caught Dagda's indrawn breath as his gaze moved back to her chest and then to the vee between her legs. "You're going to make me admit it, aren't you, Morrígan?"

"I would expect no less, Dagda."

His lips lifted in a parody of a smile. "I know this, wife, which is why I came prepared." He reached inside his tunic and held an object aloft. "And this is evidence enough."

When Morrígan caught sight of the ruby gem, her heart froze at its significance. Her ring. He'd kept it. All this time, he'd kept her gift—her claim as his wife. Barely breathing, she watched as he slipped it onto his finger, permanently proclaiming to one and all that she was his—because once on his finger, only death could remove it.

Seeing it on his hand for the first time erased her hesitation, and with a smile of her own, Morrígan replied, "You were right, husband. It is enough."

"Then come toward me, wife."

She shook her head, heart pounding. "No. It is your turn to worship me."

He stared at her for a beat, then inclined his head and took the final few steps toward her. And as his hands finally touched her body, Morrígan's heart cracked open, and a sliver of hope ignited within its center.

KRAA-KRAA!

The familiar corvid cry cut through the frenzied screams of battle, catching Morrígan's attention. She turned sharply to the left, twisting her torso to keep her seat upon the war horse and instantly spotted the Fomorian soldier bearing down on her with malicious intent. A rogue soldier, no doubt tasked with destroying the dark sorcerer of the Tuatha.

A crow swooped past her left shoulder in a deadly dive down the hill toward the oncoming enemy. With claws outstretched, the bird raked its talons across the face of the soldier, carving a deep channel from his left eye to his right cheek. The Fomorian roared, face twisting into a snarl of rage. Without breaking stride, he raised one hand, palm out, and released a torrent of fire at the retreating crow.

"Badb!" Morrígan screamed at her sister.

Hearing her portent, Badb banked sharply, wings snapping out to swoop to the left, the fire missing her by a wisp of air.

Incensed that he'd missed his prey, the Fomorian roared again and turned his sights back to Morrígan. Malevolent chaos rampaged in his deadly gaze. He wasn't done, not by a long shot.

She hadn't reckoned on giving away her position this early in the battle. On her king's orders, she was meant to be out of the main skirmish, biding her time, waiting on the right moment to strike the incoming fleet, and this rogue soldier was a nuisance that would cost her the element of surprise. It was too soon to act, but that decision had been made for her; this soldier was a distraction that must be dealt with now.

Changing the battle plan, Morrígan gripped the reins of her horse in one hand and lifted the other, palm up, to the heavens. Almost absently, she felt the sharp sting of claws in her left shoulder as her other sister, Macha, took off in flight to join Badb above.

Connected internally by their sibling bond, she heard her sisters' urgent cries. *Kill him,* they cried. *Now!*

Morrígan knew it for the truth. Already, too many of their people lay dead or dying; the vibrant green grass of their homeland was awash with the lifeblood of the Tuatha.

From her position on top of the hill, Morrígan had watched the invading giants arrive on their shores and observed their growing fleet lining the horizon. With her crow's eye, she'd confirmed that every ship carried at least fifty Fomorians, and even though her people had the numbers, they didn't have the strength—not when their enemies were three times their size.

The Fomorians were sea raiders—hostile, monstrous gods who reveled in darkness, death, and drought. Everything her people weren't...except for her sisters and her.

The crows shrieked again, their piercing cries insistent this time. *Morrígan—now!*

Badb and Macha were violence and chaos; they thrived on destruction. But Morrígan—she was war personified, she was death and darkness itself, and she didn't need her sisters to tell her that now was the time. The darkness had already spoken.

Gritting her teeth, Morrígan fixated her gaze on the Fomorian soldier who continued to rush toward her, even as her hand lowered from the sky and twisted darkness spewed forth in a vicious torrent of pain that flooded his chest.

Comic surprise etched his features, and he came to a sudden halt. As if in slow motion, he looked down at his chest to the hole of live, writhing darkness that twisted with a menacing energy. His eyes snapped back to hers, and Morrígan saw his acknowledgment that his time on this earth was done.

Not breaking that gaze, owning everything it entailed, Morrígan released a soft sigh. The action was an ignition. A fireball in his chest roiled, spinning with a velocity that caused the feathers of her black cloak to flutter. Then on a victorious whine of power, the Fomorian exploded.

Morrígan felt the splash of hot liquid flicker across her face. She blinked, and as her vision adjusted, the Fomorian was no more, the only reminder the acrid burn of flesh in the air.

Badb and Macha cawed in triumph, whirling overhead in twists and turns. Morrígan ignored them, acutely aware that her position on the hill was now compromised. The release of her power had alerted other Fomorians, and countless numbers of them were now racing in a mad scramble up the hill.

But they weren't her immediate concern. She had two tasks to fulfill, and the first must now be attended to with all urgency. Ignoring the enemy soldiers running toward her, she turned her attention back to the ships on the water.

Morrígan closed her eyes, centering her power. The runes appeared in her mind's eye, and she began to chant. Her gift responded, the darkness building inside her. As the chant came to a close, she opened her eyes, her irises no longer their usual green but now black—the color of death.

She pursed her lips and slowly exhaled. A twisting, writhing tendril of darkness shot forth and arrowed down the hillside—not toward the oncoming soldiers, but to the sea below.

With her crow's eye, Morrígan followed its unerring path to the shoreline. As it hit the waves, there came a huge boom of sound, sea spray and sand scattering on impact. But that arrow of darkness was neither swallowed by seawater nor did it sink into the sand. Propelled by Morrígan, that arrow continued to push outward against the inexorable tide.

The sea rumbled in response, a low groan of sound that whispered across the land. Morrígan's horse shifted, its hooves trying to find purchase on the trembling ground. But it did not bolt—it knew its mistress well.

Watching that arrow, Morrígan repeated the chant again,

her voice low and hoarse as she fought purchase against the pull of gravity. She felt her forehead bead with sweat. Turning the tide was a lofty request—it went against the bounds of nature, and Morrígan knew that if she had been standing on her own feet, she would have fallen. This was the strongest magic she had attempted thus far, and it tickled the edge of madness.

The sea swelled again, pushing against her arrow. Gritting her teeth, Morrígan called upon another surge of her power and held firm. Painfully slowly, the swell that carried the waves ashore began to turn. Noticing her progress, her sisters cawed triumphantly above, then swooped down to resettle on her shoulders. Almost absently, Morrígan felt their talons dig into the soft skin. Ignoring it, she continued to direct her power, and the sea finally responded.

Beginning from the shoreline, a new swell close to a furlong, began slowly to move out to sea. Soon enough, that swell became a huge wave that moved relentlessly toward the Fomorian ships amassed on the horizon. Pushing higher and higher, that swell eventually came upon them.

With her acute hearing, Morrígan could hear the cries of startlement and the screams of terror from her enemy. It did nothing to melt the ice around her heart. Her lips lifted into a cold smile as she squeezed her hands into tight fists, finally releasing her hold on her magic. In response, the tsunami she'd created suddenly exploded with a turbulent ferocity. Ships and men scattered in all directions, ripped apart by the force of her wave.

Morrígan watched with dark elation as the water churned like a frothing, writhing beast and swallowed her enemy.

It wasn't until her sisters pecked at her shoulders and

flapped their wings agitatedly in her ears, that she allowed herself to be pulled back to the present. The sounds of the battle returned, and Morrígan turned to scan the writhing bodies on the battlements below, watching as they twisted, rolled, thrust and parried—dirt, blood, and sweat flying in a dark, crazed dance for survival. With her experienced eye, Morrígan could see that even though the Tuatha now tripled the number of Fomorians, they were still struggling to dominate the battle. There was also the enemy almost at her back, now a hundred meters from her position on the hill.

Morrígan knew they must turn the battle in their favor; completing her final task would ensure that it happened. So, coiling the last vestige of her powers to her chest, she kicked her horse's flanks and galloped down the hill toward the oncoming enemy.

Her long, midnight tresses and her cloak of black feathers rippled behind her, exposing the indecent lightweight shift that did nothing to shield her woman's body. It was a guise: a suit of armor that was as tough and durable as any soldier's chain mail—for her magic and battle skills were not just her only power; she also had her body.

As she hurtled toward the battle, Morrígan's right hand crept to the hilt of her sword. Grasping its familiar coldness in her palm, she pulled it from its sheath, and with a piercing war cry, plunged into the fray, swinging it with all her might. The giants' blood ran thick and fast down her shining silver blade. She determinedly pushed onward to the center of the battle, her blood screaming with ecstasy. The blade rang with truth and violence, devastation, and destruction. This was what she was born to do—this was what she was destined for.

She could hear Badb and Macha creating their own havoc as she thrust, parried, and stabbed. It became a movement, a devastatingly dark dance of death, and she—the Morrígan—was the ultimate winner.

Morrígan left a trail of bodies in her wake and did not relent until she came upon her quarry, Lugh, the current king of the Tuatha. His head whipped toward her, no doubt feeling the familiar darkness that heralded her presence.

"Morrígan!" he shouted above the din of the battle. "Finish it! Finish it now!"

That confirmation from her king was enough to release her hold on her humanity. Throwing her sword to one of her people, she leaped to her feet on the back of her horse, opened her arms wide, and embraced her heritage.

There was a flash of light before smoke curled thick and blinding, and from within the swirling darkness a crow rose with a victorious scream of release.

SHE WAS THE MORRÍGAN. She was the crow.

Her sisters cawed above her. *Come join us,* they cried.

Morrígan didn't hesitate, flapping her wings to join her sisters above. Together, they dove among the enemy, swooping and pecking, flapping and scratching, creating further chaos amid the storm of battle. Morrígan found vulnerable flesh between the kinks of armor, eyes that were not shielded behind helmets, and naked hands on hilts. The sounds of the battle rang in her ears, and her blood cried out for more.

It was hard not to fall unreservedly into her other form, to forget who else she was. But in her mind's eye, she held tight to an image of a man, a man whose love she craved. It was enough to reign in the blood lust and turn her mind to the last task at hand: find Indech, king of the Fomorians.

The target reinforced, Morrígan ducked and weaved among the soldiers until she felt the foreign shift of power just ahead. Then suddenly, there he was.

The leader of the Fomorians was larger than average, a veritable giant among his kind. His shoulders were broad, roped with muscle, the tendons in his neck bursting with the pace of battle. His single eye turned to pierce her, seeing her through the corvid form.

He knew who she was. Knew what she sought.

Enemy now in her sights, and not one to prolong fate, Morrígan released her hold on the crow. Darkness roiled—a mirror to before—and surrounded her animal form. Soldiers, Tuatha and Fomorian alike, scattered as that smoke grew, encompassing her and the Fomorian king. A thin, gray, transparent shield grew over the two of them, enclosing them in a separate world.

As the smoke cleared, Morrígan emerged, tall and lithe, her cloak of crow feathers once again around her shoulders. She raised her head to look the Fomorian king in the eye. In turn, he assessed her, measuring her as she measured him.

"This is what they send against me?" he sneered. "You? A woman?"

Morrígan's lips formed into a cold smile. "Not just a woman—a Sovereign Goddess."

Indech snorted, his saliva flying between them. "Your people are weak, entrusting such decisions to women. Who are you to decide who sits the throne?"

Morrígan became deathly still. "I serve my people well."

Indech leered. "You serve your people with your cunt! How does that make you a goddess, when we"—he swept his arms out wide, encompassing his people—"are giants.

Masters of our own destiny. We need no woman to bless our actions!"

Morrígan's lip curled. "Your one eye makes you blind as well as stupid! My abilities do not just lie in my *cunt*," she repeated with a hard edge, "but with my power! And you, foreign king, will feel my wrath for coming to take that which is not yours!"

Morrígan flung her hands out, ribbons of midnight leaching from her palms to wrap themselves around his form. Indech roared at her challenge, and from his own hands came a red flame that spewed forth in blazing, searing heat.

Their magic collided, darkness and fire, each fighting for dominion. But one did not consume the other and Morrígan realized then that what her king had said was true; their powers were of the same matter—darkness and death personified.

Morrígan's heart stuttered at that truth and the knowledge that this enemy would test her power. But she had a promise to fulfill, and a husband to call her own. She also had a land to protect and a people to save. The stark reminder of all she had to lose was a knife thrust of motivation.

He will not win—not today, not ever!

Gritting her teeth, Morrígan forced everything she felt, everything she desired, into that thrust of her power. It was a conflagration. And painfully, inch by inch, her darkness began to riot and rebel against Indech's fire.

The enemy king's face became strained. He knew the tide was turning. He rebelled against his loss, inhaling long and deep. Morrígan felt the draw of power, knew he was pulling energy from the chaos of the battle around them. His returning thrust was strong—stronger than her own, even with Dagda's magic entwined with it. Morrígan faltered, and her legs buckled as his onslaught pushed her backward. Her retreat scared her, and she was cognizant of her fate if she did not change her tactics.

Swiftly changing her battle plan, Morrígan gritted her teeth, bowed her head, and groaned aloud. It went against everything she was to show such weakness.

Out of the corner of her eye, she saw Indech's lips stretch into a garish smile, and then he was moving toward her. Morrígan held her ground, hating the fact that she had to cower.

Easy Morrígan, let him come.

In the next breath, his form towered above her, his body blocking the light of the afternoon sun. Standing in his shadow, she craned her neck back, not once relenting her grip on her magic, ensuring her hands trembled with the effort of holding her darkness in place.

His face burned with triumph as they almost came within touching distance, his fire consuming her darkness. "You are mine, sorcerer!" Indech spat, his spittle catching her cheek.

Morrígan forced out a dry laugh, her lungs burning with the pressure of keeping her position, and said between clenched teeth, "That is where you are wrong!" She lifted her head, and her eyes were scathing as they ran down his form. "No one owns me! I am the Morrígan, and I cannot be overcome!"

Indech's face mottled into a deep purple. Flinging his magic at her, he lunged. She'd preempted his attack and finally released her hold on her own. Their magic collided in a cacophony of sound, two forces of equal strength exploding between them. But for all her plans, Morrígan hadn't prepared for the giant's lunge. She went flying backward, her spine smashing onto the wet ground below. Indech's large, heavy form squashed the breath out of her. She saw stars spin wildly behind her eyelids as she struggled to draw breath. Her hands were trapped between them, at the same height as his thighs.

He moved ruthlessly fast, his hands gripping her shoulders and slamming her head back against the ground again and again as he snarled above her. His words were incorrigible, violent insults. She'd heard them all before, every insulting word that had ever been uttered from those who were scared or jealous of her power, and they rolled off her like the wave that had crushed the Fomorians into the ocean.

Morrígan wasn't afraid until he swung a massive fist into her face. She felt the blow with a resounding impact, her jaw rattling, and her lip splitting open. She blinked dazedly, trying to hold onto consciousness. Desperation clawed at her—another blow like that would knock her unconscious and foil her rash plan. She prayed to chance for a boon.

And chance responded, providing her with an opening as Indech pushed himself up to straddle her body. His change in position brought a modicum of movement to her hands. Breath rasping in her throat, vision clouding, Morrígan focused on moving one hand to the split along her thigh. Once she had the familiar hilt in her hand, she pushed down the bile in her throat and reached out her other hand to grab hold of his shaft, squeezing it tightly.

The action was unprecedented. Indech startled, halting the movement of his fist above her head. "What the fuck is this?" he roared.

Pushing past the pain in her jaw, Morrígan rasped, "I had heard you were not men. Before I died, I wanted to ensure that I was killed by one."

Indech snarled. "I am more than a man, sorcerer—I am a god! And you should count yourself lucky to be killed by me. It is an honor not reserved for many."

Morrígan forced her face into a stiff smile, fighting her terror. One wrong move and her plan would fail—*she* would fail. "But why does it have to end in my death? I can think of other ways we can be of use to each other—our powers melded together. Besides, I tire of being a pawn for my people. I seek my own way, preferably with others who crave the call of violence as I do."

She moved her hand suggestively over his groin. The movement and the words were unmistakable.

A glint came to Indech's eye. "You are a strange woman, sorcerer, to be excited by violence."

"I am who I am," Morrígan answered simply, forcing past the pain to thrust her chest out. Her flimsy shift slipped dangerously low, providing him a view of her naked breasts.

Indech's eyes dropped, and Morrígan felt his shaft lengthen under her hands. He lusted for her, like so many others before him.

Now, the urge whispered over her skin; *now is the time.* Without second-guessing the voice in her head, Morrígan's other hand tightened around the dagger that still remained in the sheath attached to her thigh. Using every last iota of her strength, she whipped it out and plunged it directly into Indech's groin.

The Fomorian king screamed, his body pulling back from hers in a frenzied scrabble. He dropped his head to stare in shock at the dagger slammed into his balls.

Free at last, Morrígan rolled awkwardly to her feet, ignoring the aches of her body and the dizziness that threatened to consume her. Facing him, she said in a soft voice, "As I said before: I am nobody's woman."

Indech didn't seem to hear. His hands reached down to grasp the hilt of the dagger, and he groaned long and hard as he pulled it free, lurching forward as the blade retracted.

Morrígan looked upon him, unfeeling. "You should not have done that. It will only speed your death."

Indech lifted his head and speared her with a gaze full of hatred. "No, but it will give me the chance to do this!"

The dagger flew from his hand. At the last moment, Morrígan turned sideways. It pierced the flesh of her shoulder, narrowly missing her heart. Self-disgust that she'd given him the opening bloomed hot and acrid at the back of her throat. *Focus Morrígan!*

Holding her injured arm close to her side, Morrígan no longer wasted time on words. Lifting the other arm, she called on the dregs of power that she'd only just managed to hold in reserve and began to chant.

His own magic swamped by trying to heal his fatal wound, Indech could do nothing but stumble toward her. Blood ran down his pants as he took one step, then another. But he never made a third, and his movements were too slow, his body too sluggish to block her attack.

Her dark arrow of power slammed into his chest, piercing his heart with unerring accuracy. Then, before Indech had time for another breath, Morrígan squeezed her hand into a tight, unforgiving fist and called upon his death.

THE GRAY SHIELD around Morrígan and the Fomorian king died, and the sounds of battle attacked her senses once again. Her dazed stare drank in the action around her, and Morrígan noticed that with the death of their leader, the giant sea raiders were finally being overcome by the Tuatha.

She tilted her head back, relieved to catch sight of both Badb and Macha. Morrígan breathed deeply, now able to acknowledge that her duty to her king and her people was done. She'd fulfilled the promise cemented by her union with Dagda. A union that had given her and her husband another chance—a chance for a marriage that would no longer be in name alone.

But on this affirmation, Morrígan felt a whisper travel across her skin. The sinking in her stomach that accompanied that whisper was a portent, one Morrígan had felt many times before. It was a clarion call from nature—a demand to balance the scales. Because like all gods, expending her power came at a cost, and with her powers, that cost was always the same. Thus, that whisper was an indication that one of her people would die today. The question was: who?

Heralding that omen, Morrígan's gaze roved over her people and halted on two figures fighting at the front lines. Her heart stopped as she recognized who it was that she looked upon. One of them was her grandfather, the previous king of the Tuatha, and on his right, fighting next to him, was Dagda.

"No!" she whispered, her voice a thin thread of sound as terror gripped her heart. *Not them! Anyone but them!*

But her protest was for naught because nature always claimed its due, and Morrígan knew that one of these beloved men would be the recipient of that final kiss. And even as the acknowledgment settled into her bones as truth, she saw the swords of two enemies rise to swipe not only the head of her grandfather from his neck, but also to stab into the chest of her lover.

The protest ripped from her lips. "Noooo!"

Even in the midst of battle, Dagda heard her call. He

turned unerringly to face her, shock written all over his features as he clutched one hand to his heart. In that moment, Morrígan saw the devastating truth of his wound and knew she wouldn't lose only her grandfather today, for Dagda had been pierced with an injury no healer could fix.

The hope that had finally begun to take wing in her chest flickered dangerously...before irrevocably guttering out.

CERNUNNOS & THE WINGED CHANGELING

Cernunnos
AND THE Winged
Changeling

CORINA DOUGLAS

DEDICATION

This one is for you, Piper.
You are the sweetest girl: kind, emphatic, and caring.
As you have a love for all things animal, this one is for you.
All my love,
Mum xx

CERNUNNOS & THE WINGED CHANGELING

The crunch of leaves and other detritus on the forest floor was inordinately loud in the sudden silence. Brenna paused in mid-step as she noticed how preternaturally quiet her surroundings had become. A shiver of foreboding ran down her back. Gone was the rustle of insects underfoot, the scamper of paws through the trees, the flight of numerous birds and their carefree, trilling song. Instead, there was now a hushed silence, heralding that something...or someone, was coming.

This awareness had her pulling back from the mind of her spirit animal who was flying through the trees ahead, chasing a squirrel. Brenna sent her tawny owl a hurried message to find safety before consciously pulling back into the present moment. Her vision blurred, and for the precious seconds she transferred back into her physical body, Brenna prayed that whatever threat now came was not already upon her.

As her sight slid back into her own body, she glanced around the forest. As far as she could see, there was nothing out of place. However, the hairs lifting at her nape told her otherwise. The crawling across her skin intensified. Brenna knew her only option was to hide, for she knew who walked this kingdom—and what he was capable of. They all did.

Cursing silently under her breath and refusing to acknowledge that her hands were shaking, Brenna dived behind a thicket of brambles nestled underneath the thick girth of an oak tree. She focused on stopping her ragged panting and contemplated using her druidic power to erase all traces of her presence. But using it would only create a signature on the air—making it even more obvious she was here. No, she would have to rely on stealth alone and hope he would not detect her position.

There was a shift in the air, and a sudden crisp breeze arose. It carried an icy finger, a seeking tendril of power. Brenna knew what that entailed, and she clamped her lips shut, urging her breath through her nose—slowly, surely, and very quietly.

The whispering breeze turned almost suddenly into a rustle of leaves, and then the very ground began to tremble. The sound built into a crescendo, a drum beat of pounding hoofbeats, and within moments the harbinger of that preternatural power was upon her. The sight that greeted Brenna was mesmerizing—she could not turn away had her life depended on it.

A stunningly gorgeous male sat astride a powerful great white stag.

With her mouth suddenly bone-dry, her eyes roved over his form.

His body was lithe and firm, not a wasted ounce of flesh upon his frame, and his torso rippled with the movement of his body. Her gaze moved up his corded neck to a face that captivated her every thought. His green eyes sparkled like the forest in full splendor, lush and vibrant, but it was the antlers that crowned his head of rich dark curls that captured her unwavering attention.

He was more than she'd imagined him to be, more than she'd thought possible. And as she stared at him in all his glory, Brenna understood he really was the true king of the forest, crowned by nature herself.

He was Cernunnos, the Wild God of the Forest.

Cernunnos guided the great white stag without any bridle, his legs squeezing into the beast's sides as he directed him forward a few paces. The stag, in response to some unknown signal, came to an abrupt halt a few feet away from her.

The Wild God's face was chiseled into an expression of remote coldness as he barked, "Come out!" He had a voice hewn from gravel and a tone that brooked no argument.

Brenna's stomach dropped. Her game was up, her position behind the brambles now one of shame. How had she thought to hide from him? For what awaited her on that majestic, four-legged beast was no ordinary man, but a god.

By some miracle, her feet didn't stumble as she rose from her crouch. Forcing herself not to prolong the inevitable, Brenna raised her eyes and her gaze instantly locked with his. The power of their connection was like a physical blow, her breath catching painfully in her chest as she gasped aloud.

Stupid, stupid, stupid! I shouldn't have come!

But Arial needed sustenance; her tawny owl was starving. The winter had been harsh and unyielding; the creatures Arial usually consumed had vanished. Brenna had been desperate to feed her; Arial hadn't had fresh meat in at least three days.

She had hesitantly entered Cernunnos's domain, aware he dwelled here, too tempted by the knowledge the Wild

God of the Forest kept a section of his land free from winter's harsh grasp. She'd thought to ease her hunger, but her rash actions had caused whatever life she shared with her companion to be narrowed to the span of the following moments.

Heart hammering, Brenna didn't flinch when Cernunnos swept a leg over the stag and dropped to the forest floor. His leather-booted feet were almost soundless as they fell upon the brambles, and she couldn't stop the color rising in her face as her gaze helplessly followed his long, lithe legs, encased in black leather, all the way up to his naked, muscular torso. Her gaze was arrested by the intricate tattoos decorating his chest, arms, and back, and her fingers twitched at her sides with an undeniable urge to run her hands over his skin.

Flushing now, she dropped her gaze to her own booted feet, even as she felt his gaze narrow on her face. A tingle crept across her skin—an awareness that he was perusing her form as she had his. The air felt electric, and she tried her hardest to still her racing heartbeat, sure he could hear it.

Hunted. She felt like the prey, and he, the hunter. The analogy was apt, given Cernunnos was known to take vengeance on those who plundered the flora and fauna of the forest.

Swallowing hard, Brenna felt his gaze rise slowly back to her face, silently demanding her attention. She lifted her eyes to fixate on his aquiline nose. It was a strong nose, proud and perfect, but when his lips moved next, she couldn't help dropping her gaze to his mouth.

"Who are you?" Cernunnos demanded. "And more importantly, what are you doing on my land?"

A shiver ran down her spine at his guttural growl.

Praying her voice would remain strong, she forced out, "I am a druid from the village. I came looking for food."

Cernunnos cocked his head to the side, green eyes narrowing. He looked cold and removed. "The village is a two-day walk from here," he returned sharply. "You are one of my sister's people. This is my land. Its bounty serves only my subjects. Why would you come here, knowing that merely roaming my lands would invoke your death?"

The gravel-hewn voice was even more threatening because of its remote tone. It was as if the Wild God of the Forest cared naught for the outcome of this meeting, and that if he needed to kill her, he would. In Brenna's mind, she knew he wouldn't think it abhorrent but rather an inconvenience.

She swallowed again, forcing her lips to move. "The food is not for me, but for my companion, Arial."

Here, Cernunnos stilled, his face tightening. Brenna had the sense she'd surprised him; that he hadn't another was here. She lifted her hand in pleading, clarifying quickly, "For my spirit animal."

He blinked, those rich green eyes almost quizzical. "Spirit animal?"

Cernunnos's abrupt, harsh tone caused a shiver to lace her spine. She'd heard about the Wild God of the Forest. They all had. How he preferred animals to humans, even above his own kind, shunning his otherworldly brothers and sisters so he could dwell here among the forests in the lowlands of the mountain range. Cernunnos was a recluse, avoiding everyone and everything except his duty and his domain. It was said the animals were the only creatures he spoke to, that he preferred their company to men, and going by the tone of his voice, the unused roughness of it, as if he also struggled to formulate words, she suddenly understood there was a wealth of truth behind those whispers.

Untamed and wild.

The thought brought another surge of adrenaline, and her heart rate kicked up a beat at the thought of being held by someone like him; of being loved and cared for by someone like him. Without being told, Brenna had the sense that to earn this wild god's love would be akin to basking in heaven and hell all at once. There was no doubt in her mind that he would be fiercely protective, passionate, and all-consuming—a hellfire that could either kill her or birth her anew.

"Well?" he barked impatiently, the growl apparent in his tone.

Brenna flushed again. What was she doing thinking such thoughts? And of a god, no less! Such a tryst would be profanity, one that would see her killed—maybe both of them. Clenching her fists at her sides and berating herself at her own silly notions, she said, "Arial and I are tied as one, linked together by a connection that was forged through death."

"Explain." The simple word was relentless.

Her voice stumbling, Brenna shared, "Arial saved me. I—I was trapped under a rockfall. Had been for most of the day and half of the night. Arial heard my cries for help and came to perch nearby. I made a connection with her. L—like you, I have a natural affinity with some animals, but it was the first time I'd made a connection with an owl. Usually, I can only talk to the smaller creatures, like the mice or the insects, but our connection was effortless. Arial understood what I needed through the images in my head, and she flew off to get help. My brother came, Arial leading the way. He removed the rock to free me, and we've been together ever since."

Cernunnos's face was expressionless, but his emerald eyes were burning with some unknown emotion. "And how did you make this connection?" he questioned coldly. "You are my sister's child, are you not?"

Brenna did not take a step back at that forceful gaze but rather held her ground, fixedly staring at his nose...her gaze soon dropping once again to his mouth. "Yes, I follow Cailleach, but this anomaly in my power isn't the only one."

As soon as the words left her mouth, she felt sick. Why had she said that? She'd never told anyone about the full extent of her powers.

Cernunnos tilted his head, his dark curls swaying gently in contrast to the proud antlers on his head. She could feel his green eyes intent on her face, the pressure unyielding. "And what are these additional powers, druid?" he pressed.

Biting her lip, she ground out softly, "I gravitate toward earth and water." She couldn't help flicking her gaze up to his eyes, just catching the flicker of surprise that crossed his face, so swift it was as if she'd imagined it.

"A healer with earth magic and the ability to converse with animals?" he mused. "You are truly blessed then. But your parentage leaves me questioning who you truly follow. You are clearly more than just Cailleach's child. Is this why you thought you could traipse across my lands? That because you have an affinity for the earth and the animals, it is your right to intrude and take that which is mine?"

Brenna felt the blood in her body freeze at the change in his tone. "No, no, I did not! I came here out of desperation. Arial is starving! This winter has been fierce. It has depleted our resources. So much so that we have nothing to spare. Even the children in my village are starving. I had no choice but to take her elsewhere to feed. Please, please do not punish her for this transgression. This was my idea. Punish me instead, just please do not punish Arial."

Cernunnos straightened, his body tensing. His words were slow, deliberate. "You would take the punishment in her place?"

Without hesitating, Brenna nodded. "In a heartbeat. She came here on my orders. I told her to hunt here. The fault is mine."

"And what of yourself?" Cernunnos asked in a deadly quiet voice. "Did you also come here to plunder the fruits of my forest?"

"No!" Brenna cried, her voice firm even though her body now held a slight tremor. "I came here only for Arial. I have rations." She fumbled, reaching into her pocket for the dried strips of beef she'd carefully hoarded over the autumn. The contents were meager, but they were enough to solidify her claim. To her surprise, his lips loosened from their thin, hard line, almost as if he wanted to lift them in the semblance of a smile.

"Well then, for this transgression, I will give you a warning and one warning only. For if I find you in my territory again, I will not give you a measure of doubt next time. Be forewarned, blessed druid, because no one enters my territory unannounced and uninvited without surviving the altercation."

Brenna's muscles locked, and the tendril of fear that raced down her spine was sharp and piercing. She understood all too well what Cernunnos would do if he caught her again.

Before she could profusely thank him for sparing her life, he continued, "And for the courage it has taken; for the fact that your motives held true and you only sought goodwill for one of my creatures—even if this owl does not normally reside on my land—I leave you both with a gift." He pointed imperiously to the ground at her feet.

Brenna followed the gesture and felt her heart skip a beat at the sight of two dead rabbits, the scent of iron fresh on the air.

She didn't question how he'd delivered them or how he'd killed them, because she knew the Wild God of the Forest wouldn't answer her. Instead, she inclined her head and dropped into a low curtsey, more than aware of the boon he had awarded both her and Arial. "Thank you, my lord, for your generosity and humility."

He didn't bask in her gratitude. Rather, he ground out harshly, "Call your owl and be gone from these lands— immediately."

Brenna felt the sudden blast of his intense dislike as if she'd fallen into the searing heat of a fire. It was in such blatant contrast to his generosity that all she could do was bob her head and remind herself that this man—this god— was subject to nothing and no one, and she was lucky to have been granted life *and* food on this foolhardy mission.

Cernunnos did not wait to see if she would fulfill his bidding. He vaulted upon his giant stag, the antlers of both beast and man standing tall and proud and, by some unknown signal, they galloped away on pounding hooves.

Brenna watched his retreat, her heart racing with a mixture of fear and a strangely alarming tingle of desire and awe.

CERNUNNOS CAREENED BLINDLY FORWARD, his eyes unseeing of the forest splendor. What in the Mother had just happened? Who had that been? That woman...that *druid*? Her visage had pierced his soul, twisting his insides into a turbulent current that flailed against the tide. He'd felt something—a connection, a draw so strong and powerful that he felt as though he'd been punched in the gut. And her scent—sweet jasmine tinged with a hint of honey—it had been his undoing. She had smelled heavenly, almost like a homecoming.

He should have taken his vengeance and slaughtered her then and there. Made an example of her insolence and a statement to her people to never enter his domain uninvited ever again. But it was her beauty that had initially stopped him cold. Ethereal and otherworldly. He was not normally drawn to pretty things, but she'd been a star from the night sky, bright and shining.

Her long, silken hair had shone in the dappled sunlight, sparkling like honeycomb. In sharp contrast to the green foliage of the forest, her skin had been pale and unmarred, as perfect and breathtaking as his dark fae sister. But it was her eyes, the color of a new fawn's, that had caused his breath to catch. Lustrous and full of shining splendor, they had been rich with love and laughter—rich with life.

Her visage had fairly crackled before him, even cowed as she was, petrified of his actions. He'd scented her fear on the breeze, sharp and pungent. However, during his questioning, it had taken him but a moment to realize that her fear had never been for her but for her spirit animal—the owl.

His brows drew together, and he clenched his thighs against his steed. The majestic great white stag came instantly to a stop, his hoofbeats halting under the crunch of brambles. Cernunnos slid off his favored beast and leaned against his sweating hide, absently rubbing at the long neck of his friend. "Who was that woman, Eiros? Did you feel the air change like I did?"

The great stag turned his head, dark eyes flashing. The expression on Eiros's face was almost comical, his lips peeling back into a wry sneer as his voice was heard in Cernunnos's mind. *"She was mortal and is not of your concern."*

Cernunnos heard the disdain in his beast's growling voice. "I'm not so sure about that."

However, mortal she was, yes, and that fact had him baffled. Why would he respond to a mortal in that way? She had druidic magic, but she had more than that if she could communicate with her owl. Of course, the owl was one of Cailleach's favored animals, yet the woman had carried more than his fair sister in her blood. She was like a shapeshifter, yet not. That meant that, somewhere along the line, her parentage had been tainted by another— potentially his fae sister, Morrígan. He was sure of it.

Stepping back from Eiros, Cernunnos planted his hands on his hips and turned to survey his domain. It was now eerily quiet, aware that its master was here. He used his senses to probe the land and its inhabitants. Satisfied that all was well with the creatures and the forest itself, he turned back to his stag and confessed, "It felt as though I was meant to meet her."

In fact, even as he said the words, Cernunnos felt the flicker of a memory stir against his mind: the image of a flaming bird, its fiery countenance ablaze in a show of otherworldly power. The image was unmistakable, for all his siblings knew of this creature. It was the Phoenix—the Custodian of Creation, and his father. He could still recall the exact day of their last meeting some ten years past. A visitation from the Phoenix was rare and always came without forewarning.

Cernunnos's father had surprised him while walking through a section of the lowlands on his weekly rounds through his domain. He'd been carefully observing whether the spring rains were clearing the debris from his rivers and streams as they should, that the beavers were safe and secure, that the fish were leaping, and that the birds had migrated back to their nests. As he'd traipsed through his land, observing and checking, the Custodian of Creation had appeared in his path as if from thin air, those red, orange, and yellow feathers ablaze with eternal fire.

Cernunnos had immediately halted, a deep-rooted knowing so ingrained within his being as to who and what had appeared in his path causing him to instantly bow his head in respect. "Father."

The Phoenix hadn't wasted any time with pleasantries. He spelled out in his powerful, melodic voice in Cernunnos's mind, *"I have come to warn you of a dalliance in your future, one which you must heed."*

"What is it, Father?" he'd asked aloud, not at all shocked by the Phoenix's clipped welcome.

The flaming bird had cocked his head, an arrogant cant to his chin as he'd peered down at Cernunnos with flames dancing in his eyes. *"Your withdrawal from others will soon come to an end, my son. As the eldest of my children, you must mate, and soon. I have foreseen who is in your future. A winged changeling will be your undoing."*

Cernunnos had just stopped himself from scoffing at his father's comment, barely holding himself together throughout the rest of their short interaction. And when the Phoenix had gone in a sprinkling of embers and fireflies, Cernunnos had rolled his eyes to the heavens before continuing on with his task.

But days later, he had contemplated the Phoenix's words.

A woman? He'd had no need to chase women, no need to have one permanently in his bed either, not when they came in search of him—wanting to see if he lived up to his reputation as the Wild God of the Forest. His dalliances in his younger days had gotten him into this mess. The women who'd left his bed had always come back for more—oftentimes, too many. Their persistence, along with the political nightmare he'd had to wade through as his siblings fought over power and land, had ultimately caused him to flee society in search of peace and balance.

Yet, he'd never forgotten his father's words about a winged changeling. And that mortal woman who he'd just met...she'd held a connection to an owl—a winged beast! Recalling that memory and the Phoenix's words had Cernunnos murmuring to Eiros with a touch of wonder, "My father foretold this meeting ten years ago."

Eiros jerked his head back, the long, curling bone-white antlers flashing in the speckled light filtering through the forest canopy. *"The Phoenix? Why did you grant her leave then?"*

He knew why, but he couldn't tell Eiros that he'd been poleaxed, struck by her beauty and slammed by her presence. She'd been a goddamn shining light! *Good. She'd been good.* He'd sensed it almost immediately. She'd been not only a woman with power, but a woman with goodness shining from her very soul. He, on the other hand, was wild, harsh, and unforgiving, a mar to her beauty and all that she was.

And he finally admitted to himself right there and then that he'd let her go because if he'd stayed any longer in her tempting presence, he would have taken her to his bed... possibly even to his home.

At that remembered ache of need and at the strangeness

of its intensity, Cernunnos curled his hands into fists and admitted to his beast, "Because she tempts me more than I can control."

At this, Eiros's words were incredulous. *"You? The one who cannot be tethered by any woman?"*

Cernunnos felt a crooked smile tip his lips. "Yes, it is foreign and unsettling, especially when I cannot face the company of most of my siblings." He turned away, surveying the canopy of the trees above and catching sight of a buzzard as it flew overhead, squawking a warning to the others around that their master was here.

Eiros jerked his head back, swiveling it left and right as he, too, surveyed the domain he watched over with zealous passion. Snorting, he turned back to Cernunnos. *"That is because they talk too much and are insecure in their motivations and themselves. Their druidic children also bicker, squabbling about territory and material goods. Here, life is simple. Your children are the beasts. Your realm is a paradise. As far as I'm concerned, you are the level-headed one."*

Cernunnos felt his tentative smile bloom. His beast was pigheaded in many respects, but he'd earned that right through his endeavors, not only by Cernunnos's side, but also through his own feats. Eiros wasn't his second for nothing. "You were always biased, my friend."

Eiros pierced him with a haughty stare. *"Never forget it."*

Cernunnos gave him a mocking bow, his heart lifting even though his thoughts were a minefield—and totally fixated on the golden-haired woman who shone like the north star.

BRENNA HURRIED THROUGH THE FOREST, her breathing and steps uneven as she followed an internal tug toward her spirit animal. In order to communicate, she needed to get closer to Arial and obtain the tawny owl's attention.

As she ran, the dead rabbits slapped against her thighs, a blatant reminder of the generosity of the Wild God of the Forest. She gasped for breath as her stomach twisted and churned. She couldn't understand why she had responded like that, and to him of all people—*him,* Cernunnos, the Wild God of the Forest! She'd behaved like one of the village girls who only ever talked about the strapping young lads strutting about like peacocks as they came into their prime, like some ninny who had no other thought in her head other than to climb into a man's bed. What was wrong with her? She was not like this!

Yet, she felt alive. So utterly, incredibly alive. Unlike anything she'd ever felt before. It was as if Cernunnos had ignited a smoldering flame she hadn't known existed. Her skin fair tingled, her mind buzzed with thoughts and feelings, and her heart—it raced. Not with fear, no, but with anticipation, as though something bigger, something *more* was within reach.... And all because she'd met him—the veritable king of this domain.

Cernunnos.

His name was a ripple through her mind, creating not just its usual feelings of respect and awe but also longing. *Gods!* Her face flushed, Brenna bit her lip and determinedly hurried forward, her mind returning to her spirit animal. She needed to find her. Now. Before the sharp edge of Cernunnos's generosity that she carefully balanced upon became a falling star.

Coming to an abrupt halt, Brenna focused on her internal connection with Arial and tugged on their bond.

Instantly, Arial responded. Her tawny owl was adept at communicating, and an image high in the treetops blazed in Brenna's mind. She could feel as well as see Arial's attention fixed on a squirrel currently scampering up and down a pine tree, its face bulging as it carried several nuts in its cheeks.

"Arial, it is time to leave. Now."

Arial blinked, long and slow, and a hoot of denial was heard in Brenna's mind. *"Not now. I have sighted prey."*

Brenna's mind turned firm, her emotions strong and unbreakable. *"No, Arial. Now! I have food—gifted from Cernunnos himself. He has ordered us to leave immediately. His generosity will not last. Come to me—now!"*

Brenna felt the owl jerk back in surprise, her feathers ruffling. *"He found you? And you live?"*

She swallowed. *"Yes, it was a true blessing from the Mother."*

"No, not from the Mother, but from the wild god himself," Arial corrected.

And on the whisper of her owl's reply, Brenna found herself lifting off from the tree branch in a swooping glide. She felt the fresh, brisk breeze whistle past her cheeks and smelled the early growth of spring in this ethereal forest domain as Arial banked and flapped toward her.

Satisfied she was returning, Brenna blinked and pulled back from her spirit animal, coming back into her own mind. The world tilted alarming for just a moment before the nausea eased. Moments later, Arial appeared, diving low toward her, claws outstretched in welcome.

Brenna raised her cuffed arm, the leather malleable yet tough and marred by countless claw marks. Arial settled upon her raised arm in a flawless maneuver before jumping to her shoulder where she nestled against her cheek in welcome.

"*I missed you.*"

Despite everything, Brenna smiled. "*And I, you.*"

"*The rabbits smell delicious. I assume there is no time to eat before we leave?*"

Brenna's voice was firm. "*No. We dare not linger.*"

ON THE RETURN TRIP HOME, Brenna was consumed with a myriad of remembered images. She felt overwhelmed, her senses saturated by her meeting with Cernunnos, his earthly scent, his commanding presence, and his otherworldly power. Arial seemed to sense that she was distracted, for the tawny owl stayed close, often returning to perch on her shoulder as she hurried back to the village.

When they stopped to camp in an abandoned dirt cave, a safe haven often used on her travels, Brenna finally deemed it safe to partake of Cernunnos's gift. She started a peat fire, not just to cook some meat and dry the skins, but also to warm them during the night.

Even though Cernunnos's forest had been glorious, abundant, and in full bloom, the world outside of his domain continued to cycle through the seasons, and here and now, it was still winter. One of his duties was to manage the cold season and guide them through its tempest. However, over the years he had become more and more reclusive, preferring to remain in his forest, ignorant of what went on outside of his boundaries.

Brenna had heard the stories for years, of how he had been withdrawing as the seasons passed. She'd also heard her people talking about the possibility of their own goddess, Cailleach, taking up the mantle of winter. Of course, the rumor had come from one of Morrígan's people and was most likely devised by their fae goddess, given it was well known she did not like Cailleach.

Brenna shuddered. The role of winter contained unimaginable power, and with winter also came death—a ravaging of not only the land but its inhabitants too. She wasn't sure if their gentle goddess could survive such a role, and yet, she understood that something needed to change. The winters were becoming inhospitable. Too many of their elderly, sick, or weak were dying from starvation or winter ills. Cernunnos needed to do something. But first, he needed to take notice and soon, because this year, the winter had hit them hard.

It was harsh and unforgiving. And as of yet, Cailleach had done nothing to ease the burden, not answering their prayers to consult her wild brother to make him see what was happening to their land and people. Brenna suspected it was because Cailleach loved him. Their goddess had a deep-rooted respect for Cernunnos, and it was more than a sibling's love. After meeting the Wild God of the Forest himself, Brenna could understand that fascination and that loyalty. Cernunnos commanded respect and earned it.

With the smoke curling around the dirt cave and threading through the strands of her golden hair, Brenna skinned the rabbits mechanically and methodically, taking extra care to ensure there were no nicks. The skins would be her present. The meat, however, would be for Arial, despite that Cernunnos had said one rabbit was for her, the other for her owl. She was strong; she was unbending. She could and would survive on her dwindling larder and the frozen roots she scratched from the earth. After all, she'd managed thus far on her own after her family had succumbed to a disease that had ravaged their village, and she would survive for a lot longer.

It was imperative that Arial had meat, though. The tawny owl couldn't survive without it. Winter would hold on for another few weeks yet, and the meat, though dried, would sufficiently sustain the muscle and sinew the owl still held.

The fire sizzled as a drop of fat spat upon the meager flame. The aroma was enticing, and her mouth watered. Arial, similarly affected, flapped her wings even though she'd eaten her fill of fresh meat only an hour prior.

Her spirit animal spoke into her mind. *"Thank you, my friend, for all that you risked."*

Brenna sent her a smile as she rested upon the log. Arial's eyes, large and unblinking, were fixated intently on her movements. "You would have done the same for me," she returned softly.

"It is true; however, my assistance is limited."

Brenna shook her head. "Not true. Your presence brings me joy every day. More than you know, Arial."

The tawny owl brought her purpose in life and chased away loneliness. With Arial, she was also unafraid, able to face the darkness that hovered at the edge of winter.

Brenna poked at the skins again, fingering their density. They were only slightly damp. The fire had sped up the drying process, and if it stayed alight for what remained of the night, she could very well begin darning a new hat or a pair of gloves tomorrow evening when they arrived back at the village.

She turned back to Arial, running a hand over her feathered back in a gentle caress as she said aloud, "Sleep well, my friend. Daybreak will be here soon enough."

The owl blinked. *"It will be no chore on a full belly."*

Brenna smiled again, her heart and mind happy. With one last glance at the skins and the fire, she curled onto her side on the cave floor and closed her eyes as soon as her head hit the pillow of her arm.

THE DAWN WAS bright and beautiful, though deathly cold. The only noise as they tramped back over the plains was the crunch of the icy snow beneath her feet. Even Arial seemed hunched upon herself, her feathers ruffling regularly, as if she feared they would become so cold they would stop working completely. Brenna sent her off into the air every so often, forcing her to beat her wings and push back the chill.

Soon enough, after hours of traipsing across the frozen wonderland, the sight of curling smoke became visible around the bend of the lowland mountain trail. Her village. Seeing it had her feet quickening, the promise of a bed and shelter spurring her on.

In another hour, Brenna could see the thatched roofs sagging under the weight of the snow. Her heart, as it always did, sunk at the sight of the limited smoke streams curling from the roofs. Too few. She fervently hoped these last few weeks of winter would pass quickly and ease their burden; she did not want to tend to any more patients who had no hope of surviving winter ills.

Dawn had just broken across the horizon when Brenna entered the circle of thatched huts. Using her magic, she shielded both her own and Arial's forms from view, including their scents and that of the rabbit skins, so they could enter the village unseen. It wouldn't do for the sentries to pick up on a fresh kill, not when more than half of the village inhabitants were starving. There was only so much generosity she could give before she or Arial suffered even more than they did.

Everyone had been tolerant of her owl's presence so far, but if they knew she hunted and killed for it rather than gifting the meat to others, she didn't think Arial would be allowed to remain here. There was also the fact that she was worried one of them would kill Arial to fill their own belly....

Brenna spied her lone hut on the far outskirts of the village, almost remote in its distance from the others, and breathed a sigh of relief that the shutters were still closed tight against scavengers. She quietly walked around the back and raised her palm against the rear wall of the wooden roundhouse. There came a low groan, almost a sigh of wood resettling, and a door popped open, exposing her bedroom. She quickly entered, waving her hand in a mimic of before, and pressed her palm once more against the wood. The door swung shut, the invisible edges becoming smooth and unmarred from both outside and in. Only then did Brenna release the sigh of tension that she had carried since her encounter with Cernunnos. Her shoulders slumped with relief. She'd made it back alive. Against all odds, she'd returned, and with not just both her and Arial's lives, but also with fresh meat and skins for a new hat or gloves.

Birds began to twitter outside as she set about starting a fire. Sleep beckoned, but first, she needed to ensure the hut remained warm. Given they'd stopped their trek, the cold would soon seep into the building, crippling both of them while they slept and recovered. Her task would not be done until the fire had been stoked and banked so they could get a few hours of solid rest. The rabbit skins also needed to be hung up so they could dry for use in the coming days. Her movements were methodical, automatic, and even in her half-asleep state, she had the fire roaring with the limited supply of wood she had left.

Arial found her perch and settled upon it. In Brenna's mind, she could feel the owl's satisfaction, the sense of being replete. It had been a while since her friend had had a full stomach—and fresh meat at that. Brenna allowed herself to bask in the feeling of being able to provide for her friend, knowing she had granted Arial a chance to see the winter through.

She lay down on her straw bed beside the fire and trained her gaze on the smoke that curled up to the top of the thatch before it escaped through a small hole in the roof and out into the dawning world outside. Succumbing to tiredness, her eyes eventually fluttered closed. However, the last image that remained in her mind wasn't of her cabin or Arial. Rather, it was of a strong face, fierce and cunning, with emerald eyes in full earthly splendor, and a set of smooth, sable antlers that crowned the regal head of the Wild God of the Forest.

A BARRELING CRASH and an angry commotion had Brenna snapping awake, her hands automatically reaching for the dagger strapped to her thigh.

"There she is! Get her!"

Without a chance to understand what was happening, hands reached down and roughly grabbed her wolf skin jerkin, wrenching her off the bed and throwing her toward the open door. The room was a riot of sound and movement, numerous figures looming in the smoke from the fire, causing everything to become a blanket of confusion.

Brenna heard Arial flap her wings, then screech—not in alarm, but in attack.

"Arial!" she cried, her stomach churning. *What was happening?*

Fingers bit into her upper arms, unrelenting and cold, as a voice leaned down and growled into her ear, "Don't think to fight us, witch! You'll live to regret it."

Witch? The voice was familiar. Brenna turned her gaze to the man, feeling her face blanch of color. "Ygrid? What is going on? Why—"

"Enough! We will not listen to your talk. You are poison! You have disregarded the rules of our people, crossing boundaries that shouldn't be crossed. But all things come full circle, and today you will pay for your misdeeds!"

"Misdeeds? What misdeeds?" Brenna cried, her last words a grunt of pain as a booted foot slammed into her lower back. She went sprawling face-first out of the door and into the snow.

Arial screeched again, and Brenna heard the unmistakable sound of her swooping before she just caught sight of her diving through the door. Relief that her friend had escaped her captors was short-lived as she lifted her head and saw who was now around her. They closed in, their faces tight, anger a writhing beast across their features.

Ice slithered inside her veins as six men circled around her. She took a breath, one more, two. It was instinct to attack but that wasn't her way. Not when she didn't know the full story. Besides, these were her people. She'd grown up with them. Telling herself to remain calm, she cried, "Stop! This is madness! I know not what you accuse me of. At least tell me what this is all about."

Ygrid sneered at her. "Don't give us that! Stop trying to hide what and who you are. We know all about your clandestine activities—who you've visited, what you've done! Whore!"

Brenna felt her mouth drop open. "Wh-what?"

She had no clue what they spoke about. "I have whored myself to no one," she bit out vehemently, a worm of anger beginning to loosen her tongue. "I am innocent of this crime."

"Bull!" another of the men roared.

She turned to face him. Sven. A man her age. They'd grown up together, even shared their first kiss together. "Then what is it I have done exactly, Sven? Tell me, or else this inquisition and this attack is for naught."

His face twisted, his blue eyes, usually bright and fresh, now frosted and cold as ice. Brenna could also see disdain in their depths—disdain and hate.

"You know of what we accuse you of, Brenna," he returned in a hard, unforgiving voice. "You lay with the wild god. It is sin to bed our scions."

Her stomach dropped. "Pray tell, how did I do this thing?"

"The evidence is obvious," another man growled, his tone glacial. "You were missing for two days. Don't tell us you weren't, either. Petre came looking for you and found your hut empty. And here, we find you have returned with rabbit skins drying over the fire! There has been no sign of such animals for months now. Only a gift from the gods would ignite their presence. How else could a woman like you receive these gifts when our hunters, tried and true, cannot bring home a single kill, no matter how small the rodent?"

Brenna's heart skipped a beat. She had thought no one had seen her leave or return to the village. She'd also laid wards around her house to deter anyone from entering.

As if he'd heard her thoughts, Ygrid said, "Petre knows your scent well, given you tended to his wife. And as our only healer, he had need of your skills. His wife died yesterday because no one could prepare her brew—because *you* were missing. She died needlessly."

Brenna froze, her limbs beginning to ache in the snow as her clothing became damp. Anger spurred her reply. "I left a concoction for Mildred," she shot back. "There is a supply in her cupboards. Her children also know how to make the remedy. How is her death my fault? Have you looked at Petre? Have you questioned how she died? Was he out drinking mead again, digging himself an early grave and shirking all his responsibilities? I will not take that blame. It was not my fault!"

"How dare you!" Petre growled. He squatted down to his haunches, his face mere inches from her own, and his left arm swung back and across her face in a vicious backhand.

Brenna rocked sideways, her cheek burning, the flash of pain at her lip a clear indication that it had split. She flung her hands out at the last moment, catching her fall before she sprawled face-first into the icy snow. Her ears rang and her blood pounded, anger now an avalanche fueled by years of disrespect from the man. She lifted her head and screamed, "You have just proven your worth! I say again that I will not own Mildred's death, for it is not mine to carry! And if you seek to punish me for a crime I did not commit, I will only warn you once—I will fight for my freedom, and I will take no prisoners."

Petre sneered. "You? A woman? A healer? What can you do to me, apart from whore yourself?" His eyes speared her form, traveling with horrible intensity over her furs, as if imagining her naked body underneath. His lip curled as he added with a leer, "Although your body does leave me wanting."

Brenna shrank back, feeling the snow hard and unyielding at her back. "You will not touch me!"

"Who is there to stop me?" he returned. Around him, the men murmured at his words, some with discomfort, but others with agreement.

Brenna felt ice slide down her spine—and not from the snow. The feeling was soon followed by a whiplash of rage. She would neither be cowed nor beaten. Not by these men —men who would wrongly accuse her without first finding out the truth.

She clenched the snow between her splayed hands, fisting it into a hard ball. Her head lifted, her gaze fixating on Petre. "How dare you?" she spat. "Has the cold addled your brain? Has starvation made you into a beast? I am not chattel. I am my own woman, and you will not use me. I will only ask once—let me go, for you have wrongly accused me twice now. I will say it again: I did not bed Cernunnos, nor did I kill your wife."

Brenna made sure to turn her face and gaze at each of them in turn, allowing some of her power to show. Ygrid shrank back at the preternatural glow that hit her fawn-colored eyes.

"Who—? What are you?" Ygrid breathed, his own eyes widening.

But Brenna was past negotiating. Her anger was now a writhing water snake, frenzied and fluid. "I am Brenna, and I will not be cowed by you or anyone!" Her hands flew upward, her fingers uncurling as they did so to fling her hands in a vicious arc around her. What sprayed from her hands wasn't crusted snow, though, but rather a torrent of ice arrows, the snow transformed into vicious weapons. They pierced the leather jerkins of her captors, sinking with deadly accuracy into the soft points between their shoulder blades and clavicles, and there they stayed, both ends of the shafts sticking out of both sides of their bodies.

The men groaned and shouted, their hands grasping for the ice. Brenna took the moment to scramble to her feet, her bare knees scraping the crusted snow. She used the moment to raise both her palms to the dawning sky. With winged creatures in mind, she cried, "To me!"

In response, the sky erupted, the new blue dawn becoming shadowed with the flutter of a thousand wings. Birds of all breeds flew toward her captors with deadly intent, diving at the men.

Ygrid had enough of his wits to raise his arms and shield his body as he raced off to his thatched hut. The others, however, stood their ground and were attacked for it.

Not one to glory in violence, Brenna left on racing legs, running into her own hut once more. She swiftly grabbed hold of her leather bag and went straight for her food stores, throwing in the meager rations she had left. Grabbing a blanket next, then some flint, a few small tools for foraging and survival, and her makeshift bedroll, she finally shoved her freezing feet into her still-damp boots and left the hut.

Arial, seemingly waiting for her mistress, flew straight past her and back into the cottage, screeching, *"The rabbits!"*

Heart in her throat, Brenna stopped midstep, waiting on her owl to return. With relief, she saw some of the men had followed Ygrid's lead and were also racing off to their own cottages, the ice shafts protruding from their shoulders.

In the next moment, Arial returned, dropping the two rabbit skins into her outstretched arms with a warning squawk. Brenna caught them and shoved them hurriedly into her pack before racing on, shouting internally to her spirit animal, *"Good girl, Arial! Now fly—to the trees!"*

She couldn't stay here. The tether holding her to the village had been broken with the men's accusation, and then permanently cemented with her returning attack. Without thinking of the finality of her situation, Brenna raced for the forest at the edge of the village, retracing the path she'd walked only hours before. However, this time the dawn wasn't beckoning but high overhead.

For a moment, she hesitated, exposed in the blinding sunlight, and wondered what she was doing. Reentering the forest in the dead of winter, all alone, was asking for death. But that moment only lasted a mere trifle. She reminded herself she had the skills to survive—she could hunt and forage, she could also heal and knew the signs when illness struck. It was very clear there was nothing left for her here. She had given to this village her whole life, in food and via her gifts, healing many of the people from illness or near-fatal accidents. She'd stayed awake many nights caring for those that often didn't repay such kindness, and with the loss of her parents, her only family, she was alone.

No, there is nothing more for me here.

With the hesitation now gone, her legs moved again, and soon Brenna was racing past the cottages, ignoring the blatant stares and outcries of the people. Her eyes remained fixed on the looming forest beyond the last thatched roof.

Arial swooped in her path, left then right, swinging this way and that in silent demand to hurry.

"I'm coming, Arial. Flee!"

The tawny owl ignored her, swooping once again across her path to look back behind them. Then she screeched, causing Brenna to stumble at the sound of alarm. *"Run!"*

Arial screamed into her mind. *"There are four men behind you!"*

Brenna whipped her head around. Sure enough, there were four men gaining on her, and they were not the ones she'd speared with ice arrows. She recognized neighbors and other men she'd grown up with. Her heart broke at the truth behind their chase. How could they turn on her so quickly? How could they think she was blessed by a god? She was different, yes, preferring her own company and that of her owl, but they had no knowledge of her gifts or that she could speak to Arial. All she'd shown them was her healing power. But...had someone been watching her all this time? Following her into the forest while she foraged for herbs and medicines? Witnessed her experiments with the animals and plants?

"Run!" the owl screeched again. *"Faster!"*

Brenna put her head down and used every last ounce of strength to maintain her pace. Just a little farther and she'd be there. She just had to get to the forest. Safety lay in the trees; there she could use her powers to camouflage herself.

Her legs were burning and her chest was screaming as she sprinted. Just before she entered the dim interior under the snow-crusted trees, she spied Arial swooping upward, climbing to the canopy. The loss of sunlight was blinding, and Brenna's vision blurred. Feet stumbling, she careened forward, unwilling to stop. They were close. She could hear the men's crunching footsteps and the harshness of their breathing.

"Stop! You will not escape destiny, witch!" one of them cried.

The word threw a cold stillness over her heart and immediately had her rage rekindling. Who had been spreading lies about her?

"The Hearne told us all about who and what you are. You can't outrun us. We are the fastest hunters in the village."

She stumbled. The Hearne...they had turned their fearless hunters on her as if she was a rabid dog? How was she to outrun them? They were powerful, skilled, and relentless. She couldn't escape on foot, but she could use her magic to conceal herself. All she needed was to find a quiet place to rest. She could wait them out. After all, she was prepared with food rations and blankets.

Arial, as if sensing her intention, screeched in her mind, *"Yes! I will await you in the trees. Quickly, hide!"*

Brenna's gaze swept left then right, trying to find sufficient cover. There! Straight ahead was a thicket of dense trees and bush with enough branches and surrounding trunks to create a dark, shadowed haven for her to hide within. She sprinted toward it, her leather boots squelching, breath gasping loudly in her ears. Heart racing, she ducked around the bushes, not caring that the brambles scratched her face or that her clothing was now muddy and damp.

Pulling herself into a tight ball, she wove a rune upon the air and gently coaxed the plants and forest detritus to crowd closer. There was a rustle of leaves, the soft groan of tree limbs, and the sound of a thousand tiny feet scurrying through the dirt. As the forest drew her close in a lover's embrace and erased her last few steps, only then did Brenna's chest loosen. She peered through a gap in the bush, back the way she'd come.

She'd hid not a moment too soon, for the men were suddenly right there, their limbs muscled as they raced toward her. Their faces were drawn tight, their eyes narrowed in concentration, and Brenna saw their real intent like windows into their souls: They intended to hunt her down just like an animal. It was there for all to see.

With bated breath, she waited, her blood roaring in her ears, as they suddenly came to an abrupt stop. Then, Artair, her closest neighbor and someone who she'd helped many times with hunting wounds, flung out an urgent, commanding, "Halt!"

The others stopped in their tracks.

Brenna's heart pounded as she saw Petre among them, his shoulder strapped with a rough bandage flooded with fresh blood. *He* was part of the Hearne? By the Mother! Brenna knew he wouldn't be partial, not after the insults she'd thrown at him, and she mentally kicked herself for not causing him further injury.

"What is it? There is no one here," one of the men said brusquely. "She is getting away! We must continue the chase. She's a woman; they tire easily."

The concession had her breath freezing in her chest. Some of their women had gone missing recently, supposedly caught in a storm, or they'd simply left, seeking food, never to return. Was there something more sinister to these events? Had they all been accused of witchcraft too?

She shook her head. That wasn't her problem right now —escaping these men was. The Hearne were not known as the fiercest hunters in her clan for nothing.

Petre spoke again, his voice quiet and deadly. "No, she is here. I can smell her."

Indeed, Brenna could see his nostrils quivering, and a puzzle piece clicked into place—Petre had druidic abilities, and going by the faint taint in the air, he'd been using his power for more than just sustaining the balance. It was him who had smelled her leaving the village, him who had smelled her returning, and most likely him who had also smelled the rabbits...and possibly the wild, musky odor of the Wild God of the Forest.

Brenna's fists clenched. Hiding would do no good. Not with his skills. And she was not one to cower. No, she would meet them head-on, just as she had Cernunnos.

With a gentle touch, Brenna wove another rune with her fingers in a tight, intricate circle and breathed softly, "Arise."

In response, the branches, brambles, moss, and insects all withdrew in a soft murmur. The sound drew the attention of the men, all four heads whirling to fixate on her position. Swallowing hard, Brenna held their gazes as she carefully rose from her crouch and took a few steps forward. Close enough to admit her presence, but not close enough to indicate she came to them willingly or that she surrendered.

She was conscious this moment was a mirror of yesterday. Yet, strangely enough, even though she'd faced one of the most powerful beings in the world in her last altercation, it felt like the odds of living through this experience were even less in her favor.

"That's right, come out, little rabbit. There is no escaping the hunt," Petre sneered, his face molding into something unrecognizable, no longer the boyhood friend she had grown up with.

"No." The word was quiet but forceful.

"No?" another growled, and as she turned to stare at him, Brenna felt as though she'd been punched.

Simeon. Her cousin through her father. Someone she called family. It was a lifeline. "Simeon, please, cousin— help me! You have to understand I didn't do what I am accused of. I can exp—"

"Quiet!" he snapped. "You are no one to me. Do not call

me cousin. We do not share blood—not with the taint you have brought to our family name and to our village."

Brenna felt the blood drain from her face. Any feelings of fealty she had left dissipated at his words. If her own family did not believe her, there really was no sense in continuing this journey. Heart hardening, she let the magic she'd contained roil to life inside her, and her hand lifted, the palm alight with green and blue light...

CERNUNNOS GROWLED. He'd heard more than enough. As the accusation was flung at the golden-haired woman, a lightning bolt of pure agony seared through him. Her own family had disowned her—for a sin she had not committed!

It was enough, more than enough, to warrant his rage—enough to step in and save her. For he knew her with everything he had. He *knew* her. She was not of these people but one of his own. His woman. As if carved from his true, secret desires. Such a woman did not belong with these men, that village, or that family. No, she belonged with him, and he wasn't leaving without her.

But not before he illustrated what hurting his woman meant.

With the mere flicker of a thought, Cernunnos made himself suddenly appear, literally popping into thin air right before the men. Even as he caught their shocked disbelief at his sudden appearance, his mouth was opening and he was roaring.

The sound was thunderous, full of red-blooded anger, and only he and Eiros knew the ravaged noise was more than his anger, for a touch of fear was apparent to his own ears, cemented by the wild pounding of his heart.

They scrambled back in a flurry of limbs and gasps, one shouting his name, another visibly frozen in place, his limbs were trembling. The scent of fear in the air was unmistakable. Not dampening his power, Cernunnos let it roar forth in a crescendo of wrath as he said in a voice riven with thunder, "This woman is under my protection. Leave her be or you will face the consequences. You know what I am capable of—heed my warning."

He knew he didn't need to spell it out, not when all their eyes were now riveted upon the bone antlers sticking out of his head, but he wanted one of them to buck against his constraints, wanted an excuse to turn their lives into dust. The roaring in his blood demanded vengeance for the way they had treated his woman. He was also conscious that he was visible to the golden-haired beauty behind him, and he had to walk a fine line between his natural bestial instincts and his humanity. He also did not want to lower his standards to match these human filth. But as he stared at them, willing them to do his bidding, one of the men had other ideas.

Tall and muscled, a dark-haired man pulled his dagger from the belt at his side and waved it threateningly at Cernunnos, his face twisted in a sneer of disgust. "Why should we listen to you?" he spat. "You are just as tainted as she is. You slept with one of our own—it is against the bounds of nature!"

Cernunnos couldn't stop the snarl that erupted from deep within his very being. "We did no such thing! And even if we had, it is no business of yours. Who are you to cast blame?" Cernunnos looked him up and down, his lip peeling back in distaste. "I know exactly what type of man you are—you show loyalty to no one but your own endeavors. You will never be happy with your lot in life, always thinking there is something more, something better. I pity whoever you cast your shadow upon."

The man's face was bone-white, the brackets around his mouth a clear indication that the insult had hit home. "You know nothing!" he ground out. "You live outside of our people, hiding away in the forest. People talk of your power, but I have seen none of it. Who do you rule over? Beasts and insects, trees, and bush. Pah! Child's play. Why should we respect you and yours?"

The explosion in Cernunnos's chest was lightning quick, a flurry of such rage that he didn't even feel it coming before he was once again roaring, his hands bunching by his sides. Without further thought, he launched, not bothering to use magic, taking satisfaction in the crunch of his fist striking the man's chin. His opponent didn't have a chance to retreat, not against his quick reflexes, and the expression on his face was one of stunned surprise before Cernunnos smashed his fist into his chin.

At the last moment, even though he deserved it, Cernunnos pulled back from hitting his nose because he knew that one hard hit would push the bone right into his head and kill him....and he was conscious his woman was watching, her body trembling and pale, her eyes wide and haunted, all sense of her own attack snuffed out. His gentle fawn did not need to witness this violence. He would protect her from it and the ugliness these mortals endured.

The blow threw the man backward, the crunch audible in the waiting silence. Even the forest around them had gone quiet, watching and listening to its master. Cernunnos leaned over him and ground out, "Your only warning has been used up. One more word, one more movement in this woman's direction, and your life will be over. Choose now and choose wisely." He lifted his head and turned to the other three. The one who'd soiled himself was still trembling, his teeth clacking together in the eerie silence. The other two, however, wore horrified looks, but the respect was clear as they bowed their heads, eyes lowering to his torso.

One of them, the one his woman had called Simeon, asked in a small voice, "You did not sleep with my cousin?"

The words brought a small sound from behind him, but he kept his gaze on the threat ahead as he replied, "No."

"Well, how did Brenna acquire two rabbits then?"

Brenna? Was that her name? Cernunnos didn't look at her, though he could feel her pain like an invisible scar. What had they done to her before he'd found her? Why had they accused her of such a thing? Had his gift created this angst? Without questioning Brenna, he knew she had denied the accusations, and it was clear these men hadn't listened.

This had him rearing to attack them again, but with teeth ground together, Cernunnos held on to his wrath and said evenly, "Because of her courage and the journey she made to ensure her animal survived this inordinately long winter, I rewarded both her and her owl with a rabbit each."

Simeon's face slackened at the words, and his eyes darted to Brenna. Cernunnos could see remorse there as well as sadness.

But this man's regrets were not his to own, and he was here for no one but the woman—Brenna. It was a name which suited her. And it answered his questions behind her birthright because Brenna meant little raven. It was a clear indication of her heritage. She was as he suspected—one of Morrígan's children. However, the women gifted with such a name were usually dark haired.

It was no wonder why she was special. Brenna was a

child of both of his favored sisters—Cailleach and Morrígan. Both strong women—one quiet, one brash, and both unbelievably beautiful. Brenna had captured enough of the spirit from each of these two goddesses to shine all on her own.

Finally, Cernunnos turned to look at her for the first time. Her fawn-colored eyes were wide and luminous, horror and shock apparent, but on top of it all was also wonder and a small touch of what made Cernunnos's stomach warm in an unfamiliar way—pleasure. Brenna was pleased to see him; glad he had come. It wasn't until then that something loosened in his chest, and the tightness he didn't know he'd carried since their initial meeting slowly began to release.

He'd been worried she didn't feel their connection like he did, that she wasn't as consumed by thoughts of him as he was of her. But her face, her expression, and now the step she took toward him—it all told him a story, and a feeling of such profound relief flooded through his body. The Phoenix had been right. A winged changeling would change his life forever. Because he knew in that moment as she calmly walked up to him with no hint of fear, that this woman would be his salvation and his undoing.

He waited, still and silent, just like the men, as Brenna walked right up to him and placed her small, fine-boned hand onto his forearm. His skin electrified at her touch, burning with heat. He wanted that small hand to run over his body, his torso, and into his hair. Imagined it against his cheek and then...and then... He blinked as her voice cut through his vision, addressing the men before them.

"The Wild God of the Forest has spoken true. I have done no wrong apart from seeking to feed my owl. You wrongly accused me of a deed I did not commit. That said, I wish you no ill will, but I would ask that you clear my name of this wrongful taint."

Simeon cleared his throat. "We apologize, cousin. Petre told us he was certain of what had happened. We believed him as he's never been wrong before."

Cernunnos followed his gesture to the fallen man. "Why would you believe him?" he questioned softly. "This man is clearly no leader. Can you not see his ilk? His stain spreads." Cernunnos waved at the three of them, and the whisper of coercion that had been upon them via Petre's magic was gone in an instant.

Simeon shook his head and blinked along with the other two men, once, then twice. Then as his eyes looked upon the golden-haired woman who was his cousin, Simeon said with deep regret and a touch of bewilderment, "I am sorry, Brenna. I don't understand why we would accuse you of witchcraft." He looked at his fallen comrade, his voice taut as he added, "It is obvious Petre had his own personal vendetta. I do not take lightly to being manipulated, and I wash my hands of him. Please, I beg you to come back with us in peace. We will personally see that your name is restored as well as your home."

Cernunnos froze. "You destroyed her home?"

The man tensed at his tone but said truthfully, "Just the door. We will fix it immediately upon our return." He held out his hand to Brenna. "Come, cousin."

Cernunnos stood there silently, his whole being crying out "No!" He did not want Brenna to leave. After all, he'd followed her here to...to...what? What had he followed her here for in the end? To see her? To confirm if these feelings for her were real and not a figment of his imagination? All he knew was that his drive to be with her remained. In fact, it had only intensified with the man's words.

Cernunnos knew only one thing in that moment—that Brenna wasn't leaving him. She would not return to that village; she was coming back with him.

He opened his mouth to speak his intention, but Brenna cut him off with, "No, Simeon, I am not returning."

Simeon's mouth dropped open. "Not returning? But where will you go?"

Brenna shrugged. "I know not where. But this incident has cemented that I do not belong here. I've never belonged—not since my parents died. I am...different from you all."

Simeon stared at her for a beat, seemingly about to argue, but as he opened his mouth again and caught her gaze, he slowly nodded. Resignation came over his face. "Where will you go then?" he repeated.

Cernunnos felt his body still as he waited with bated breath. He turned to watch the woman beside him with an intensity that bordered on panic.

Brenna did not look at him as her lips lifted into a smile. "I know not, but I am certain I will be fine. I have lived on my own before. I am not defenseless and have sufficient knowledge of foraging and hunting to survive what may."

"But what of your patients? We have no other healers in the village."

"That is not true," she said with a shake of her head. "I have trained Beth well. She will be a great healer."

"But she is not more than a child!" Simeon protested.

Brenna looked at him with a raised brow. "She is older than I was when I began healing our people."

For a moment, Simeon looked shocked, then he truly looked at her and said, "That is true. I forget how adept you are." His mouth tightened, and he gave her a sharp nod. "Alright, cousin, I guess there is nothing else to say except that I'm sorry, and that I wish you well on the journey ahead."

Brenna's face tightened with anguish and a touch of grief. "Thank you, Simeon. And I, too, wish you well on the journey ahead."

Cernunnos sensed this sudden emotion was because a chapter of her life was closing. He wanted to set Brenna's mind at ease, to tell her that she'd be stronger for leaving these people behind, but it wasn't his place to say that, not here and not now. There were too many people present, and he was bristling to get away to the safe harbor of what he knew and understood. Away from jealousies, desires, and materialistic gain—all that he'd hidden from years before.

At a nod from Simeon, and a curt command to carry Petre, the men moved forward to hoist Petre's dead weight over their shoulders and silently headed back the way they'd come, back toward the village. Cernunnos was darkly satisfied that they were carrying one of their own and not his woman.

Soon, they were alone. He breathed in his first relaxed breath since he'd come across them all and felt the commotion they'd left behind slowly easing upon the wind. The creatures and the insects began to move again at their natural pace, no longer tense and waiting, terrified of being caught in a skirmish that would have assuredly ended in death with their king at the fore.

Cernunnos turned to face Brenna, making a conscious effort to dampen his power. The otherworldly glow around his body dimmed, but he knew it would remain in his eyes. The tension around her face had lessened, and he sent her a tentative smile, the action unnatural but coming more easily than he'd believed. "I suppose you are wondering why I am here?" It was all he could think to say.

Brenna visibly swallowed. "I had been wondering if you were a figment of my imagination," she breathed.

The concession stopped him short. It told him more than she knew, and his heart began to race. "I am real," he returned softly. He couldn't help his feet moving to close the distance between them, or the hand that lifted from his side, fingers reaching for her.

She fixated on that movement, her eyes following his hand, and slowly, just like a newborn fawn, she trembled as his fingers finally found hers. He grasped that small fine-boned hand carefully, as if he held something so delicate he knew any amount of pressure would make her break, and said with everything he felt, "I do not know what this is between us. All I know is that I cannot stop thinking about you, and that I needed to follow you and find you. I had no idea what I would do when I saw you, but now, after witnessing what has just happened, it is clear that I cannot let you go." He squeezed her hand now, the nerves beginning to show as he said softly, "And you are coming back with me—to my forest."

Her mouth dropped open, shock crossing her features once again. "I...I—" She swallowed. "I do not know what to say. I can't deny that I feel something for you. Or that I, too, cannot stop thinking of you. But to return with you to your home? You are a god! I am a mortal druid. We are not suited —you heard them! It is madness! I—"

"No!" Cernunnos barked. "We *are* suited. It has been foretold. And, believe me, I am well aware of what is acceptable in this world and what is not. But I cannot deny this"—he waved his hand between them—"thing between us. You belong to me. It is as clear as night and day, the stars, and the turning of the sun. You are coming back with me. Now."

Without hesitation, Cernunnos turned to where he had first emerged from the trees and whistled sharply. At the command, Eiros appeared, his coat shimmering with iridescent light as his white form blurred into existence. The giant stag lifted his head and roared, a sound that had the birds lifting off from among the trees.

Brenna stumbled back a step, a small sound mewling from her throat, and Cernunnos tightened his grip again, leaning down to whisper, "It is okay, my lady. He is merely staking his claim as my second in command."

At her indrawn breath and stilted nod, he turned to the great white stag and barked sharply, "Eiros! Stop that. She is impressed enough without your bellowing!"

His stag looked at him, eyes narrowed in disgust. *"You ruin all my fun. I am merely impressing upon her what you give her with your offer. After all, she will also become my lady as well as yours."*

The comment stopped Cernunnos short. Yes, if Brenna came with him, she would be the queen of the forest, of all this domain. And he realized that he wouldn't have it any other way. He couldn't be with a woman who was not his equal, and with her soft heart and inherent skills, Brenna would earn that right all on her own—even before his creatures knew of her ability to converse with her tawny owl. "In that case, you will willingly carry her."

The stag lowered his head in agreement, no hesitation to his stance. For that, Cernunnos was thankful. Eiros had always followed him faithfully, and after spending the previous day arguing, he had finally convinced the stag that this woman was no passing fancy, that this was an inherent need that had to be fulfilled for him to go on.

And that one day he'd agonized over whether to follow her or not had been enough for him to understand that he couldn't let her go. And after witnessing him lose his mind, Eiros had also understood. So, with all due haste, they'd ridden out first thing that morning. And arrived not a moment too soon.

The reminder of what had just happened was enough to have his limbs tightening, his chest squeezing in preparation for another roar—but not with Brenna in his hands, not with her shining light by his side. He would protect that untarnished glow forever.

Turning to her again, Cernunnos said, "I know this is sudden, that this is wrong in the eyes of some, but I cannot deny what is between us, and I would like you to return with me to my home." He took a breath, mindful he had not asked her yet, and added softly, "Will you come?"

The offer was direct and sincere. He would pressure her no further; he could do no more.

Brenna stared at him, her gaze locking with his, and the connection between them was like a knife thrust into his chest—not of pain but like a lock turning. It had such a sense of rightness to it that he added, "Please."

The concession was one he'd never made before, and Brenna seemed to sense it, her body trembling again. Her mouth opened, and the words she uttered were breathless. "I will come with you."

Her response had his breath halting, his knees going weak, and for a moment no sound or movement escaped him. In that split second thereafter, he felt a smile such as never before light up his face. "Thank you."

Not giving her time to second-guess her response, he said to Eiros, "Bend for your lady."

The stag moved dutifully forward and dropped gracefully on his forelegs. Cernunnos kneeled and cupped his hands. "Please jump up, my lady."

Brenna hesitated for a moment before doing as requested. Her foot was light, her body even lighter, and Cernunnos felt his member twitch in anticipation of what she was like beneath her clothing—clothing he would one day rip from her body. He felt the truth of it arrow straight to his groin, and the agony of not unwrapping her now was almost his undoing. The path to that journey would be pleasurable itself, he knew it to his bones.

Putting that undeniable urge aside, he gently lifted her upon Eiros's back, then jumped up behind her, satisfied that he was in a position where he could hold on to her for their journey home.

He wrapped his arms around her waist and gently pulled her back against his chest. When she came willingly, softly, and the smell of her intoxicating scent wrapped around him, Cernunnos finally felt the tension he'd been carrying evaporate into the mist of the surrounding forest. With his heart pounding erratically in his chest at the significance of what he'd just won, Cernunnos turned Eiros in the direction of home. And as they took off at a steady canter, his precious cargo held securely in his arms, he did not fail to notice a tawny owl in the forest ahead, her wings spread out in soaring freedom.

DAGDA: A NEW DAWN

DAGDA

A NEW DAWN

CORINA DOUGLAS

DAGDA: A NEW DAWN

The fires roared, their flames licking into the ebony night. The resulting fireflies twinkled and danced on the crisp autumn breeze, caressing the dancers who yielded to the beat of the drums and the intoxicating trill of the pipes. Samhain was once again upon them, and everyone gathered had come to celebrate the lowering of the veils between the worlds. It was a time to reconnect with loved ones, a time of joy, a time of celebration.

Dagda moved with abandon, his head flung backward, his arms wide, as he embraced the whirling lights of the innumerable stars in the dark sky above. The drumbeats were a stampede in his blood, his temple pounding in time with his heart as the rhythm of the music carried him onward.

The night air was rife with the sounds of merriment—the crack of wooden cups being thrown together in numerous resounding cheers, the slosh of mead as it was dipped into barrels and tipped back without a sense of scarcity, the tinkle of laughter and soft conversation, the snap and crackle of countless fires blazing in the open meadow, and most obvious of all, the rhythmic slapping of flesh against flesh as the people succumbed to their base desires, taking whomever they wished to culminate with in this one night of freedom.

Dagda whirled again, his eyes on the trailing lights in the sky above when he felt the mead in his cup spill over the arm of his tunic. He paused, suddenly realizing his thirst and lifted the cup back up to his lips. As he tipped the contents back, he stumbled, and a smile stretched across his face as the world continued to whirl softly around him, even though he'd come to a standstill. The mead was taking over, fueling his bloodstream and inhibiting his movements.

Finally.

It had taken hours to reach this point—hours of careful, deliberate manipulation. For Dagda wanted to be drunk tonight. He wanted to dull the pain in his chest, that now familiar ache that threatened to loose his fists in a flying rage. He'd been well aware that tonight's festivities would not leave him such an opportunity, not when everyone was fixated on celebrating, and more importantly, falling into the pleasure of a sexual joining with whomever they damn well pleased. There would be no recriminations tonight by either party, no matter who they chose to fall together with. And tomorrow, when Samhain had ended, life would continue as it always did...until the following year.

But not for him. For him, the nightmare would continue, regardless of the occasion. His wife would be required to seal the promise of kingship at any time it was warranted, and in the most intimate of ways—by using her body as a vessel to legitimize the power of their new king...just like she was doing now.

Dagda grunted, the sound pained even to his own ears. Angry at the reminder he was trying his damndest to drown out, he abruptly turned to the nearest mead barrel again. Swooping his cup into the brown liquid, he brought it up to his lips and tipped the contents down in one fell swoop. Yet as he swallowed it down, the mead did nothing to diminish that last image of his wife.

He squeezed his eyes shut and hung his head, feeling the constriction in his chest bloom with renewed strength. *Breathe, man! Focus! Morrígan is only doing what she is required to do. She has a duty to fulfil.*

But the litany he'd repeated five times before felt meaningless tonight, empty. For he had seen the look on her face when she'd walked past him. How her blood-red lips had parted in anticipation of what her evening with their new king would bring. And there was no denying that the newly anointed High King Bres was beautiful—a glistening, golden male with flawless skin, of muscled breadth, and long, flaxen hair.

With the loss of Nuada's hand, their old king had been less than perfect, and so their people had turned their eyes to other candidates. Out of them all, Bres had been chosen. Half Fomorian, half Tuatha Dé Danann, he seemed the most natural choice to cement the rift between their two peoples. But Dagda had his doubts. From what he'd seen so far, Bres was a wolf in a sheep's skin. He was beautiful, yes, but he was most definitely vain, and the stories Dagda had heard did not give him confidence in the man's reign. He felt sure that time would tell; Bres would eventually show his true colors...but right now, he could do as he wished. And who he was doing was his wife.

What had angered Dagda more than he'd thought possible was the look in Bres's eyes as he'd turned to receive his trophy—utter delight and pure sin. And the look he'd sent Dagda thereafter perusing his wife had been pure provocation—as exemplified by the hand he'd swept behind Morrígan's back to clasp her ass in what could only be a possessive movement. His wife had immediately tensed, yes, and she had swiped his hand away with a hiss of outrage; but Dagda had also seen the glint of anticipation in her eyes, and he knew that the sexual challenge Bres offered would intrigue her. Dagda knew well that Morrígan liked to lead the sexual act, and if Bres was already trying to stamp his dominance over their union, there was no doubt she would meet that challenge head-on. And he was only too aware of *exactly* how his wife would respond during their coupling.

Dagda's fists clenched at the unfairness of it all. He—having to share *his* wife! Why Morrígan? Why his wife?

Yet he knew why. She was powerful beyond imagining, a true warrior, and not just on the battlefield but also in the level of her sexual prowess. To Morrígan, the act of sex was a weapon in itself. It enabled a transference of her power, and if the receiver could not handle who and what she was and the resulting power she had to give, they died. It was a true test for the leader of their people, and Dagda had not wished as fervently as he had before that Bres would fail that test this eve. Yet his wishes had gone unfulfilled, because only hours before, word had come that Bres had survived his first culmination with Morrígan, thereby cementing his new position as their king.

The confirmation felt like ashes in his mouth, because deep down, Dagda had known with a sinking feeling in his gut that Bres was more than capable of taking all that Morrígan had to give. It had been evident in his arrogant swagger and the confident way he carried himself into that fateful ceremony. It was another blade in Dagda's gut, another cut along the fragile bond that held him and

Morrígan together, and the sixth time he had to watch her leave that room with another.

Argh! He threw his cup into the mead barrel, the resulting spray of brown liquid sparkling in the firelight. Breathing through his nose, he began to count to ten, slowly, and he forcibly pushed that last image of Morrígan and Bres away. *Let it go, man. Tonight is a celebration. Take a little of that for yourself.*

Feeling a measure of his control return, Dagda turned to take in the surrounding revellers. They were gathered in a meadow close to his residence, the full moon plump overhead and the stars' bright beacons in the sky. The cool autumn air was rife tonight, but the numerous fires that were laid out in a shining blanket as far as the eye could see were doing a fantastic job of pushing it back. There were some five hundred people here tonight, and at a glance, he could tell that at least half of them were naked. The firelight flickered over their bodies, enticingly hugging the curve of a breast, the sharp planes of a toned stomach, a muscled buttock.

Most of the people gathered around him were druids, but his kin were also here—other gods who had chosen to celebrate with their children, Cernunnos and Cailleach, his two favorite siblings among them. The only one missing from the gathering was Morrígan. Again, a pining entered his blood, and the anger, the pain, the humiliation, the heartbreak—it all rose again, tearing his soul anew.

No, no, no! He could not escape it, no matter what he tried. It appeared alcohol would not be his savior tonight. He had to try something else…. Yet nothing came to him but the mead in front of him. So he reached out and filled his cup again and again until he felt the rhythm of the drums and the pipes yearning to carry him away. But before he could take more than three feet, a hand on his arm stopped him. He looked up, a warning on his lips, but the harsh words he was about to loose were swallowed when he saw his white sister.

"Dagda," Cerridwen said softly, her voice a soothing lilt over the sound of the music. "How are you this eve?"

"I am well, sister. As you can see,"—he spread his hands around him—"I am rejoicing with my people."

A small smile tilted her lips, and she inclined her head gracefully. "Just so, brother, and you look well for it." Her eyes searched his as she added, "Much better than this morning, I see."

He tensed. Cerridwen had been there as they'd crowned the new king. She had also watched as Morrígan led Bres from the room, and no doubt had seen his wife's eyes shaded with a lust she couldn't hide. He glibly lied, "I don't know what you are talking about, Cerridwen. I couldn't be happier that the Tuatha Dé Danann will be led by such a fine, perfect, young man."

The emphasis on perfection was not lost between them.

Her bright blue eyes considered him, and he felt the depth of her assessment as she pressed, "Even someone Morrígan admires?"

He couldn't hide his indrawn breath.

Cerridwen's gaze softened, and her lips twisted into a soft smile. "She is happy tonight, Dagda. Tonight, it does not feel like a chore."

Jaw clenching, he glanced away, his gaze skittering past her shoulders to a naked couple fornicating on the dewy grass behind them. The sight did nothing to calm him, his body tensing even further.

Cerridwen's soft voice cut through the red haze of his

memories. "You will also find something you are lacking tonight, brother."

He jerked as the words cemented, and he cut his gaze back to hers. "What do you mean?"

A mysterious smile held her lips. "A chance of happiness will be offered to you tonight...if you are open to receiving it."

Dagda swallowed. He knew, as they all did, that Cerridwen's words were not to be taken lightly. Like a lot of their siblings, his white sister was prophetic; she saw things that would come to pass. "What do you mean, Cerridwen? Speak plainly."

"You know I cannot, brother. The visions are cloudy for a reason."

"Then why tell me this at all?" he bit out in frustration.

She shrugged, her delicate shoulders lifting under her white dress. The breeze kicked up in that moment and her golden hair and white skirts billowed past her as she replied, "I am not our father, but I couldn't ignore how you are feeling. I can taste your grief like a ripe fruit permeating the air. It felt wrong to not share what I have seen. Take heart that a measure of happiness will be yours tonight, Dagda, but only if you will allow it."

His heart tripped. What did that all mean? And a measure of happiness—in what? With whom? He had to know, even if Cerridwen couldn't plainly tell him. He demanded, "Just answer me one thing then, Cerridwen—is my wife coming tonight?"

Her blue eyes instantly shadowed, and Dagda knew the answer even before she moved her head from side to side. "No, not her, but another. Someone you admire."

The response had his brow furrowing, more confused than ever. But before he could question his sister further,

Cerridwen had gone, her white dress a puff of cloud as she moved swiftly through the meadow, weaving in and out of their children until she was lost among the flickering shadows and twinkling fireflies.

HOURS LATER, Dagda was still moving, his body swaying to the beat of the drums. However, his feet had slowed their crazed dance, his body more languid now than frantic. The pace of the revelry had come down to a gentle simmer, and a lot of the dancers had fled, their naked forms flickering in the shadows as they found the person they wished to culminate with.

He took a generous swig from the wooden cup in his hand, swallowing the honeyed mead. As the cup was lowered from his lips, he caught sight of his wild brother—his tall, curved horns shining darkly in the fire's light—as he entered the forest on the edge of the meadow. He saw Cernunnos hesitate at the treeline, his form just visible as he tilted his head to the side. It looked as though he was in conversation with another.

Dagda squinted, trying to pierce the shadows. It surprised him to find it wasn't a person who had captured Cernunnos's attention but a creature—an owl to be exact. This was further cemented by the soft hoots that he heard on the breeze. And to Dagda, it looked and sounded as though the owl was talking back to his brother. *What the...?*

But before he could call out to Cernunnos, his brother was moving and in the blink of an eye, he was lost in the shadows of the silent giants. Dagda sighed softly in quiet defeat. It was well-known that his eldest brother preferred the animals and the solitude of the forest rather than spending time with their people, but that did not mean that his absence didn't hurt. Dagda missed their early days when they were mere boys kicking around and annoying their other siblings, when Cernunnos chose to spend his time with his family rather than in solitude.

Deciding that tonight he couldn't withstand any more sad memories, Dagda's gaze shifted from this brother, this time seeking one of his sisters. There! He caught sight of Cailleach's distinctive moonlight hair, wrapped in its tight, customary braid as she twirled around in a dance similar to his own moments earlier. Her bright silver eyes were wide, her face happy as a tinkle of laughter escaped her bow-red lips. She looked rich with happiness, rich with life, and his heart swelled to see her so open and carefree. Her usual shy demeanour was replaced with a wild abandon, no doubt helped along by the mead they'd downed.

He moved toward her, determined to spend what remained of the evening with Cailleach when two men, both young and limber, circled her with intent, one in front, the other behind—like crows to a feast. A protective rage immediately gripped Dagda's heart. She was his younger sister, and if he was honest, his favourite, and he felt a fierce protectiveness against any man who tried to deflower her. Cailleach was untouched, and he preferred to keep it that way. He took a step forward, one, then two, but before he could take a third, there came another hand on his arm, firm and strong, which pulled him to an abrupt stop.

His face twisted into a snarl. He whipped around to face the perpetrator. "Who is stupid enough to halt my movements on Samhain?" he growled.

But who he stared upon wasn't a warrior as he'd assumed, or even a male for that matter, but a whimsical, soft, delicate woman who glowed with a warmth that shone from within. His heart lurched as he recognized who she was—a woman who he'd discreetly watched far too many times; a woman who had his loins tightening every time he was within her presence. *Boann.*

She didn't shy from his harsh demand or the threat that was inherent, but instead offered him a blooming smile, warm and inviting. "Dagda, isn't it?"

Her voice was musical, the soft notes lush and soothing; a voice that he'd heard could make a man weep. Boann had a giddy smile on her lips, a slight sway to her body, as if she'd caught his arm in mid-flight. Her eyes sparkled with a mirth and mischief that most were portraying this eve, and at the sight of that innocence, Dagda's thoughts immediately lightened, his heart momentarily lifting the burden it carried.

Realizing that the silence was now dragging between them while he stared at her in a strange fixated awe, he bowed his head low and returned swiftly, "My lady, I apologize profusely. I assumed you were one of my children. To what do I owe the pleasure of having a woman so lovely as you stop me in my tracks?"

She smiled wider and it transformed her face into an artist's canvas, a masterpiece that stole his breath away. Her eyes sparkled a rich umber, and her long, dark hair fluttered in the light breeze, a halo that teased around her womanly body. She was an enigma, at once beautiful and feminine, while at the same time knowledgeable and wise. Their people loved her, for she was a goddess of poetry, fertility, knowledge, and creativity. She was also their previous king's wife.

The reminder had his gaze shifting past her shoulders; and there, sure enough, was her husband, Nuada, the recently besmirched former king of the Tuatha Dé Danann.

Dagda couldn't help lowering his gaze to the man's right arm, which was cradled against his chest in a white sling. A bandaged stump peeked through the cloth, right where his hand was supposed to be.

"I was watching you," she said with a mischievous grin, the words causing him to glance back at her. She angled her head toward the forest, in the same direction that Cernunnos had gone, adding, "I knew your intention was to follow your brother, so I thought I'd come and stop you. There is too much fun to be had to hide away so soon this eve."

She'd been watching him? For how long? And how had he missed her? Clearing his throat, he said in a voice raspier than he would have liked, "Tonight I had need of him."

One of her delicate brows lifted in question. "Why? It is well-known that Cernunnos does not like to take part in all this revelry."

"That is true, but tonight I needed his touch."

Her umber eyes glittered with surprise, and her gaze became intense. "A man's touch? But I thought you preferred women?" she blurted out.

He started, his mouth dropping. "What? No—yes! I mean, yes, I prefer women," he stammered. Then, taking a breath and feeling like an ass, he said more calmly, "What I meant to say is that I needed my brother to act as a distraction. I knew I could guarantee his undivided attention this eve...if he'd chosen to stick around."

She glanced around him then. "Why? Where is your wife? Surely, Morrígan could support you tonight?"

He caught the innuendo of the type of 'support' that Boann was talking about. Morrigan was noted for warming the beds of others, and very well so. Her sexual prowess was renowned by all, sung in bawdy and shining songs alike—

along with her victories in war. Oh yes, his wife had many
sterling qualities, and many duties that left his needs in the
dust.

Dagda cleared his throat. "Morrígan is otherwise
occupied tonight. She has duties to attend to."

Boann made a small noise, discreet but audible none-
the-less that it had his eyes cutting once again to hers as she
said softly, "So the Tuatha Dé Danann decided on Bres's
succession to the throne then? We missed the ceremony.
Nuada was...tied up with the healer."

Dagda nodded, accepting the obvious lie without
question. Nuada had lost his kingship because he'd lost his
hand. They all knew it. Just as they all knew that his wife,
Morrígan, was currently fornicating with another. The
words didn't need to be said and, in fact, there was nothing
else to say.

Boann shuffled on her feet, her light-yellow dress
swaying in the raw breeze as she added hurriedly, "But that
is nothing compared to the duties that Morrígan has to
fulfill. I am sorry."

He nodded, still quiet, and looked past her shoulder at
her husband again. Nuada was knocking his cup back,
swallowing the mead with wild indulgence. When he
lowered his drink, Dagda caught the slight shuffle of his feet
as the man stumbled sideways, knocking into the young,
nubile woman standing next to him, who was barely
clothed in the crisp autumn air.

Dagda couldn't help but wonder why he was dallying
with that woman when he was wed to the curvy beauty by
his side. Boann was stunning beyond belief and with a sweet
countenance to match.

"You are as trapped as she is, aren't you?" Boann asked
suddenly, cutting his musings short.

For a moment, he just blinked, but as he digested the comment, he felt the ashes of her pity. "Why do you say that?" he asked, his eyes intent on her face, which now had a rosy blush to it in recognition that she may have been too forward in her statement.

"I—I . . ." she broke off and looked down at her feet. Shuffling, then taking a breath, she glanced up and said with a forthrightness he hadn't seen or heard before, "Because I understand being married to duty, and having that responsibility can strain any relationship." Blowing out a breath, she turned, catching sight of her husband, and added, "Nuada and I...I have often believed that we share the same relationship that you do with Morrígan—tied to duty and other's desires rather than our own."

When she turned back to face him, and he saw both the sincerity and the despair there, Dagda swallowed, pushing back the sudden lump in his throat. "You and Nuada are growing apart?" Is that why he was with that other woman and not with this gorgeous woman in front of him?

She glanced back at him, regret and a haunting sadness in her eyes. "He no longer sees me. I am simply a common fixture in his support network. His wife, yes, but no longer his lover. There are many others who would do whatever required to warm his bed at night—and he will let them. The loss of his hand has only reinforced that need to have others fawn over him, especially now that he has lost the kingship."

Dagda was stunned. He hadn't seen or heard of Nuada straying from his wife, but then he hadn't seen him in nigh on two years. Dagda could still remember the man's wedding to Boann, a spectacular, whimsical occasion that he thought had truly showcased the love they'd shared. He'd thought theirs had been a true match—one like his and Morrígan's had been. But given what his relationship with his wife had now become, Dagda supposed that anything was possible. There was no denying that Nuada's role had been a heavy one, leading their people in war against the Fomorians not once but twice—and with the second resulting in the loss of his hand and subsequently his kingship.

Dagda considered her, wondering if Boann had initiated their withdrawal, or had it been Nuada? By Boann's account, it was her husband that had sought more. And what exactly Nuada looked for that was more than Boann could give, Dagda didn't know, for the woman before him was perfect in every way—curvy, mischievous, fun, playful, and warm.

Boann was watching him closely, and Dagda realized he hadn't replied. "I'm sorry," he said simply. "I don't understand why he would stray from a woman such as you."

Her eyes widened at his compliment and her features softened in quiet thanks at his support. "I am sad and have shed many tears," she admitted, "but I have finally admitted defeat, for what has broken between us cannot be fixed. There have been too many transgressions to forgive his actions."

"There really is no hope of a reconciliation?"

She shook her head. "Not a true one. We are still wed but it is in name only and I am weary of the game we are forced to play. But tonight, there are no restrictions. As you know, Samhain is a time for celebration, a time of no inhibitions, and tonight, Nuada will do as he pleases. The veils will be lowered between the worlds and also between us." She indicated the woman that Nuada now had his arm around. "It is only a matter of time before he takes off with that one, and on this occasion he won't be discreet about it."

Dagda inhaled sharply. Oh yes, if Boann had been

subjected to this for the last few years then she would well understand how it felt to watch one you love be with another. He felt trapped—trapped and hurt. So hurt that it felt as though a blunt knife was twisting in his side, tearing his guts apart, just like when he watched Morrígan lead each new ruler to her bed. *Just as she was doing now...*

He considered Boann, wondering at her position and his own at the same time. Again, he couldn't help but see how she blazed like the fires that burned around them. She was stunning, a curvaceous beauty that perpetually glowed from within. And her countenance, it was sweet and kind. She also had intelligence, an intuitiveness that he knew had served Nuada well time and time again as she'd stood by his side. He couldn't understand it. How had Nuada turned from what she had to offer? Certainly, that woman on his arm was nothing compared to Boann.

He impulsively reached out and grasped her hand, twining his fingers with hers tightly. "The words seem irrelevant, and I know they won't take your pain away, but for what it's worth, I'm sorry."

Her eyes went wide, unshed tears visibly welling in the corners. "Thank you," she whispered. "And for what it's worth, Morrígan is a lucky woman."

The words were a lance, both painful and heartwarming. Dagda squeezed her fingers. "And Nuada is, too, if only he could see that. I am sorry, Boann."

Her eyes shone. "Me too, Dagda. Me too."

Releasing her hand, he said huskily, "Enjoy your evening and may you find happiness in tonight's festivities."

Her smile was shaky, yet still warm at the same time. "And you," she whispered in reply before turning to walk away, her long, yellow dress whispering around her curvaceous body in a silky caress.

Dagda watched her disappear from view, conscious that he could feel his heart tripping in his chest, and he couldn't help but wonder if Boann was the one that he was supposed to spend the night with.

HOURS LATER, he was kicking himself at his stupidity. Of course the woman he'd claim tonight wouldn't be Boann! He hadn't seen or heard anything from her since their chance meeting earlier that night. They had a connection, yes, and a shared understanding, but nothing more. He was looking into things. Cerridwen was known to be wrong at times; it was likely that tonight had been one of those times.

The sky was lifting, changing in color from a deep indigo to a hint of a blush to the east. Dagda could feel the temperature plummet, and a soft gray mist was permeating the air. It would be a cool fall day, but one that held a hint of sunshine—a new dawn.

The revelry had been reduced to a mere trickle, with only a handful of people still around. Nuada had left long ago, slipping away with no sense of discretion into the boughs of the nearby forest. The hand he'd lowered to rest around the waist of the nubile woman he'd been familiar with earlier had been a blatant proclamation of how their night would end.

His head pounded from the act of imbibing too much mead and his feet were sore, but it was his heart that felt bruised the most, battered and pummeled with repeated abuse. He knew as the new dawn rose that he couldn't carry on like he had. Something needed to change.

Dagda could feel the trickle of the otherworldly beings who'd shared in the night's festivities now slowly winking out as they disappeared back behind the veil. He'd said his goodbye's earlier to the comrades he'd lost in the war with the Fomorians, and also to his siblings too. The hole in his chest only felt larger and emptier right then, as he understood it would be another cycle of the seasons before he saw their wraiths again...and in another year, yet more would be on the other side of the veil. Life and death, like all things, were inevitable; a cycle of birth and growth that quickly melded into death and decay. But it was the way, the balance of life, and Dagda was more than aware that he, too, would one day fall victim to that same cycle.

But not today. Today was a new dawn and he needed to find a new path.

A giggle slipped out of the mist to his right, and he decided there and then that he'd done enough moping over the course of the night. Morrígan would still be busy, so there was no need to hurry home. Besides, she would welcome the extra space to finish up her...duties. So instead of turning toward home, he veered left into the forest and began his trek toward his lodgings at Glen Etin, aware that it would be as empty as his arms had been last night.

No! I can't think like that any longer! It was a cruelty to continue to dwell on what Morrígan had done last night. He had to let it go. *It was her duty,* he told himself again. *Just as I have my own to attend to.*

It was ironic really, that he'd come to love Morrígan. He could still recall their joining. Neither of them had wanted it. Neither of them had hungered for the other, yet they'd been forced into marriage in order to protect their people. Their combined power—ignited through the act of sex—granted their people such power that they had squashed their enemies. And somewhere along the way, he'd fallen in love with who and what she was—and she, him. The overlong linger of her eyes, the lasting touch, that squeeze of his hand when he felt a semblance of emotional pain—they were all signs that she loved him. And he her—with a fierceness that had taken his breath away.

But their love had been tested right from the start. There was no denying it. In the last ten years, that love had been weakened by the stares and the whispers, by the cool smiles of the men or women that Morrígan led away with a sashay of her hips, by the knowledge of everyone around him that they knew his wife gave her body freely to others just as much as she gave it to him.

Boann was right. He was trapped in this marriage, blinded by the emotional cruelty that he endured every time his wife led another to her bed. He was a wreck; half of who he was, insecure and melancholy. He was also lonely. Far too lonely for a man of his caliber. He was changing, and into someone that he wasn't proud of.

Dagda felt hopeless at that moment but also more powerful than he'd felt in a long time, because he understood then and there that this way of life couldn't continue. He knew the power to reverse his position was in his hands. He held the reins of life, and if he didn't take control and push his steed on another path now, the future laid before him was already written in the stars—years of more pain, heartbreak, and humiliation.

Cerridwen had given him hope last night that someone in the coming days would help to ease his pain. That someone would offer him the solace he needed—the closeness that he craved with his wife.

His steps now felt purposeful, less heavy and aimless as he wandered through the forest, carefully sidestepping slumped forms, either alone or entwined with others. The peoples soft snores permeated the air, mixing with the newly arisen sounds of bird calls and animals and insects underfoot. The world was awakening and he supposed he was too. He picked up the pace now, almost at a trot as he headed further into the forest toward his lodgings.

The wooden construction was upon him before he knew it, but what stopped him in his tracks at the sight of it was the fact that his chimney was smoking. Had Morrígan returned already? Had she, too, experienced her own epiphany at how they were pulling apart? Did she miss him as much as he missed her? He raced inside, but who he found standing in front of the fire wasn't his wife...but Boann.

A small, tentative smile was on her lips, those umber eyes bright with a heavy dose of nervousness as well as determination.

"Boann?" His tone evidenced his confusion.

"Dagda," she returned in that soft, velvet voice.

When she offered nothing further, he asked, "What are you doing in my home?"

She ducked her eyes to the floor. "Isn't it obvious?"

He stared at her, feeling his brows tighten. What? He didn't understand. Or...did he? Was she here for what he assumed she was here for? But what of their discussion last night? What of how she felt about Nuada? Choosing the path of honesty, he said softly, "When a woman enters a man's home, they only desire two things: companionship and sex, or to steal from them. Are you here to steal my cauldron, or is it the former, Boann?"

"What do you think?" she returned smoothly, her eyes now back on his.

He assessed her, wondering at her sudden uncertainty. Could he really assume she was here for him? And just as he'd desired last night since hearing what Cerridwen had to say? He took a chance. "I would like to think that it's not the cauldron, Boann, not when you have similar powers."

Her soft tinkle of laughter was light yet trembly, as if she were testing her own confidence. "That is true," she returned, "but we all wish for more power at times, don't we, Dagda?"

He swallowed and took a step toward her, one of his hands lifting by his sides. His fingers reached for her cheek. She didn't move, but her face lost that smile and her body became as still as stone. She allowed his movement, and when his fingers touched her soft skin, he felt his own body become rigid. This was happening. Here and now. He felt it right in his chest. It wasn't time to speak in innuendoes any longer; he felt too raw for light banter anyway, especially after last night.

"Are you here then, Boann, to claim a measure of happiness for yourself?" he breathed, his voice low but audible in the still silence.

Her eyes did not leave his, unflinching, and her voice was stronger than he would have imagined when she in turn breathed out, "Yes. I crave the touch of a man who would love me."

He froze. "And you think I love you, Boann?"

Her head moved slightly from side to side, her eyes still not leaving his. There was no flinch in her gaze, no apology or cowering. "No, you do not love me," she answered in return, "but you will. I see it."

His stomach plummeted then, bottoming out to his feet, and he felt his vision reel at her admission. He would love her? More than Morrígan? Right then, he didn't think it was possible. But then, like Cerridwen, Boann was also touched by the gift of sight, blessed with visions of the future. And from what he'd heard, her visions were accurate almost every time. "Is that of your making or mine, Boann?" he asked softly. "Because you know I still love my wife, don't you?"

She nodded. "I know, Dagda. But that love you hold for her is a mere flame to what it once was. You hold on to the memory of your initial love, to the promise of what it could have been. If you are honest with yourself, you will realize that that flame has been spluttering for many seasons, and the only reason you hold on to it still is because of the promise of those initial memories. It took me time to see that I did the same, time to see that I feel differently about Nuada now compared to what I did then. I was trapped and stuck in a cycle of loneliness and heartbreak. That does not mean that I do not love Nuada, but rather that I love his memory and what we once were...just like you will come to remember Morrígan."

He didn't like her words or her theories. Dagda hated her for telling him what he thought he felt and knew, and his hand clenched on her cheek, his fingers imprinting against her soft skin. She gasped, a tiny little noise that parted her lips, but she did not complain, merely waited, looking at him. He felt the challenge in that stare, as if she'd said the words aloud—that he had to believe her. That she was right.

They remained like that, stuck in stasis, staring into each other's eyes until eventually he released her, taking a step back. He couldn't deny that the truth she'd said aloud was already emblazoned across his heart. He'd felt its coming even before Samhain, felt its burn as he'd watched Morrígan lead their new leader away. What Boann had just said aloud was what he'd shied away from—what he'd known with this morning's new dawn.

His head dropped, his hands falling to his sides. Defeat

felt heavy in his chest, as well as a profound sadness. He'd lost a love he'd thought was true—a love that he'd believed would see them through until they crossed into the Other. But duty had slowly destroyed that love by the role that Morrígan had played, and he was not a man who could drop all sense of self-worth by continuing to allow it to happen. He was the Dagda; jovial, fun, and happy—not this melancholy, half-alive Celtic god who meekly allowed all to bed his wife. His wife—the one who should solely be his!

Yes, Boann had it right. He still loved Morrígan, but when that emotion flowered in his chest, it wasn't an image of who Morrígan was now, but of who she once was when their love had first blossomed—when her role only entailed bedding him alone to attain a shared power. But with the end of that first war with the Fomorians, she had become their Sovereign Goddess, and her sexual union was deemed more important to the future of their people than his needs had been. And even though Morrígan claimed it was her duty, she had made the choice to accept that role rather than decline it. Looking back, Dagda knew that was the first step toward what was now their inevitable parting.

"Dagda?" Boann cut into his musing, her voice tentative now. "Are you okay?"

He shook his head, still refusing to meet her gaze.

It was her hand that reached out now, small and fine-boned, delicate blue veins marbling her porcelain skin. The strength of her grasp surprised him as she gripped one of his hands, her fingers entwining with his. "It hurts, doesn't it? Seeing the truth for what it is."

He said nothing but he did not turn away from her comfort.

"Nuada and I, we are ahead of you and Morrígan. We knew the truth of it within the first few months of our union. But you and Morrígan, you are too tied to your duties, too consumed with the tasks laid before you. I know you cannot leave her; your marriage is cemented like ours is until you cross into the Other. But I have seen the future and I know what is to come. This emotional parting will hurt, but not as much as you believe right now. Not as much as what you have already experienced in the last decade. In hindsight, your separation is inevitable, as is Nuada's and mine."

"Is that why you're here?" Dagda suddenly asked her, head whipping up. "To offer solace as we go through similar paths in life?"

She shook her head. "No, that is not why I am here. I am here because you hurt, but also because of my own selfish reasons. I saw you on the day of my wedding for the first time, and even though I'd just been married to Nuada and was supposed to be irrevocably in love with him, I felt something fly through me swift and sure when I first laid eyes on you. I can't describe it, but I knew it was wrong—especially on the day I was married to the man I was in love with. I denied that feeling and those emotions for years, but my eyes have always strayed to yours when in a room, Dagda—to a man that they shouldn't. I've felt the potential of our union for a long time, and I denied it as much as I could, refusing to accompany Nuada to your gatherings. But I can't deny these feelings any longer, not when you, too, are hurt and drowning. There is something between us I crave, something you have that I need...and the reverse of that is also true."

Dagda felt speechless. He'd never dreamed that Boann felt this way, especially because he'd been well aware that she hadn't accompanied Nuada on the occasions he'd visited his home. He remembered feeling that sense of disappointment when she hadn't been with him, and he'd written it off as an appreciation for a beautiful object, an appreciation for her intelligent conversation and whimsical beauty. But had it been something more? He couldn't deny as he stood next to her now that he felt more than a tingle of desire.

She was luminous in the new dawn light streaming through his bedroom window, shining like a bright beacon. Her features were soft yet open, and her honesty was fresh and welcome. He had had enough of politics and snide innuendoes. It wasn't his scene, not like it was Morrígan's. His wife had been bred to lead a court, bred to be a leader, and she played the role naturally.

Dagda was conscious that Boann was waiting, her lips slightly parted, a hopeful light in her sparkling eyes, and he hesitated, realizing that what Cerridwen had said last night really had come true—Boann was offering him a chance at happiness, a chance to find something that he alone could cherish. He could feel the quickening in his loins, the anticipation of their joining, but he was conscious that this connection they held was more than physical. It was also emotional, an understanding laid on shared foundations, each of them burned by the love they had for another—a love that had died in the face of duty.

He told himself that Boann deserved the respect of an honest response. His gaze ran carefully over her face. Her skin was as soft as down under his fingers, warm and inviting, and now illustrating a slight blush against her porcelain palette. "Boann, you have given me so much just now, and a lot of what I hadn't thought I needed. Our meeting last night was short, but it held a lasting impression on me. You parted the veil that I'd been hiding behind; you made me see what it is my life with Morrígan has become. I realized that what I've been doing is not living, that what I've been feeling is not happiness, and who I've become is not someone I am proud of. You were right. The love that Morrígan and I shared was crippled from the start. We enjoyed a brief interlude of true love, reciprocated by us both, but watching her lead others to her bed has destroyed my confidence in our bond. I cannot stomach it any longer, and I just needed someone to point that out in order to move forward."

Her features had turned hopeful, her eyes sparkling even more than before. She seemed to be holding her breath. "And?" she breathed. "What of my invitation?"

He felt the warmth of her breath travel over his wrist, and he moved his hand to slide slowly behind her head, twining his fingers into her dark brown locks as he leaned in close to say against her lips, "And I accept your invitation to find a measure of happiness. I think it would be a crime if we did not find solace in each other."

She pulled back sharply, her mouth now inches from his. "Solace? Is that all?" she shot back. "You believe I will be a vessel to disguise the hurt you go through while your wife beds another?"

His other hand reached out to grasp her shoulder and he stared right into her eyes as he said, "No. Solace is a small part of the equation, for desire and a sense of admiration were always the first two emotions that I felt when I first saw you. Those emotions haven't dimmed, Boann, but rather strengthened in the last twenty-four hours, and after this discussion, I'm hopeful that we will find not only solace but also love in each other's arms."

Her face came alight and a smile such as he'd never seen on any woman bloomed across her lips. "Well in that case,

Dagda, let us use the opportunity afforded us right now to begin the path to healing."

His answer wasn't verbal, because with one last image of his wife in his head—entwined with another in their bed—he wordlessly tugged Boann close and captured her lips in a searing promise to make good on that path.

WINTER SOLSTICE

Winter Solstice

Corina Douglas

CHAPTER 1
TRITUS
3RD CENTURY BC, ANCIENT SCOTLAND

Cailleach came back from her work of wielding wild weather and storms in the soft, hushed whisper of the hide lifting and closing. Her feet didn't make a sound as she hung up her hammer and unlaced the heavy robe that lay around her shoulders.

Tritus remained quiet and still in the bed as she walked over to the fire pit and had a small bite to eat. Cailleach barely grazed the meal he'd left her, for after only two short bites and swallows, she was done and off to wash her face in the chuckling stream.

The fire crackled and popped quietly in the middle of the cavern, casting a golden, warm glow over her petite form. Cailleach might be small of stature, but she carried a mountain of power that contradicted her size. Many had learned the hard way that his woman was not to be trifled with. He observed her quietly as she finished her ablutions and then moved to their pallet.

Tritus lay still as a stone as she stood over him in the near darkness. But that position was hard to maintain when a hard jolt of desire rippled over his skin as the dress she wore swished to her feet in an elegant drop of sound, leaving her milky skin and slim body a feast for his eyes. His breath hitched, his groin twitching, and before he knew it, his member was standing ramrod straight, straining against the furs.

Cailleach let out a small giggle. "Still awake, dearest? Did I not satisfy you earlier in the day? I thought the time we spent on the carlin stone would have eased any cravings until the morrow."

His hand reached out for her, snagging her wrist, and he tugged her soft, pliant body on top of his—right where he wanted her but not where he needed her. Not yet. His tongue seemed stuck to the roof of his mouth, and he forced it to relax, his eyes taking in her gorgeous face. For the umpteenth time, he blessed the gods for this woman as he said, "I will never be satisfied when it comes to you, Cal. You never quench my thirst, merely bank the flames."

The smile caressing her lips arrowed straight to his heart as she bent down and kissed him. Her lips were lush yet demanding; a sweet, intoxicating mix. Tritus let their tongues dance together, his hands unable to stop roaming over her body. Her skin was warm under his touch, something he was always in awe of. It appeared that Cailleach never felt the cold, even when the wind was bitterly chill and the act of breathing would produce a white wisp of cloudy air before him.

His woman, this Goddess of Winter, was everything she conveyed—a deity of unparalleled raw power and infinite courage. Like a sharp-edged sword, she was beautiful yet vicious. But for all her outward confidence, her reign as the Winter Goddess was ultimately a duty she was condemned to fulfill, an obligatory mantle of power that came with the knowledge that this world was a never-ending cycle of life and death. It fit uneasily around her shoulders like a misshapen cloak.

Cailleach melted into his touch, one of her hands slipping between their bodies to push the furs aside. Her gasp was audible when she found he was just as naked as she.

A smile tipped his lips as her wide, silver eyes met his. "I've been waiting for you," he murmured, tightening his hold across her back.

Her fingers were bold as she palmed him in her hand. "I can tell."

The words were mischievous, all traces of her prior exhaustion gone, and Tritus suddenly decided that what he'd intended to say to her could wait until the fire within him had been quenched. He could also feel her need, the signs Cailleach no longer hid from him—the hitched breathing, the restless movement of her legs as they twined around his, the slight tilt of her hips as she tried to get closer, and the gentle swelling of her breasts as they pressed against his chest. His woman had needs, and he was there to satisfy them.

For a long moment, there was nothing but the sound of flesh sliding against flesh, a throaty groan, a soft gasp. And when Tritus finally slipped inside her, he held her close and rocked her gently in a sweet embrace, his eyes never leaving hers as he poured everything he felt for her into their linked gaze. The tears glistening her cheeks with their joined release brought a pleasure-pain that only briefly satisfied the yearning he had for her.

When their breathing returned to normal, Tritus tucked Cailleach close to his side, wrapping his arm protectively around her shoulders. The fire emitted more soft crackles and a gentle hiss, bathing them in a warm cocoon of privacy.

With their bodies replete and his lover boneless and quiet, Tritus decided now was the time to share what was on his mind.

Nerves fluttered in his stomach as he wet his lips, but he forced the words to come. "Cal?"

"Hmmm?" came her soft, sleepy reply.

His mouth suddenly dry, Tritus hesitated, but before he could begin, she spoke.

"Before meeting you, this feeling of desire was always a mystery to me," she mused, reaching out to rub a hand over his chest. "I could not understand why my siblings would shirk their duties or forget all else when they were captured by another. But after meeting you and experiencing this feeling myself, I now have great empathy for them. I can understand why they would forget all else but the need to satisfy this call of the flesh."

Tritus felt she expected him to laugh at her response, but the words cut him to the quick. "Don't cheapen what we have, Cal. What I feel for you—what we create when we join together—it is more than just a claiming of our bodies. Its strength lies in the emotions you elicit, in how I feel around you, and who you make me want to be. It is not at all about scratching an itch!"

Her head lifted off his shoulder, and her sparkling, silver eyes pierced his as she laughed softly. "All right, it was said out of turn. I apologize, Tritus. You're right; what we have is more than I'd ever thought possible." She laid her head back down on his chest, one hand stroking down the planes of his stomach as she admitted, "I am still coming to terms with what we have—what *this* is. It consumes and frightens me all at the same time. You've given me unimaginable happiness and a purpose outside of my duties. I have no idea how I once lived without you. Life is…more than it ever was before."

He knew exactly what she was saying. "I understand, Cal. I feel the same way." He tilted her chin toward his and pressed a hard kiss to her lips. The action stirred his groin again, his body tensing, heart and blood once again pounding through his body, and he groaned. "By the Mother, Cal! You are a temptation I cannot resist."

Her lips curved against his as she teasingly grazed them over his own. "I find that I do not want that to change, lover; I quite enjoy the moments of the flesh." Her hand trailed down his chest again and deliberately, unerringly, between his legs. Her hard stroke had him once more going stiff as a board.

He groaned again. "You are a witch," he hissed between clenched teeth. "But tonight, I must show restraint. There was a reason I waited up for you."

"You mean for more than what we just shared?" Cailleach cut in with a raised brow. She laughed coquettishly, like a young girl on the cusp of full womanhood, a girl who has learned the secrets of her own body. Then, reading his nervous silence, she pressed a hand against his chest and pushed back to stare at him closely. Her face was golden in the light of the fire, her hair a burning curtain of moonlight as it swung to cradle her high cheekbones. "This sounds serious."

Tritus reached out a hand to cup her cheek. "It is serious. I've come to notice the turning of the seasons. It is almost midwinter. Across the salty sea, in Gaul, my people take the time to celebrate the last days of the longest nights. We celebrate the rebirth of the sun and its perilous journey to bring life and light to the land once again. It is a wondrous time,

Cal, celebrating this momentous event. It's filled with magic and the excitement of youth. I can still remember the first time I was old enough to join in the solstice festivities." Tritus smiled at the memory, his eyes on his woman but his vision elsewhere, remembering the little boy he used to be, eyes wide with awe as he watched the preparations for the twelve-day festival.

Cailleach lay back down beside him, but at a distance that allowed them to maintain eye contact. "You are talking of Yule, aren't you?" she whispered, one of her hands now tangling in his long, dark hair. "The time that my people celebrate my waning power. The turn of the season."

Her words and her soothing fingers against his scalp cut his reverie short, and Tritus refocused his gaze on hers. "Yes and no," he said softly, an awareness at his neck that told him he needed to tread carefully here. "We do celebrate the same festival, it is so; but I do not believe you should associate this event with your waning power. The seasons will change regardless of your assistance, and the sun will continue to rise whether winter comes or goes. What my people celebrate is the earth's change toward the light, yes, but it's more than that, Cal—it is a time to come together with loved ones, a time to stop the bone-weary work we are subject to day in and day out, a time to rejoice with others, and a time to remember those we have lost. It is tradition."

He rolled to his side, propping up his head with one hand as he reached out to touch her hip with the other. His fingers curled against the bone, his hold firm and claiming. There was always a need to touch, to slide his hand along her skin. He didn't halt that proprietary need, and neither did she.

Yet her next words were edgy, strained. "And are you bringing this up because you would like to continue this tradition? Would you like to visit a village and participate in the holiday cheer?"

Her body had gone rigid under his hand now, and Tritus suddenly realized she'd misinterpreted where he was going with all this. "No, Cal, I do not want to visit them alone!" He sighed. "I've made a mess of this, haven't I?"

He moved closer and pulled her toward him, his arm going all the way around her back to tangle in her thick, moonlight hair. Holding her serious silver gaze, he said clearly, "I want *us* to participate in the holiday cheer. As in, you and me, together. I want us to have our own traditions, a melding of our values. I've been thinking on it for a while, Cal, and the only tradition I hold a sense of attachment to is Yule. With the change in seasons and with the break you are afforded in your duties, it makes sense to spend that time together. In the short time I spent at that druid village before we met, I became aware that your people also celebrate this momentous change in the seasons, and I would like us to continue that tradition—together."

Her face had changed as he'd stumbled along, the tense cant to her features relaxing as she understood that he didn't want to celebrate Yule alone. And now, with one of her eyebrows arched, a suspicious glint came to her eye. "And is there more to this celebration that you are holding back? Is there an end that you wish to achieve? Because I'm sure that if you heard of how my people celebrate Yule, then you would have also heard it is a time of fertility."

Tritus felt his heart kick in his chest. And not from the truth of her comment, because he knew well that Yule also brought luck with fertility, but because her voice wasn't as warm as he'd hoped it would be at the prospect of what they now broached—the subject he'd wanted to discuss the most. The idea of a child had been on Tritus's mind more and more these last few months—another soul to share their happiness, to amplify what it was that he and Cal shared. He supposed it was the pendant that had done it, seeing it nestled so possessively between her breasts.

He was the first to admit that since they'd consummated their relationship, he'd been a territorial beast, overprotective and passionate. He had, however, restrained himself from being controlling. Tritus wasn't stupid; because as much as Cailleach showed him her vulnerability, he knew he was the only one to see that side of her. The only one she had opened her heart to. He was glad he made her happy, and he wanted to see her even more so, but observing the pendant against her chest every day had him thinking of what else could one day lie there...and potentially make them even happier. A child would be the epitome of their love, a welcome addition he'd cherish. And knowing what he knew of Cal, Tritus understood deep in his soul that she would make a wonderful mother.

The idea had been solidified during his last journey to the nearby village. While selling his wares, Tritus overheard the men talking of their plans to bring in the Yule log, readying themselves for the coming winter solstice. The news shocked him at first, for it was late autumn at the time, and the midwinter feast had felt a long way off. But then he remembered the traditions that came with the seasonal change, the months of planning they required, and he'd had a yearning for those old feelings again—the anticipation and magic of time spent with family and friends as they rejoiced and reveled in the memories of the loved ones they'd lost.

An old man with a grizzled beard had jabbed one of the younger men in the ribs, a wide smile stretched across his aged face as he'd teased, "You be getting ready early so ye woman is well prepared for the lovin' she'll be receivin', I suppose, Finn?"

The young man's face reddened as he stammered, "I ain't laying with her just for sport, Yemen. I have good intentions, ye know. She is a woman of me heart. Always has been."

The old man had clapped him on the shoulder. "I'm just jesting, Finn. I know ye intentions are pure. It's the other young'uns without a woman I be worried about. Come Samhain next year, and we'll have fatherless sprogs running 'round again. It's good that ye men have ye sport, but you must be sure the outcome of such sport doesn't make the woman ye choose bear ye bairns on 'er own. There was too many bairns last year that no one claimed, and I can only take so much under me wing now me daughter has brought her own brood home."

Finn nodded vigorously. "I know, Yemen, and it's you I must thank for steering me on the path of celibacy until I knew my choice for certain. I can promise ye that any bairn we are lucky to conceive this winter solstice will be fathered and claimed by me."

The old man had smiled at Finn with a big toothy grin. "Good. I have taught ye well then—or I suppose me wives have." Yemen chortled mercilessly at the young man's features that were now puce and nudged him in the ribs. "Come by and see me later if ye will; I have some tips on how to please ye woman if ye think you're not too cocky to learn some secrets from an old man."

Finn reddened even further, but Tritus could see by the light in his eyes and the tone of his voice that the young man was eager to take up old Yemen's offer, and he'd confirmed his suspicions by replying, "Aye, I not be too proud to hear what ye know. After all, what other man in this village can boast thirty grandchildren?"

Yemen chuckled. "Easily done if ye can please four wives, lad."

The old man then turned back to Tritus with a big grin on his face and finished his trade, switching a handful of oat seeds for one of the new, sharp daggers he had made only last week. With a nod and a jaunt in his step, Yemen had returned to his roundhouse on the village edge.

Tritus watched him go before serving the rest of the men who had come to trade with him. As he exchanged his weapons and pendants for more seeds and tunics, and even a delicate bone comb, a sudden immersive thought had churned in his mind, stirring his blood. It was then that he was struck by the thought of having a child with Cailleach —a winter solstice baby. Someone they'd love and cherish. Someone to complete their circle and enrich the happiness they shared.

But as he now stared at Cal, who had again tensed beside him, a pinched look to her features, Tritus wondered if he had erred with that idea.

The Winter Goddess cleared her throat and suddenly sat up, pulling at the furs to cover her luscious nakedness. That move alone had a flutter of nerves settling in Tritus's stomach. *Too soon,* he thought. *Much too soon.*

"What is it, Cal?" he asked gently, reaching for her hand. This time, it felt stone cold in his.

Her words were small, brittle. "Am I not enough, Tritus? Is that it?"

His jaw dropped. "No, Cal, of course not! You are more than enough. More than life itself. I feel—" He broke off, groping for the right words. They all felt inadequate. "I feel *I* am not worthy of *you*."

Her brows drew together. "We've been over this already. Do not bring that up again, Tritus. Please, tell me what is really on your mind."

He jerked upright, matching her pose with his own, and reached out to hold both her hands in his. "I'm not doing a very good job of this, am I? What I'm trying to say, albeit inadequately, is that I would like us to have a child. It would bring me much joy, and I think you'd make an excellent mother."

Cailleach had gone as still as stone. "A child?" she whispered.

He nodded, his fingers tensing on the fine bones of her hand. "Yes. A child. Yours and mine."

Tritus waited, heart beating erratically, sure she could hear its pounding in the tense silence. His statement stretched, the words hanging between them. "Cal?"

She swallowed, her throat bobbing. "I—I...you have surprised me," she finally shared in a small voice.

Tritus snorted, recognizing the bombshell his proposal must have been if she was not thinking along the same lines. "I suppose I have. Although, I assumed a woman thought of these things before a man," he softly teased.

When she didn't respond, not even lifting a corner of her mouth, he tugged her hands, silently requesting she look at him. When her silver gaze raised and captured his, Tritus said softly, "Is the idea abhorrent to you, my love? If it is, please know that I will be happy if it were just the two of us. It's just that you make me feel more than I've ever felt before. You make me dream of a great life together. I—"

"Stop!" she hissed, one of her fingers now pressed tightly against his lips. "You do not need to explain yourself. Your intent is clear enough. I just...I am not sure if I am ready,

Tritus. That and the fact that I have no idea if I can have a child."

He paused, watching her closely. "Can't...or won't?"

Her eyes flared liquid silver, the irises swirling and coalescing with the temper that rose in her blood. "Can't, Tritus. I have never lied to you."

He shook his head. "I don't understand. How do you know that you can't have a child?"

Her lips pressed into a line, and she looked away, her gaze now focused on the fire that continued to crackle softly in their warm haven, a mockery of the atmosphere now shared between them. Not for the first time, Tritus thanked the gods for this cave. Its walls protected not only his woman, but also provided a place for them to celebrate their love and desire and their precious time together, ensuring all intruders and their prying eyes were kept away.

"Cal?" he prompted in the face of her continued silence. "Why can you not have a child?"

She shuddered and, keeping her gaze on the crackling fire, said in the merest whisper, "Duty comes before all else in this lifetime, Tritus. My father is most possessive of his children; the Custodian of Creation decided he did not want to deal with numerous personalities that held gifts of his making. As such, he curses those of us who get with child."

"Curses?"

Licking her lips, Cailleach explained, "If I fall pregnant —and that's a big *if*, Tritus—I have been told I'll hold no power. Nothing. That means the world as we know it will be under duress. The seasons may not turn as they should, the renewal of life and the death of that which is old and aging —none of it would come to pass. This means it is a gamble to fall with child, and, between my siblings and our cousins, it is a decision we must not take lightly."

Her words were a shock. Of all the responses he had anticipated, this was not one of them. Tritus mulled over what she had said. His fingers absently rubbed the back of her hands, caressing, reassuring, reminding her that he was there with her, that she wasn't alone. It was a habit he'd nurtured, for he had recognized that this winter diamond was rough at the edges because she needed to be. The safety and security of her previous life had been stolen by her loyalty to her brother, the Druidic god, Dagda. Cailleach had told Tritus the story of how she came to be the Winter Goddess, how winter's mantle had been forced upon her as punishment for that loyalty. He knew that in order to survive her role, Cailleach had needed to protect herself by changing who she was. By being less trusting, less open, less vulnerable—like a flower that had wilted into something less beautiful than what it truly was.

Tritus had vowed to himself that he would change that. He would be someone Cailleach could rely on, someone she could be vulnerable with. He ached for her and for all she'd lost in more ways than one. And now, with this latest revelation, Tritus realized that fear held her in its grip—fear of losing her power as well as fear of any recriminations from her siblings.

Carefully, slowly, he said, "I can see why the thought of getting with child would drive a wedge of fear, my love, but fear should not prevent you from doing what you want. There are ways around the duties you are required to fulfill, not the least of which could be offloading them to others— even to me. Given the assistance I've provided in the last year, you know I am not without skill, nor are we situated in a place of risk. But if you are worried that being with child will make you vulnerable, you needn't, Cal. Together, we are strong." He gestured around the cave. "This is also the best home anyone could ask for. Solid and secure; a haven for us all."

Her hands tugged against his, and then her touch was gone. She pulled the furs higher, clutching them against her throat. It was a wall, Tritus realized. A wall between them. And her next words confirmed it.

"I am not ready for children, Tritus. I possibly never will be. No matter how much you guarantee that you will look after us and keep us safe, I cannot take that risk. My family is power-hungry and others more so. Our union is also abhorrent in the eyes of many. Even if they understood you are Cernunnos's son, I would lose everything I have, even my position in this world."

Tritus couldn't respond. The words fell between them, stones in a still pond. The fire chose that moment to spit and hiss as the remains of the log he'd put on earlier crumpled into ashes—just like the hope that died in his heart. Slowly, he clarified, "You're saying no to children... forever?"

Cailleach opened her mouth, then shut it again. Her forehead wrinkled, her face straining under some internal pressure. Licking her lips, she shared, "Not forever, but not anytime soon, Tritus. There is an immediate threat—the druid most of all. He—"

"Talorgan is nothing, Cal," he bit out, feeling a worm of anger that only arose when mentioning the man. "He is a jealous fool not worthy of our time."

Her lips pressed together. "You may think that, Tritus, but I can't deny my innate need to watch him. He is dangerous. I feel it."

Tritus felt his chest stir with fury. How dared that man affect her so? Before that time on the mountain, he had only seen Talorgan once before, on a trip down to the village he used to live in. The druid had been argumentative, seeking him out to taunt and tease. Not once had Tritus engaged, keeping what he and Cal had a tightly-wrapped secret. He suddenly realized that the Druid's year of punishment on their mountain home had just ended. No longer was Talorgan required to carry out his tasks here at every full moon. His greedy attempt to kill the second stag had been finally paid for.

Relief flooded through his body at the thought. Tritus was thankful he would never have cause to see Talorgan again unless he ran into him while visiting his sister or his parents. Tritus had avoided the village as much as possible in the last year, only visiting when there was word that his parents were sick. His friend, Drust, had been his eyes and ears, watching over Tritus's family in the time he'd been gone. He was incredibly thankful for the gift of Drust's friendship, but not a day went by that he wondered how Drust and Talorgan could be twins. Except for Talorgan's left eye—which looked like a fractured starburst of color, the blue iris coalescing with flecks of yellow, red, and turquoise—the druid and Drust were identical, right down to the blue whorls tattooed on their faces. Yet, there the similarity ended, for their personalities and the gifts they possessed were different. One excelled in Druidic power, the other in physical strength and the skills of a warrior. Tritus had long come to understand that they were two sides of the same coin.

However, for all his posturing, deep inside, Tritus had to admit that Cailleach's fears about Talorgan weren't misguided. During his last interaction with the Druid, there had been a prickling of his nape as he'd felt the weight of matters unfinished between them—a feeling of fate, the inevitable turn of a wheel. To what end they were entwined, he did not know, but he had hoped that with the end of Talorgan's punishment, he and Cailleach could move forward, away from the Druid's influence.

Shrugging off the memories, Tritus now said softly, "I agree with you that Talorgan is dangerous—to an extent. I do not deny it, but there are many threats in this world, both perceived and imagined. Threats are a fact of life, Cal; something we face every day. The bigger question is, do you trust in the way I look after you? I hope you know I will not let anything happen to you or a child we might be blessed with."

Cailleach swallowed, eyes wide, face pinched, but her sharp nod agreed with his comment. "I believe you, Tritus, I do. But I have been forewarned of dark tidings." She grimaced, and he caught a trace of fear flitter across her face. "Because of this, I do not wish to bring an innocent child into the mix."

"What dark tidings, Cal? You can tell me." Tritus could see her distress, and it concerned him. He burned for her to share with him—anything to ease the burdens she carried.

Her tongue darted out to wet her lips, and her glance skittered away to the fire. "I cannot say. It is family business; it does not affect you."

A shadow chased across his heart. It was almost inconsequential, a flutter of movement that could have been anything, but deep inside, Tritus felt his intuition sit up and take notice. He *knew*. He knew deep inside that there was more to her response than she was letting on. But he also knew his woman, and it was pointless to question Cailleach further; she would tell him in her own time...or not at all.

"Fine. You can keep your secrets for now, but I will learn them later," he warned. And because he needed his answer, he pushed, "Aside from these dark tidings, though, what would your answer be? If none of these worries were present, would you want a child?"

Her fingers curled tightly around the furs, her knuckles going white. For a moment, Tritus thought she wouldn't answer his weighted question, but then she said softly, "There is no guarantee we would be blessed with new life, as it is rare for my kind to fall fertile, but I...I am not averse to it." She lifted her head and speared him with her gaze. He could see the luminous sheen in her eyes as she added in a whisper, "Such a gift would be more than I ever dreamed to receive."

Her answer released a soft internal sigh in his chest. However, with that answer, Tritus realized he had one of his own. The timing of his proposition was wrong, he could see that now. He reminded himself that they had years ahead of them—years to enjoy one another before a child was welcomed into their world. And as he thought more on it, Tritus realized he wasn't sure that he was ready to share Cal just yet.

Assessing her body language and the stiff cant to her face, he gently reached out and drew her into his arms, his heart stinging at how rigidly she moved. Pressing her face into his chest, he kissed her on the top of her moonlight head and whispered, "That is enough for me, Cal. Only when you are ready, I promise."

At first, Cailleach lay stiff against him, but at those words, her body relaxed, the tension melting away and her arms encircling his waist. She turned and pressed a kiss against his naked chest. "I love you, Tritus. Never leave me." The words were fierce, her grip now strong, and Tritus could feel the desperation in her hold.

"I'll never leave you, Cal." He rubbed his hand up and down her naked back, soothing her as if she were a frightened child. And, as her grip eventually relaxed and loosened, he added with his chin resting on top of her hair, "But you must know that I don't accept your 'no' completely. Even if there will be no talk of beginning a family this Yule, there will definitely be a celebration. You will be coming with me on my next trip to the village. This year we will begin our own tradition of celebrating the season."

Again, she tensed in his arms, and he growled firmly against her hair, "There is no argument on this one, my love. You deserve to celebrate the solstice, and I would be honored to share it with you. Besides, you can't deny me—not after you've just shot down my other request."

A breathy chuckle left her lips. "Well, as it appears you cannot be swayed, you have my permission to make your plans. Your determination is almost palpable, Tritus."

He felt relief that she'd taken his feigned growl in the way he'd hoped she would, and an even greater relief that she'd agreed to celebrate the solstice with him. His arms tightened around her petite body, her nakedness now warm against his own, and he pulled her back down to lie beside him on the pallet. Dragging the furs over their bodies to create a cocoon of warmth around them, he whispered, "When it comes to you, I have great visions, Cal. And I promise you, this will be a winter solstice you won't forget."

CHAPTER 2

TRITUS

3RD CENTURY BC, ANCIENT SCOTLAND

With the first rays of dawn, Tritus turned away from the cave and began his long trek to the village nestled at the base of the mountain. As he left the safety and security of their enclave and entered the hushed silence of the forest, he couldn't help but think of when he would see Cailleach again. It was difficult to be apart; her safety preyed constantly on his mind. At times, he found it ridiculous, given she was so much more powerful than he. She was a goddess, for goodness' sake! How in the heck could she not defend herself? But there was a vulnerability to his woman, and she went to pains to keep it under wraps. The thought brought a small smile to his lips, because Tritus could still remember the first time he met her.

He first laid eyes on Cailleach while out on a hunting trip upon her mountain. It was an earth-shattering meeting. She appeared as the Winter Goddess, the ugly crone who called in the winter, wielding storms of imaginable power— storms that brought death and destruction, but which also removed decay and damage, making way for new growth.

As the crone, Cailleach had come upon them suddenly and warned Tritus and his two hunting companions, Drust and Talorgan—one his best friend, the other already a foe—that they might each take only one deer that day. The warning was indisputable, and the punishment final, but for all that, one of their party had not followed her decree. Talorgan had attempted to take a second deer, even after Tritus intervened to warn him against doing so.

To their horror, the Winter Goddess reappeared, and her anger was a precursor to the punishment to come. However, for some reason, Cailleach had given Tritus the right to determine the Druid's punishment, and he'd been in a quandary, because he knew Cailleach expected him to claim Talorgan's life as just punishment. But Tritus was more than aware that such a decree had the power to undo his friendship with Drust. As a result, he made a fateful decision that day—he had not asked for Talorgan's life but instead chained the druid to a year-long punishment of nurturing the land.

Tritus had thought his time with the Winter Goddess would come to an end after she accepted his punishment. But he'd been wrong. Cailleach had realized that he could see under the veil of her disguise—to the woman she was underneath. Not the tall, ugly crone who personified death itself, but the woman she really was: young, beautiful, and unsure of herself. During that hunting trip, Tritus had come to realize that the others didn't see Cailleach as he did, and he'd made a slip during their discussion, calling her beautiful when the others saw her as someone who was clearly not.

The slip had intrigued Cailleach. She'd also seen him as a threat. Because, aside from her siblings and the other gods, Tritus was the first to see more than the ugly crone, the first to talk to her in a manner that was not solely anchored in fear and repulsion. Her curiosity led her to seek him out the night before they were all to return to their village, and what followed was the unearthing of a long-held mystery—a mystery that involved the truth of Tritus's own true heritage and how he would inevitably become tied up in the Winter Goddess's future.

Cailleach made him a proposition. She asked him to stay with her so he would be able to understand how much of a threat he could be to her and her own. And for some reason, with an intuition greater than he could understand, and along with a hungry, fixated desire that coursed through his veins, Tritus had agreed. There had been no denying he felt an inexplicable pull toward the woman...this powerful Winter Goddess.

A fragile trust developed between them, slowly at first, and then with the coming of that first spring, his emotions for her changed, becoming a raging torrent. Astoundingly, her desire for him matched his own, and they found themselves connected on a higher level, aware that they had both been touched by Fate, their paths so entangled that it was hard to determine where one began and the other ended. In his own mind, Tritus didn't see them as having individual paths; rather, he saw them as one rope that held two interconnected braids, both strands tightly entwined in a strong, unbreakable bond.

He wasn't prepared for how momentous and otherworldly their eventual sexual union had become, nor had he ever before felt anything akin to what he felt for this woman—not for *anyone* in this life. Cailleach was his everything, the other part of his soul, and the sensations and feelings evoked in their private moments were like precious jewels he kept close to his heart.

Now, as his feet crunched through the snow, making a sharp sound in the still air, he held those feelings close to his heart as he allowed his thoughts to wander again, reveling in a recent memory. Cailleach's hands had been hungry last night, her grip tight. Her lips had carried an urgent passion, an unwillingness to let go, and when he kissed her goodbye this morning, her words drove that message home.

"Be as quick as you can," she whispered. "Don't tarry overnight at the village. Every moment without you is intolerable."

He lifted a hand to caress her cheek while his other possessively fisted the long strands of her moonlight hair. "Do not think for one second that I don't feel this same urgency and passion, my love."

She sighed and leaned into his hand, turning her cheek to place a soft kiss in the middle of his palm. "It is the only beauty of this curse Morrígan placed upon me. Only my true mate was meant to find me under the veil, the only one able to see me. She has no idea that the curse of the crone was a gift in the end, a gift I will treasure for the rest of my life. It appears that my brother, Dagda, chose well. We also have him to thank for bringing us together. "

"The rest of your life?" he repeated, one dark eyebrow raised. "You talk as though we are on limited time, Cal. I do not plan on going anywhere—ever."

Her eyes widened, and she looked abruptly away to stare out into the winter wonderland beyond the entrance of their cave to the pine trees bowing low under their heavy raiment of snow. Her words were soft and full of emotion, her voice choked as she responded, "And I, too, my love. You are my everything."

For some reason, her words brought a faint chill to the

back of Tritus's neck. Had he imagined the flicker of pain that crossed her features before she'd looked away? No, she was just as nervous as he was that someone would chance upon them together. That this someone, and one druid in particular, would see what they had become—no longer goddess and subject, but irrevocable, all-consuming lovers.

He had pulled her in close for a final embrace, pressing her soft curves against his long length, and deeply breathed in her scent, locking that intoxicating mix of pine and frost into his very being. Tritus felt as though he could hold her thus forever, never letting go. But the knapsack over his shoulder was a weighty reminder that he had wares to sell to the villagers, and in return, gifts to bestow upon her. He also had plans for the upcoming solstice holiday. It was a time to celebrate what they were to each other, a time to celebrate what they had, and an opportunity to cherish their joyous moments by establishing traditions and creating lasting memories.

So, with one last hard kiss upon her lips, Tritus had whispered goodbye to his winter goddess before releasing her from his arms. Swiftly turning on his heels, he began his trek down the mountain, afraid that if he looked back, he wouldn't continue.

Tritus had felt her intent gaze on his back right up till the moment he'd entered the dense, shadowed forest of snow-drenched trees. He knew she would not follow. Cailleach still found it difficult to show her vulnerability, but he could feel her presence whispering around him in the stirring caress of the chill breeze, in the rustle of the leaves on the trees, and in the actions of the curious, inquisitive animals who stopped to stare at his passing. Even now, their eyes were upon him. And it wasn't until he left the cover of her mountain and began to traipse across the open meadows nestled at its base that he felt her spirit finally leave him in a gentle, airy embrace with the softest brush of her lips across his cheek.

"Goodbye, my love," he whispered in reply, his heart already yearning for his return.

CHAPTER 3
TRITUS
3RD CENTURY BC, ANCIENT SCOTLAND

Tritus took a deep breath before leaving the safety of the trees and walked confidently toward the small village nestled at the base of Cailleach's mountain. The children saw him first. A little girl with long, auburn hair trailing down her back in a tangled mess was the first to give a cry and announce his presence. She ran up to him, her dirty, grass-stained feet running effortlessly over the wet grass, skinny white limbs flashing under the hem of her bedraggled shift.

Tritus, hiding his misgivings and his concern, bent down to his haunches and opened his arms. "Bryn!"

The little girl flew into them without so much as a pause, her wiry arms coming around his neck in a fierce hug. "Tritus! I've been waiting for you. It's so close to Yule I didn't think you'd keep your promise."

Tritus wrapped his big hand around the little girl's head and then gave it a comforting pat before trailing his hand down her snarled locks. "Oh, Bryn, you should know by now I always keep my promises."

The girl only clung to him tighter. He continued to hold

her in his arms, conscious that she needed the contact. Tritus looked over her head to the other children, noting some had come closer—but not too close—to stand and watch them with suspicious eyes. In the distance, he could see two older boys racing off to the thatched huts. No doubt they were away to warn the inhabitants of the village that the mysterious Gaul had arrived to trade with them once again.

"Did you bring it?" the little girl whispered softly under her breath, her hands now clutching his tunic with desperate fingers.

Tritus felt the object in his pants pocket weighing him down. Even though he had brought what she'd asked for, and even made it to her careful instructions, he still had misgivings about giving the weapon to Bryn.

Her request had seemed to make perfect sense at the time, and Bryn had been very convincing the last time he'd come to the village to trade. So convincing that he'd promised to make her what she'd requested. But now that Tritus held the young girl in his arms and felt her frailty and innocence, he was conflicted as to whether he should give her the knife or not. Surely she didn't need to go out and fend for herself? Surely the village watched over her and her brother and hunted and trapped game for them both, even when their father couldn't?

Still, for all these last-minute misgivings, Tritus realized he couldn't deny Bryn now, not while holding her in his arms. So, pushing his thoughts aside, he replied, "I did," as he discretely slipped the little knife into one of her small hands.

Bryn pulled back, eyes shining, and not with tears this time, but with trust. A smile bloomed across her rosebud lips as she slipped the knife into the pocket of her shift. Her other hand reached up to cup his chin. Looking into his face, she whispered, "Thank you, Tritus, I knew you would."

Her reaction gave him immediate pause. It spoke of a girl who was not a child but rather a young woman, and he wondered at Bryn's true age. She was small of stature, fine-boned and delicate, her long, unkempt hair shadowing her pinched, white face—which, he noted, was looking angular and haunted. For all that, Tritus could see she would be a true beauty when she was older, a rival to Cailleach's starburst of flowering innocence.

He'd thought Bryn only ten summers, not a girl on the verge of womanhood. But that question was wiped away like a leaf in the breeze when she stepped back and he got a full look at her angular face. There was no hiding the look in her eyes—the trusting warmth and the desperate hope. But that wasn't what caused him to freeze. There were bruises marring Bryn's face; large, purple ones that didn't come from climbing a tree or tumbling down the mountain. And, as his eyes traveled over her body, Tritus also noticed that on the girl's right arm, peeking out from under her rough shift, were four dark splotches—more bruises that could not be mistaken as anything other than finger marks.

The girl had been beaten.

Tritus's indrawn breath was sharp. His eyes lifted back to the bruise on her cheekbone, and he lifted a hand to gently brush the backs of his fingers across her delicate skin before gesturing to the marks on her arm. "Bryn—who did this to you?"

The girl's gaze immediately fell to the ground, her eyes shuttering closed. "No one. I fell out of a tree."

Tritus felt his stomach turn at the obvious lie. "Is that how you also got those marks on your arm? From a tree?"

Her head jerked stiffly from side to side. "Petyr had to

help me down. There was no other way around it. He did not mean to bruise me."

"Petyr? Your brother?"

She gave a sharp nod. "Yes, he saved me from breaking my neck. I can carry a few bruises for such a gift."

Tritus didn't say a word. His intuition was raging; he knew she lied. Jaw tight, he forced out, "Well, I will have to meet your brother and thank him for saving you."

Bryn's face blanched, her body shifting and her eyes skittering over her shoulder to look at the other children now closing in. "Petyr will be working now, but I will pass on your message."

Tritus opened his mouth to question where her brother could be found, but the other children, who had carefully stood back until this point, came close, effectively cutting their private conversation short.

"You're back!" a dark-haired boy exclaimed. "Did you bring more pendants to trade with today? My father would like to give one to my mother."

Turning away from Bryn, Tritus forced a smile at the boy. "Of course. I remembered your previous request, Podrick, and I used my time wisely between visits." He patted the knapsack over his shoulder. "There are about ten new pendants in here."

The boy's eyebrows rose to his hairline. "Oh! Is it possible to pick one out now?"

Tritus shook his head. "You know the rules of trade don't allow for that, Podrick. We'll have to make my presence known and give everyone a chance to approach. I hope you and your family accumulated enough seed over the autumn to barter with?"

He nodded eagerly. "Yes. The women here have been in a right fit getting enough seeds together to trade with you.

They are jealous of those who received a pendant on your last visit." He smiled smugly. "I think you'll be well pleased with what's on offer today."

Tritus patted him on the shoulder. "Good. My woman will be truly thankful if she gets what she wants."

"Your woman?" Podrick asked, an eyebrow raised. "What woman would live with a nomadic trader? How do you provide for her and keep her safe?"

The question caused a genuine smile to tip Tritus's lips. He thought of Cailleach and her all-consuming power and answered truthfully, "My woman does not need protecting; she looks after her own."

The boy snorted, his face disbelieving. "You jest! Mother and all the other girls here are vulnerable. They need guards to protect them while out foraging. Some can't even go to the creek to gather water alone for fear of something happening. How could your woman fend for herself?"

It was true that there were dangers about, animals and otherwise. He knew that well enough, given that his people had raided these shores a short year prior. They'd pillaged and fought to earn their right to live alongside a village just like this one. Not wanting to raise suspicion, Tritus answered carefully, "She grew up with many siblings who taught her how to hunt and forage."

By the look on his face, Podrick didn't seem convinced, but Tritus was well aware no one would believe the truth of who and what Cailleach was. And there was no way he could let word of his lover's true identity reach the ears of others. Even talking with these children, Tritus was ever conscious of the shadow over his and Cailleach's past, of the sin they were committing. That she, a goddess, and he, a simple mortal, were together was a sin in their eyes and a

punishment worthy of death. Their greatest threat was
Talorgan.

It was just over a year since that fateful hunt, just over a
year since Tritus had found *real* happiness with the Winter
Goddess. Cailleach was his everything, his one true reason
for living. Her soul was so firmly entwined with his that he
had no idea how he'd gone on so long without her. She was
as necessary as the stars in the sky; a scaffold of love that
held him bound in an eternal prison he had no wish to
leave.

Tritus didn't need others to tell him what they shared
was rare. This emotion between them was more than love, it
transcended the realm of reality, just like a forest fire that
could raze everything in its path. At the same time, their
love was also a soothing balm, like the cool brook that could
chase away a dry, arid summer. For all that, their
relationship wasn't easy, though. It was filled with the
anomalies of her power and the temptation of the flesh.
They were both new to relationships, new to this scale of
emotion, and their budding love needed careful nurturing,
along with honesty and passion—both of which he was not
afraid to offer.

Tritus glanced at Bryn, now standing among the other
children, her head at least a foot taller than the others. They
had gathered around her in a protective circle, and seeing
that made the worm of worry in his heart ease somewhat.
"Shall we see who's ready to trade then?" he asked them in
an attempt to change the conversation. "I have only a few
short hours before I'll need to begin my journey home."

"You're not staying this time?" Bryn asked, her face
pinching.

Tritus hesitated. He'd heard the plaintive cry in her voice
and he wanted to say yes, but Cailleach awaited him. He'd

promised her he would only be away four days this time instead of five; that meant not staying overnight at the village this time round.

He gave her a gentle smile. "Not this time, Bryn, but I could be persuaded on the next trip if there's a cup of special mulled wine on offer."

Podrick crowed, "Oh, there may be that all right if you come in a few weeks! It's off limits right now. We're not supposed to touch the mulled wine until eight days hence. Winter solstice is coming, ye know."

"Aye," Tritus said. "I'm well aware of what's coming."

And he was excited for it. From what he'd learned in his short time with his Winter Goddess, the winter solstice was Cailleach's first opportunity to take a short breather in between her duties. It had been a busy six weeks for his love, bringing in the snow and the storms, washing away debris and rot, and clearing the land anew. He'd stood back and watched her day after day as she left the cave to attend to her duties. She returned home late each night, after the moon had reached its apex and was beginning its downward spiral. Tritus would covertly watch her enter their cave, her arrival bringing a flurry of snowflakes and a crisp breeze inside. She would hang her short hammer on the ledge by the cave entrance and then come to sit, stiff and exhausted, next to the fire to eat her evening meal. Afterward, she would join him in their bed, and even though her skin was never cold, nor did she seem to feel the ice of the winter chill, Tritus would draw her into his arms and make sweet love to her in the glow of the fire, easing her heart of the burdens she carried.

He knew it wasn't the act of bringing in the winter that caused the heavy ache to fall over her heart; it was the fact that her actions wrought inconceivable change. Winter meant death, desperation, and heartbreak, the loss of hope, and with her actions came not only consequence and responsibility, but also a sense of ownership. His soft-hearted woman, for all her power and bluffing, struggled with this stance she must take. It was a hard task she'd been given, and to be shielded within the form of an ugly crone while doing so was even harder. For the humans and animals feared her physical form, even before she spoke.

So, yes, Tritus knew exactly what the winter solstice would bring—a much-needed break for Cailleach. One that would ease her mind of the tasks she had performed and of those still left to come. It was perfect timing, because they would be halfway through her reign. When the new summer was born, her duties would end, and Brighid, her sister, would sow the land with new shoots and hope, bringing the meadows and the trees back to a lush green color and the woods alive with all manner of creatures.

The children led Tritus toward the cluster of roundhouses. The people stopped to stare at his entrance, as he was a stranger in more ways than one. He kept his shoulders back and his head high as he walked past them. Tritus could almost taste their curiosity and unease. He was conscious that, unlike them, blue whorls weren't etched across his face, his hair was unbound and flowing rather than tied back, and his clothing was cut differently to theirs, in the style of his people across the salty sea.

No, Tritus corrected himself, *they are not my people.* His family, yes, but not his people; for he'd discovered his lineage when he met Cailleach. A lineage that he still struggled to believe, even after witnessing the power his woman wielded. His father was one of her brothers, Cernunnos, the Wild God of the Forest, and his mother had been a druid who hailed from a clan just like this one.

He had seen images of his parents, memories of a time long ago. Both of them were long gone now. His father no longer walked this earth; he'd been transferred to the Other because of his dalliance with Tritus's mother. And his mother was dead, murdered by her own people for the sin of lying with a god—a sin he was committing now.

Like mother, like son.

A grimace twisted his lips, and Tritus shook the images away as his young escort stopped in front of the largest roundhouse in the middle of the village.

"Wait here," commanded Podrick, his tone now imperious with importance. "I will find Chief Braden."

Tritus inclined his head and watched as the boy slipped inside the straw-thatched dwelling.

Impatient, the children murmured and shuffled beside him, some now eager to be off, but Bryn remained silent and steady by his side, her small form pressed against his. Tritus looked down at her. This close, the bruises stood out defiantly across her cheekbone, a deep purple the color of ripe berries. His hand clenched around his knapsack. His gut told him this was no 'accident.'

The skin flap lifted, and Podrick returned with a man in tow. Tritus recognised his status not just by the silver armband around his right bicep but also the silver torc around his neck. It was very rare to see a silver torc; the elites of society wore bronze, but it was only the chieftains who wore silver.

The chieftain's narrowed eyes swept up Tritus's body and his voice was flat as he asked, "You're the trader?"

Tritus inclined his head. "I am. I have returned to trade my wares with the villagers. During my last visit, there were special requests for certain items, and with winter solstice almost upon us, this is my last visit before the holiday. I appreciate you were out hunting during my last visit, my lord, but your advisors granted permission on that occasion. I hope the wares I previously traded with are to everyone's satisfaction so I may have your permission to trade again this day?"

Braden looked pointedly at the knapsack over Tritus's shoulder. "It does not look as though you have much to trade."

Tritus smiled ruefully. "No, my lord, I suppose it doesn't, but this is not for the men this time around, I'm afraid. What I have in here is more for the women of the village. If you'd like to keep yours happy and satisfied, I have a gift she may welcome."

It had been a gamble as to whether the man would strike him for that insolent remark, but the chief's eyes widened. "You're the trader who makes the pendants?"

Tritus inclined his head, relieved that word had come back to the man. "Yes, my lord."

A sense of excitement crossed Braden's face. "My wife mentioned there was a trader who was making such items for the women. I know she'd love one as a solstice gift."

Tritus smiled. "Well, I will ensure I have the perfect one put aside for your woman. I take it that this means we will be able to commence trade today?"

Braden gave him a sharp nod. "Yes, please set up in the clearing over there. I will make my people aware that you have returned and would like to trade."

The chief pointed over Tritus's shoulder, and he turned to see a cleared area containing a circle of felled logs around a large fire pit. There were several men sitting on the makeshift seats, working on something in their hands.

Tritus turned back to the chief. "Thank you, my lord, that will do nicely. I'll be ready in just a moment."

As Braden left to speak to his people, Tritus began to move toward the fire pit, the children still following him. The men looked up at his approach, their faces curious as they took in his foreign garb and the knapsack over his shoulder. They'd no doubt seen him conversing with their chief and understood the reason for his visit.

"Ho!" Tritus called when he came upon them. "What are you working on there?"

One of the men lifted his hands, and Tritus saw that he held a piece of wood in one hand and a small dagger in the other. The wood was of similar size and width to what all the men held in their hands. With the object now facing him, Tritus could see that it was a half-finished carving of an old hag. At the sight of it, a chill whispered over his skin, and the words that came out of the man's mouth confirmed his suspicions.

"We are making the Cailleach for the burning."

"The Cailleach?" Tritus asked, choosing the path of ignorance even as he felt a sharp stab arrowing into his chest. Two emotions immediately flared inside his heart. One was fear, fear for his woman, and the other was pure male—he had no wish to see his lover in another man's hands, even a carving of her alter ego.

The man's brow raised. "You haven't heard of our Winter Goddess, then?" he asked incredulously, his gaze flicking to the other men around the fire before returning to Tritus. "The Cailleach is a mighty goddess; an old hag who rules over the winter. It is customary to shed the strength of her spirit during the winter solstice. Burning the Cailleach"—he gestured to the log in his hands—"means her spirit will be greatly diminished and will ensure the rebirth of the sun into its next cycle."

"You're also forgetting another reason why we want to

make the Cailleach weak!" yelled an old man from across the fire pit. He lifted one of his wispy, gray brows at Tritus as he said, "If the Cailleach isn't weakened, then the young 'uns won't get their fun—fun that ends with the birth of a bairn in ten moons time." His toothy grin was fixed on another lad across the fire, and the red welling in that young man's cheeks was enough to point out who the comment was aimed at.

There were whistles and catcalls, and someone else called out, "Young Euan will get his wish, I'm sure. What woman can't deny a fine strapping lad? Especially one who brings her wildflowers and special meats in the dead of winter."

Young Euan went bright red this time and ducked his head. He grunted as he dug his small blade into his chunk of wood, the face of a hag slowly coming to life in his hands.

Tritus hid his smile as he busied himself placing a soft blanket over an unoccupied log. He then carefully laid out the pendants he'd forged inside the cave he shared with Cailleach. While he worked, he mused on what the men had just shared. Tritus hadn't heard of this tradition, this 'burning of the Cailleach,' but it was clearly a custom if all these men were here carving an old hag into pieces of wood rather than out hunting or fixing the thatching on the roundhouses.

It appeared there were many similarities but also many differences between the people who lived here and those whom he'd grown up with across the salty sea. It was true Yule was celebrated here as it was there, but there were small differences, mainly to do with the many gods these blue men paid homage to. When he first arrived on this land, Tritus had been overwhelmed by the number of deities they worshiped. He'd been unable to comprehend them all, their duties and their importance; but most of all, he'd been surprised that their goddesses were given just as much jurisdiction and respect as their gods. And after meeting Cailleach, he could understand why.

Like the Gauls, these people believed the winter solstice marked the tipping of the season—the beginning of the change from winter to summer, or dark to light. These last few days before Yule were the shortest of the year, and, in a few days, the sun would change course, becoming brighter and out for longer, diminishing the dragging spirit and death of the winter.

As he laid his wares for trade out on the log, Tritus surreptitiously looked around the village, noting the sprigs of mistletoe hanging from some of the roundhouses. There was a festive spirit in the air, a sense of comradery, and he felt the familiar spirit of Yule enter his bloodstream. It had been a while since he'd celebrated this holiday, what with all the raiding and invading and the fighting he'd been subjected to these last few years. But now, with a woman in his heart and in his bed, Tritus felt that strange mixture of awe and something magical thriving in his veins. Yule was a time for celebration and a time for change, a time to cherish those still living, and a time to pay homage to those they'd lost.

He finished laying out his wares and turned to find that the men had dropped their carvings and were now crowded behind him, their faces alight with curiosity.

"Oh, so you're the one who makes those fancy pendant things?" a young man with braided dark hair asked.

Tritus nodded. "In my homeland, jewelry is favored by the women."

A cunning spark lit the young man's eyes. "Well then, I'll best be taking one." As the other men guffawed and one clapped him on the shoulder, he asked eagerly, "What are you wanting to trade with?"

"I'm looking for some holiday fare," Tritus replied. "Some root vegetables, spiced wine, and some dried herbs if you have any."

The young man nodded. "Aye. My woman made some spiced wine yesterday. She'll eagerly give you some if the exchange is for her."

Tritus smiled. "Well, you best be off then to see if she'll agree."

The man nodded briskly and raced away.

Another in the group stepped forward, an older man this time, his hair peppered with gray. "Since Alpin seems to believe his woman would be happy, maybe I should take one, too, for me Deidre." His stubby finger pointed to a bronze pendant that held the familiar triskele symbol on it. "This one looks perfect."

"Aye, Ciniod, that is a good choice," agreed another aged man beside him, this one's girth bulging under his dirty tunic. He elbowed Ciniod in the side as he said with a grin, "She'll be making your favorite pie, and not just for the solstice but the year to come!"

Ciniod gave his friend a toothy grin. "Aye, that she will, Angus, that she will." He looked up at Tritus. "What do you reckon, lad? You think this one is a great choice? I know it's not as fancy as the others, but me woman appreciates the simpler things in life."

Tritus gave Ciniod an easy smile and reached out to pick up the round pendant with the three interconnected swirls he'd carved into the bronze. "I think so. This piece has a certain appeal that the others do not. Going by what you've said, I think your woman would appreciate not only the time that went into carving the design but also its meaning."

The triskele was a common symbol here in this land. It represented the three worlds the Celts held in high esteem: the present world, the spiritual world, and the celestial world.

Ciniod grinned. "Aye, you're right. I'll take it, lad. Would you be keen on some dried herbs in return? It's well-known me Deidre's herbs are the best in this village."

Tritus beamed. "That sounds like a fair trade, for my woman covets dried herbs like nothing else."

Ciniod gave a pleased nod and ambled off with his friend to retrieve the goods they'd agreed upon.

Tritus looked at the other men, all of them younger. "Anything take your fancy, lads?"

One of them snorted. "They're the only ones with women to woo." His eyes were a bright blue and he had light red hair—a rare occurrence and considered lucky. The young man jerked his thumb at the rest of them. "We lot have no sweethearts, or anyone interested in us for that matter."

Tritus gave him a lopsided grin. "For the moment," he replied smoothly. "Just remember luck can change with the phrase of the moon. Maybe this solstice will be the beginning of that change."

The young men all snorted this time and each gave him a nod of acknowledgement before returning to their logs and picking up their carvings.

Tritus moved the two pieces that Alpin and Ciniod had chosen to a corner of the rug so they would not be sold to another. When he turned around, he saw the chieftain walking toward him.

"The announcement has been made that you are here to trade," the chief said to Tritus as he came to a stop. He ran a hand over the top of his braided hair, patches of balding skin visible in the afternoon light, and grimaced as he added, "The men and women are in a right state. They are moving as quickly as they can so they don't miss out." He looked down at the rug showcasing Tritus's wares. "I'm afraid you might have nothing to sell at the next village."

"That suits me well; I am eager to return home early today." Tritus gestured at the two pendants that the other men had chosen. "Those two off to the side have already been taken, but the others are still free. Would you like to pick one for your woman before the others arrive?"

"Aye, I would." Braden moved forward and looked over the wares for a moment before picking up a pendant that had a bright red garnet nestled within the center. "This one, I believe."

Tritus looked the pendant over. It was one he'd thought of keeping for Cailleach, but it was a cursory thought, soon forgotten, as he hadn't wanted to undermine the pendant he'd already given her.

Unlike the wares laid out on the rug, Cailleach's pendant had taken him days to create. It had all begun with the amber stone he'd found situated underground in a wet cave on her mountain. Something had led him toward it, something he could only describe as the hand of Fate. On returning home with a sliver of the amber, an idea had sparked within, and he envisioned crafting it into a gift for Cailleach. Nothing could deter him from giving effect to that thought, and Tritus had sequestered himself away, working on the pendant in secret. He'd been feverish with the task, and it had consumed his every waking thought. And, after gifting it to Cailleach, the sense that she needed nothing else but his love had stayed his hand from offering her more gifts in a similar vein. No, he did not need to hold this one for her, not when she wore something far greater around her neck.

Tritus nodded to the chieftain. "That one is a fabulous choice, my lord. The stone is eye-catching; a great piece for a striking woman."

The chief nodded. "Red is prized during the winter solstice, and although my wife will not be expecting any young bairns again, she'll appreciate the homage to the Mother Goddess."

Tritus reached out for the pendant. "It's a fine piece. Here, I'll wrap it in cloth for you."

"Are ye not going to ask me what I have to trade in return?" the chieftain asked with a raised brow.

Tritus smiled. "I do not expect anything in return. You have allowed me to trade here today; that is a gift in its own right."

The chieftain eyed him. "Aye, that may be, but these are fine gifts that ye bring. No others can offer the same, and such work deserves fair trade in return." Braden fished around in his tunic and brought out a small, wrapped package. "This is a selection of fresh root vegetables, only picked this morning. They were to be saved for the first day of Yule, but you are welcome to them as me woman knows where to find more."

Tritus was more than aware of the honor the chief bestowed upon him, as fresh root vegetables were a luxury in the dead of winter. It would also be bad form not to accept the trade. He accepted the package gratefully. "A fine trade, my lord. Thank you."

Having told Tritus he planned to give it to her on the third night of the solstice, the chief left with his wife's gift tucked away in his pocket.

After that, the other village people arrived, and Tritus

was busy trading for a time. Before he knew it, he had sold everything, and, in return, he had a bulging knapsack. He was well-pleased. He had accomplished what he'd set out to achieve—a full contingent of holiday fare. Tritus had not only planned time with Cailleach, but also a special range of food and drink to partake of over the solstice. He hoped it would be enough to convey the spirit of the occasion. But now, as he looked around the bustling village, taking in the flurry of activity, Tritus suddenly had an idea—what if he brought Cailleach down here for one night during the solstice? Hmmm.... The idea had merit, especially if she was game to witness the festivities.

With his soft blanket now rolled and stashed inside his knapsack, Tritus walked over to the Chieftain, who was busy hanging mistletoe from his door. Holly was strewn all over the roundhouse, its bright green leaves and verdant red berries startling against the white snow.

"I hear your people discourage the spirits of the dead by hanging mistletoe above your doors," Tritus said as he came up behind him. "Does it work, my lord?"

The chieftain met Tritus's gaze, his dark blue eyes confident. "Not once over Yule have we encountered any bad spirits inside our house. I think that alone speaks for itself, don't you?"

Tritus nodded. He gestured at the haphazardly laid holly. "And the holly? What is its purpose?"

"The same. Although, here in the forest, it also offers protection to the fairies and other woodland creatures who seek shelter from the cold."

Tritus felt his eyebrows rise and realized he shouldn't be surprised. These people were well-endowed in their beliefs. Here, nothing was beyond the imagination, and, as he loved a Celtic deity himself, there was no reason not to believe that there were woodland spirits and sprites around. Looking at the chieftain's house, Tritus had the sudden urge to rush home and similarly decorate the cave he shared with Cailleach, for not only was it important to carry out tradition, but the green leaves and red berries gave lushness to the setting and lent a magical feel to the village.

Tritus knew the red berries represented the sacred menstrual blood of the Mother Goddess. Along with the sun, the Mother Goddess would give life back to the desecrated winter soil, rejuvenating the flora and fauna while also welcoming the birth of new animals. It was the epitome of the never-ending cycle of life, another turn of the wheel.

"Care to help me with this, young un'?" the chieftain asked. He was holding a large sprig of mistletoe above his head, trying to wind it into the thatch of his roundhouse.

"Of course." Tritus placed his knapsack carefully on the ground and stepped forward to take the weight of the branch. As he held it in place and the chieftain bound it to the roof, he asked, "I understand that your people call this tree 'All Heal.'"

The chieftain nodded. "Aye. It holds miraculous healing powers, able to reverse the effects of poisons and heal people from all manner of diseases. It bans evil spirits, too, of both the body and the soul, and also brings good luck and blessings."

Tritus nodded. "My woman tells me it grows in the boughs of trees."

The chieftain looked at him with a raised brow. "You haven't been here in our land long, but long enough to get yourself a good woman who knows our ways," he observed.

Tritus gave him a rueful shrug. "I'm sorry, I know I'm asking a lot of questions. I am just curious about how your

Yule traditions differ from mine. You see, I have a surprise planned for my woman, and I want to be sure I get it right."

"Aye, well, all these questions make sense then, lad." The chief turned back to tie another section of the mistletoe to his roof. "To answer your question," he continued, "mistletoe is usually found growing in the oak trees around here. The druids say it carries the soul of the oak within its branches, and this is why whenever two enemy warriors cross paths under the mistletoe, they'll lay up their arms without engaging."

Tritus stared at him. "Lay up their arms? You're saying that they'll put any differences aside in the presence of mistletoe?"

The chief nodded, tying another section of the branch up. "Aye. The druids also use it in a five-day ceremony when the new moon rises following the winter solstice. They cut the mistletoe using a special golden sickle and distribute the sprigs around the village to those who need it most." The chieftain suddenly sighed. "We'll be needing it this year too. I have a few in my village that need protection from storms and evil spirits."

One word caught Tritus's attention. "Druids? I thought you had none in this village?" It was the sole reason he returned to trade here again and again.

Mistletoe now attached, the chieftain stood back to take in his efforts, hands on his hips. Seemingly satisfied, he turned to Tritus and replied, "Aye, we don't, but we have a few lads here who recently chose to pursue that path. As much as I wanted them to follow the green robe, they've decided to follow death and rebirth."

Tritus felt his stomach flip. He knew exactly whose service the lads would fall under.

"There are a few Druidic villages to the north of here,

one of them quite substantial," the chieftain continued. "As a matter of fact, I heard they recently joined with a tribe of Gauls from across the salty sea." The chieftain eyed him. "That wouldn't be where you hailed from, by chance?"

Tritus hesitated, unsure how much to share. On one hand, he wanted his whereabouts protected from prying eyes and ears, and most especially from one druid in particular. But as he thought it through then and there, he supposed it was inevitable he would return to *that* village. And who was to say that Talorgan would get wind of him, anyway? How would the druid know for sure that it was him? Tritus had no distinguishing factors except for his green eyes. They were rare around these parts, just as rare as red or blond hair. Yes, there were also the antlers on his head—evidence of his true lineage to his father, Cernunnos, the Wild God of the Forest; however, Dagda, another of Cailleach's brothers, had ensured that only Cailleach and the other Celtic deities would see them. That secret was safe from his enemy.

Releasing a breath, Tritus decided to lie to the chieftain —but not by much. "No, those are not my people. It is true we came from across the salty sea, but we made land further south. At least a ten-day trek from here, a few villages over."

The chieftain looked at him a moment longer before giving a shrug and turning to the next piece of mistletoe.

As Tritus helped him to attach the branch, he couldn't deny a sense of panic and a sudden need to blend in with these people as best he could. While Braden tied a section of the mistletoe to his thatching, Tritus eyed the blue ink carved into the side of the old man's face. An idea formed, and he casually asked, "Is there a tattooist in the village?"

Braden cut him a sharp look as he attached one side of the mistletoe to another part of the thatch and then walked around Tritus to attach the other side. "Aye, there is. A very good one too. Others come from far and wide to visit Kerr." He shot Tritus a grin. "He's not partial to traveling abroad; loves his woman too much to leave her for long, that one."

Tritus's heart kicked. "I can understand that."

The chieftain must have heard the sincerity in his tone. "Then you must have a fine woman, lad."

"Aye, my lord. She's who I sell my wares for. I attain a sense of real satisfaction in delivering her gifts on every run."

Braden's eyebrows rose. "Well, if that's the case, I don't see how ye could leave her in the first place then; Kerr refuses to."

With the second piece of mistletoe up, Tritus and the chieftain both stood back again to observe their work, as he replied carefully, "It's necessary sometimes. She is a busy woman with her own tasks in hand."

"Oh? She a healer, then?"

Tritus hesitated, then realized that Cailleach really was a healer. Bringing in the winter made the land anew, making way for birth and regrowth, effectively healing it to bring in another year of harvest and abundance. "Yes, and a powerful one too."

The chief clapped him on the shoulder. "Ye best be holding onto her then, lad. Healers are hard to find these days, especially in the winter."

Tritus nodded, a small arrow of guilt lodging in his throat at the skewed lie. He turned to Braden to ask him if it was possible if he and Cailleach could visit one night during the solstice, but there was a shout from behind and the scamper of feet, and suddenly Bryn was beside him again, tugging on his hand.

"Tritus! Come quick, we have need of you."

He took in her disheveled appearance and the tension around her eyes. "What is it?" he demanded.

"Please, just come!" she begged, tugging on his hand again.

Braden stepped forward and raised a hand. "Bryn! What is going on? This is a guest in our village! Explain yourself now."

Bryn paused, and her face pinched at the question. A moment of indecision warred. Then, aware she couldn't deny her chieftain, Bryn said quietly, "It's Petyr. He's in another fight."

Tritus flicked his gaze back to Braden, noticing the chieftain's lips had tightened.

"With Flett again?" Braden asked.

Bryn lowered her gaze to her hands, now wringing them together. "Yes."

The chieftain sighed, then gestured with his hand. "Lead the way, girl."

And as Bryn still held onto the sleeve of his tunic, Tritus had no choice but to follow along.

CHAPTER 4

TRITUS

3RD CENTURY BC, ANCIENT SCOTLAND

Bryn's legs moved quickly to keep up with the long strides of the two men, and Tritus couldn't help cringing at the sight of her skinny, naked limbs exposed to the snow. The wind had come up again and was now biting through his leather jerkin, no doubt doing damage to her thin frame. Yet, Bryn didn't seem to be affected by the cold as she quickly directed him and Braden to a clearing on the edge of the village.

It was the grunts that heralded the brawlers' presence, and as the trees parted, Tritus saw two youths circling each other, one sporting a bleeding lip and limping, and the other with a cut on his face, gasping as blood gushed from his nose.

The chieftain wasted no time. "Cease this nonsense now!" he roared, voice reverberating with a sense of command.

The two youths suddenly halted, staggering backward in shock. They whirled to face the three of them. The young man with the gushing nose narrowed his eyes on the girl standing next to Tritus and exclaimed, "Bryn! You were warned not to tell anyone!"

"You were warned not to fight!" she sharply returned. "And I hadn't intended to tell the chieftain." Bryn shot Braden a guilty look.

"Yet here he is!" the young man replied, now reaching up to pinch his nose.

The limping youth with the cut lip glared at Bryn. "This was none of your business, Bryn!" he ground out. "You—"

"Enough!" shouted the chieftain. "Leave the girl alone. She told me at my bidding. Besides, she is not the one under scrutiny, you two are!" Braden narrowed his eyes at the boys. "You two have a lot to say for yourselves. I thought this argument between you had been sorted. Why in the name of the triple goddess are you still fighting?"

The boy with the cut lip jerked his head at the other. "Petyr accused me of touching his sister."

Bryn gasped. "What?"

The chieftain looked between the two youths. "Qualify 'touching,'" he demanded.

Bryn's brother had a chagrined look on his face, his lips in a mutinous line.

The chieftain ground out, "Answer me, Petyr!"

"Yes, answer him, Petyr!" Bryn cut in. "What is this story you claim?"

The young man shot Bryn a shocked glance. "It's no story!" he cried. "Look at your arms! I saw you speaking with Flett earlier—saw him holding you there, his hands on those bruises. He's hurt you!" Petyr threw his arm out at the other yount in a sharp cutting motion. "Do not think to absolve him of his crimes, Bryn. We all know that he's already been warned to leave you alone—Father was very convincing!"

Flett hissed. "Your father is wrong! *You* are wrong! I did not touch your sister and never will! Every time I've come to see her, it has been out of concern for her welfare." He threw his hands up in disgust, lip curling as he looked at Bryn's brother. "You have no idea what's going on under your own nose, do you?"

Petyr narrowed his eyes, forehead creasing. "Are you going to lie yourself out of this predicament again?" he demanded through clenched teeth.

"I do not lie," the youth returned sharply, fists now balling by his sides.

"Petyr, that's enough," Bryn said softly. But her voice carried enough command that both youths turned to look at her. Tritus had the feeling they'd forgotten that he, Bryn, and the chieftain were still there.

Bryn enunciated slowly, "Flett has never touched me with ill intent—not in the past and not today. I tried to tell you this before, brother. You have wronged him twice now. Please, step away from this fight, Petyr. Apologize to Flett and leave well enough alone." She turned to face the chieftain, one hand on her heart. "I vow in front of you, our chieftain, that all I have said is true."

"But what of your bruises? Those marks on your arm!" her brother spluttered. "What of the bruises last week, and the week before that? You did not get them while out playing with the other children, Bryn. They were inflicted upon you."

The chieftain was looking at Bryn now, his face twisted in concern. "Bryn," he intoned firmly, "this must be addressed. I know you weren't willing to share this with me before, child, but you can see that withholding this information is causing problems. Be honest with me now, girl. Tell us who has hurt you."

But Bryn's features remained firmly closed, her eyes brittle. "I cannot," she said in a firm voice that did not waver. "All I can say is that it was not Flett." She looked directly into the youth's eyes as she added, "He has only wanted what is best for me. He is a man to be respected for looking out for those younger than himself. Thank you, Flett."

The youth inclined his head. "It is as I have been trying to tell your brother, but he would not listen, not after seeing us together earlier."

Petyr was looking between them, his face tense. "You have not touched my sister?" he asked Flett slowly, clearly struggling to believe it.

Flett shook his head. "I never have and never will," he vowed fiercely. "Bryn is like a sister to me. She has helped my family in times of need; in return, I merely sought to protect her from harm."

Petyr's lips thinned, and he looked pained. "I apologize then," he said stiffly, "for I have clearly wronged you."

Flett stared at him, his stance still tense. But, after a moment, he gave Petyr a nod, signifying his acceptance before turning to Bryn, his gaze contemplative as well as worried. "I trust that this incident gives you the confidence to share your secrets now, Bryn. As you can see, there are many here that care for you. Please, tell us what is wrong."

The girl standing beside Tritus said stiffly, "Thank you, Flett, I appreciate your kindness more than you know." But she did not say another word.

After a moment of waiting silence, the chief released a sigh. "All right, Bryn, you win this skirmish tonight. Clearly, you are not ready to share your secrets, but make no mistake that you will soon."

Tritus felt her flinch as Braden's eyes bored into the young girl beside him, but Bryn still held her ground as she stared back at the chief. Tritus said nothing, giving her the silent support of his warm presence while trying not to show how he felt. As the scene between the lads, Bryn, and the chief had played out before him, he had felt his anger grow. His intuition had been right—someone was hurting Bryn. He wanted to find out there and then exactly who that was, but given the way she had just behaved in front of her brother, a trusted friend, and the chief, Tritus knew that Bryn wouldn't relent to his probing, either. He hated to admit defeat and leave the question unanswered, but there was no use pushing the issue further if it only succeeded in turning the young woman away.

Tritus reassured himself that the four of them now knew something was wrong. He was sure Braden and the two young boys would look out for her when he was gone, and if she had not shared her secret by his next visit, Tritus vowed that he would find out for himself what was really going on.

"It's getting late, and you best be off, boys," the chief now said. "The misunderstanding has been cleared up. And Petyr—let this be a lesson to you to not jump to conclusions again before finding out if your accusations hold some truth to them. I commend you on protecting your sister's honor, but it is an empty action if it is inaccurately conceived. This is a serious error. If you were men, as a worse-case scenario, one of you could have been dead over a false accusation."

Bryn's brother swallowed and bowed his head stiffly. "As you say, Chieftain."

Braden eyed him closely before giving a sharp nod, seemingly satisfied that Petyr had understood the gravity of his warning. "Good. Now, as I said, it is time you were away, boys. We have much to prepare in the coming week. Go and see if your fathers need help bringing in the Yule log or finding more mistletoe before we lose what light we have left in the day."

Flett nodded sharply, but Petyr's reply was stiff. "Our father is away. He'll be returning later this afternoon."

Bryn tensed beside Tritus, her small body poised like a startled hare about to take flight.

The chief raised his brows. "Away? There is much work to be done here at home for the upcoming solstice. What is more important that it calls him away elsewhere?"

Petyr shrugged. "He did not say. All he said was that he'd be back this afternoon."

Braden frowned, and Tritus felt Bryn's small frame tense even more. She had turned her body away toward the trees now, as if about to flee.

The chief said, "Please tell your father to see me on his return."

Petyr bent his head in acknowledgment. "As you wish, my lord."

"Good. Now be off with you two; quickly now."

The chief turned to Bryn as the boys left in a sprint. "I was serious, young woman," he told her bent head. "There is clearly something going on here, and I am determined to get to the bottom of it. You have until the setting of the sun, two nights hence, to tell me your story. I will see no more misunderstandings between others in my village." The chief softened his words with a small pat on the girl's head. "Run along now, Bryn, back to the village. See if anyone else needs help preparing for the solstice."

Dismissing her, Braden turned to Tritus. "Now, you said something about a tattooist? Given that my work has been interrupted, I would be happy to see you to Kerr if he's home. I am sure he would jump at the chance for a last-minute trade before the celebration."

Tritus felt his heart trip in his chest, excitement now warring with apprehension. "Thank you, my lord."

For all his words of acceptance, Tritus was now beginning to second-guess whether Cailleach would appreciate his gesture. It was one thing to tell Cal he had embraced his heritage and another to return home with that heritage permanently inked on his skin. Yet, his feet were on the path now, and his intuition had never failed him before. He told himself the tattoo would be a gift for him and for her—a living, permanent example of how closely he was tied to her world.

The chief, noticing that Bryn still hadn't moved from Tritus's side, barked, "Well, girl? Why are you still here? Be off with you now! Unless you've changed your mind and you're ready to tell me the secret you hold close to your chest?"

Bryn's face blanched, and she turned and scampered away, skinny legs racing lightly over the frozen ground.

Braden shook his head as he watched her go, a frown furrowing his brow. "There is something afoot there, and I hope it will not result in any more bruises." He sighed. "That is for another time, though. Come, Tritus, I'll take you to Kerr."

"You really believe she is being abused?" Tritus asked as he fell in beside the chief.

Braden frowned as he picked his way through the trees, ducking under a branch laden with snow. A gust of wind chose that moment to pierce the forest, and the branch groaned above their heads before sending a sprinkle of fine snow down the back of Tritus's neck.

"Those bruises on that girl's arms are made by a man's hand," Braden said slowly, his voice heavy as he rubbed the snow from his gray-peppered hair. "I hesitate to suspect it was her father. Rennie has never shown any ill will toward his children; his only fault is that he spends too much time away from them." At Tritus's raised brow, he explained, "Bryn and Petyr lost their mother many years ago to a tragic accident. Rennie was heartbroken and never recovered. His grief took him away in spirit, and he distanced himself from his children. I suspect it's because the children look like his late wife, Bryn especially. However, they were never forgotten, and Bryn and Petyr have been watched over by several of my people ever since they lost their mother."

Tritus paused mid-step, his gaze assessing as it landed on the chief. "You truly think their father did not harm the girl?"

The chief, who had also paused, looked over Tritus's shoulder into the forest, his gaze unseeing of the magical, white beauty in front of him as he thought on the question. "No, I refuse to believe that Rennie would harm Bryn." His jaw locked as he added, "But if I am found wrong, there will be hell to pay."

Tritus kept his thoughts to himself for the rest of the trek to the tattooist's lodgings. When they arrived at Kerr's roundhouse and found him free and open to a trade, the chief said to Tritus, "Well, I best leave you and Kerr to conduct your trade and continue with the tasks at hand. Given your assistance with a number of matters today, I've been thinking of a way to thank you. As you showed a lot of interest in our solstice preparations, I would like to extend you and your woman an invitation to join us one night over Yule. I would also like to meet this healer you speak of, and it would be an honor to share a cup of mulled wine to give thanks for the change in season. Of course, there is the matter of where you would stay, but I'm sure we can arrange lodgings for one evening. What say you?"

Tritus felt a surge of relief that he didn't have to beg the chief for this opportunity. He had been meaning to ask Braden as he was leaving the village and had not expected the invitation to be extended. It seemed the gods had again answered his call—or rather, Fate had played her hand once more.

He reached out and clasped the chief's shoulder. "We would be honored!" he said warmly. "Thank you, that is very generous. My woman does not get out much, and I'm positive she would love to spend an evening with your people."

The chief broke out in a smile. "Good! Well, I wish you safe travels on the journey home and look forward to seeing you in a few nights hence."

CHAPTER 5
TRITUS
3RD CENTURY BC, ANCIENT SCOTLAND

The skin around Tritus's right upper arm was pinching as he began the long trek home later that afternoon, but the pain didn't detract from the inherent pride he felt as he trudged through the snow. Tritus was excited to see Cailleach's response to the tattoo. He believed it would be his best gift on his return, the spices, dried meats, and fresh root vegetables in his knapsack a close second.

There was also the invitation they'd been issued to attend Yule in the village; it was a silver lining he hadn't expected. Tritus had originally planned to bring Cailleach down to the village to witness the festivities, but in secret, away from prying eyes and ears. But being invited to attend was even better. If he could convince her, Tritus knew Cailleach could use glamor to hide her real form. She wouldn't be the ugly crone or the beautiful goddess, but simply a woman—someone who would still be beautiful nonetheless, but able to move about freely without fear of recrimination. It would be an enriching experience, one to treasure, and what Tritus hoped would be the first of many.

His steps were light as he trudged through the forest, the

sounds of the village fading behind him. In the waning light, the path ahead was dark, but there was enough late afternoon sun piercing the canopy above to discern the mistletoe hanging from the trees. The lush sprigs had been artfully wrapped around the drooping branches, a bright splash of color against the startling white snow. The mistletoe looked fresh, and as it hadn't marked the path earlier this morning, Tritus knew the villagers must have hung it from the branches while he'd been trading. It was a merry sight to behold, and he couldn't help thinking that the bright green leaves and ripe red berries were guiding his steps toward—

"Shhh! I think there's someone ahead!" came a rough, low voice.

Tritus stopped abruptly at the urgent hiss, his hand immediately going to the dagger at his side. Pulling it from his sheath, he raised it in one hand as he turned toward the source of the noise, peering through the forest. How had he missed them? He was normally cognizant of anyone approaching, of maintaining a level of stealth and secrecy at all times. Cailleach's life depended on it, as did his own if others were to find out about their clandestine union— whether they knew his heritage or not. The same heritage that allowed his eyes and ears to discern who and what now came toward him just east of the path.

Three figures. All men, and all dressed in dark clothing. One of them shouldered a large sack, grunting with a load that appeared to be heavy. The other two were crouched, one in front, the other behind, daggers at the ready as they peered this way and that.

Tritus knew the exact moment they saw him. By then his dagger was down, hidden in the folds of his tunic. He raised his other hand in greeting. "Hello there!" he called out.

"What fortune to meet on the path. Are you heading toward the village behind me?"

The oldest man in the trio stepped out of the dense forest and onto the path first. He had long, unkempt hair flecked with gray. It stood out from his head, all askew, and his eyes were small and narrow as they peered intently at Tritus. "Aye. What's it to you, traveler?"

Tritus raised a brow at his rude remark; it bordered on insult. "I'm a trader, my friend. I suppose it's no interest of mine, but I've just been there to trade my wares and thought it best to let you know you aren't far away from shelter on this cold evening." Tritus gestured at the sack over the second man's shoulders, who had now appeared beside the first. "Have you been hunting?" he asked the tall, wiry man. "It looks as though the goddess has blessed you with her gifts."

Even as Tritus said the words, his gut roiled at the blatant disregard of the unspoken rule that no large animals be killed during the winter. The beasts were starving as it was, and with that bulk to the sack, Tritus knew there was a fine chance there was a doe in there. Deer were Cailleach's favored animals; they were to be respected. Tritus knew this well, given what had happened between him, Drust, and Talorgan a year ago.

There was a muffled sound, and then a low groan came from the sack. The tall, wiry man holding the heavy load cursed, and it was then that the third man stepped out of the forest. He was heavyset with a low brow and what appeared to be a permanent sneer etched across his lips. He thumped the sack with a meaty fist. "Quiet!" he snarled at the sack. Then, turning to Tritus, he said with a leering smile, "You'd think these creatures wouldn't have enough energy to fight their destiny, but they're full of spunk, I'll grant them that. I like to think it's because we've chosen well for the solstice sacrifice."

Tritus merely stared at him, unwilling to agree with his comment.

The first man stepped forward, shielding the sack from Tritus's keen eye, and said in a hard voice, "As you can see, this is a gift for our gods—a gift for the solstice." He jerked his chin at Tritus. "What do you carry in *your* sack?"

Tritus shrugged, forcing a smooth smile across his face —his trading face. "Gifts for my woman: dried meats, spices, and fresh vegetables."

The heavyset man grinned, showing a set of chipped, yellow teeth. "Why, that sounds like a mighty feast worthy of some company. How far do you have to travel? Wouldn't want it to spoil on the return journey."

Tritus felt a lick of unease whisper across the back of his shoulders. He could feel the edge of danger like a sharp blade piercing his side. He did not trust this trio. Forcing his body to relax, he surreptitiously eyed the three men—one tall, wiry young man laden with a sack that could be easily tossed to the ground; one large, heavyset man but clearly strong; and the third, middle-aged and brawny, with straggly hair and an unkempt beard. Could he best all three? At this stage he didn't know. Best to err on the path of caution for now.

As if he were responding to friends, Tritus said with a congenial air, "There's no fear of that; we don't live far." He purposely flicked a glance up at the mistletoe adorning the branches above the path. "Besides, the mistletoe will distract anyone who intends to steal from me."

His point was not missed as the three of them raised their eyes and stared at the bright foliage hanging from the trees.

The older man with the straggly hair and bristled face, clearly the leader of the trio, twisted his upper lip into a sneer. "Well, you best be off then if your woman is waiting. Given the presence of the mistletoe, me and my men will not be disrespecting the season."

"No," Tritus agreed pleasantly, although he was grinding his teeth together in a forced smile. "It is opportune that the mistletoe has been hung to curb any unfortunate incidents so close to Yule."

The threat was inherent this time, and with a sharp nod of his head, Tritus turned back toward the path and walked on past them. With the dagger still clasped in his hand, he listened intently as the three of them whispered and snarled under their breath. He could feel their gazes piercing his back, the edge of their anger licking his heels, but he refused to turn around and look back; he had no wish to grant them the satisfaction of thinking he feared them.

Only when he had turned a corner in the path and he felt their stares drop, did Tritus quickly jump off the trail and trek carefully and quietly back the way he'd come. Crouching low in the darkening forest, he peered between the undergrowth. He saw them immediately.

The three men still weren't walking on the path but rather to the far edge of it, as if half in the forest itself. The sack on the younger man's back was wriggling in earnest now, and Tritus swore he heard another muffled moan as he watched the heavyset man growl and thump the sack again. Tritus winced at the action, feeling sorry for the animal, but he reassured himself that they were not following him and turned back to continue his journey. Cailleach was waiting, and he had no reason to involve himself in whatever was going on. The ways of the gods were sacred; he knew that better than most. But no matter how much he tried to push the incident from his mind, Tritus couldn't return to that carefree anticipation on the long journey home. It also didn't help that, more than once, an image of Bryn, with her eyes wide and frightened, crept into his mind.

When I return, I will see whatever is troubling her is put to rights, he promised himself. Although, he hoped that, by then, she would have shared her secret with the chieftain and any wrongs committed against her would have ceased.

CHAPTER 6

TRITUS

Tritus gave a huge sigh of relief when he finally dragged the Yule log into the cave and carefully placed it at the edge of the fire pit, ensuring one end of it was within easy reach of the flames. The log was so large it measured the length of their cave, the branches at its far end poking out under the hide that covered the cave entrance.

With the Yule log now inside, it felt as though he'd really brought the forest into their home, and Tritus finally allowed himself time to stand back and take in the work he'd done. Over the last year, he'd gone to the effort of transplanting and nurturing a tree inside the cave. Courtesy of his mother, his gifts lay with the flora and fauna, and he'd tenderly ministered to the seedling every day, ensuring it survived within the dark confined space. The gifts he innately carried were unearthed almost a year ago now, while helping Cailleach with her work over the winter. Tritus was surprised to find he could nurture seedlings and other plants, enabling them to thrive well beyond what was natural.

It had been at the end of Cailleach's winter reign, some

six months after they'd first met, that he decided to bring the forest into the cave. Over the summer months, he'd ensured the tiny sapling had sufficient light and water, and he'd fussed over it as if it was a newborn babe. As a result, the sapling had grown into a small tree, with a strong trunk and healthy green needles.

Now, with the smell of fresh pine in the air, Tritus felt satisfied that the winter solstice was indeed here in the cave. Cailleach had already made it whimsical and welcoming, a harbor against the harsh elements outside, but the additions he'd planned long into the night and achieved this day had brought the spirit of Yule into the room.

Mistletoe and holly now hung from the walls and ceiling, their verdant, lush, green leaves providing a sense of otherworldly energy. The red berries offered flashes of rich color, a reminder of the Mother Goddess's menstrual blood while paying homage to the gift of fertility. The small, burbling creek running along the far wall only served to intensify the magical, festive atmosphere in the room.

His lips lifted in a smile as he allowed himself to feel a measure of pride. He'd done good. All of this was a surprise for Cal, one he hoped she would enjoy.

The idea of the Yule log had come to him on his return trek home from the village. Cailleach hadn't been in the cave when he arrived back around supper time, and the disappointment had stung. He'd set about making a meal for them both as night beckoned. With the onslaught of a storm, and the eerie howl and shriek of the wind told him exactly what his woman was doing. Knowing she'd be home late, Tritus had retired to bed, and it wasn't until the wee hours of the night that Cailleach finally traipsed into their cave and collapsed in an exhausted heap next to him on the pallet. He'd been waiting for her, just conscious above the cusp of sleep, the gifts he'd traded for ready to share with her on her return. Yet he hadn't had a chance; Cailleach had fallen into a deep sleep as soon as she lay beside him.

Tritus had come to find love was a sweet poison, a blessing and a curse, but with this woman he would have it no other way, for she was his and he was hers. And so, the gifts had been left where they were, hidden out of sight in his corner of the room, now awaiting the winter solstice. Instead, he'd pulled her close and held her long into the night before falling into an exhausted sleep close to dawn. He'd awoken to find her gone, but that crushing reality had been replaced by anticipation. Because, finally, after all his careful planning, the solstice was upon them, and tonight marked the first of twelve nights of celebration. This first evening they would share alone, but he hoped she would agree to begin their trek down to the village tomorrow. He had the feeling Cailleach wouldn't be keen to join in with the villagers straight away, so he'd planned silent observation for the night of their arrival. They would sit back securely in the trees, hidden from prying eyes through the art of glamor, and simply watch the villagers and their festivities. If she felt brave enough—and he hoped she would—he wanted Cailleach to join in.

He sighed, aware he had high hopes. High hopes that were riding on his woman's decision. Turning away from the Yule log, he went to find her gifts to lay them out on the bed. It was at that moment he felt a draught enter the room, and the sixth sense prickling at the back of his neck told him she had finally arrived.

Cailleach's gasp was audible as she entered the cave. Tritus walked toward her, not wanting to miss her response. She stood just inside the entrance, her hammer dangling from one hand as she looked from the pine tree he'd decorated to the wreaths of mistletoe, then to the holly, and then around the rest of the cave. Her eyes widened when they alighted on the Yule log that extended from her feet to the fire pit, and when he saw her take a deep breath, Tritus knew she'd smelt the mix of warming spices he'd thrown onto the fire.

Her eyes, large and luminous, now turned to claim his. "What is all of this?" she whispered.

He smiled warmly at her, stopping a few feet shy of taking her into his arms. He wanted to see her face, judge her honest reaction. "Happy winter solstice, my love. Do you like it?"

For a moment, Cailleach stared at him, but then a huge smile creased her lips. "I love it, Tritus! You have brought the outside in. But I must confess I do not understand why we have such a huge great log in here. Do you need help cutting it into pieces for the fire?"

He laughed. "No, Cal. This is the Yule log, a long-held tradition of both yours and my people. We must not break it up into pieces; the idea is that we should slowly burn one end of it over the next twelve days. During that time, it will shorten naturally." He bent down and skimmed his fingers over one of the branches as he added, "Ideally, this log should have come from the same tree that we used to burn another log from over the winter solstice last year, but as this is our first occasion, I'm sure we'll be granted a pass. "

Her eyebrows arched above her swirling silver irises. "What a strange tradition, indeed!" And then she suddenly froze, her piercing gaze now looking at the ink was visible under the arm of his tunic.

Tritus had been waiting for this moment. She'd missed it last night as she'd fallen asleep, and he'd purposely left his tunic on as they'd slept. Cailleach had also awoken before he did, whispering a good morning and a promise to be back soon while he'd remained dragged under in sleep. As a result, he hadn't had a chance to show her what he'd done to his body...until now.

She whispered slowly, "What is that?" Her eyes flew up to meet his. "Is that what I think it is?"

Tritus moved closer, one hand lifting to peel back the sleeve of his tunic so the tattoos now banding his upper arm were fully visible to her gaze. He stopped a foot away from her as she perused the designs. He could feel his heart pounding in his chest. "Do you like it?" he asked softly.

Her lips pressed together, and her eyes darted back to his. "I'm not sure yet," she said carefully, her eyes still wide. "That depends on your motivation for having it done." Those silver orbs grazed over his features, unflinching and direct, as they judged his expression. "Why, Tritus? What is your reason for marking your skin?"

He had thought it was obvious, but Cailleach was ever careful; protective of herself, especially her emotions. Hard as he tried, Tritus knew she had always planned on a transient relationship, believing that what they had wouldn't be for long. And yet, at the same time, he knew she felt that what they had was forever, that this love, this emotion, which was *more* than love, was something so rare and breathtaking that they were blessed to have it. Cailleach was an enigma, and he often wondered if it was because of the rarity of their relationship that she hesitated to fully succumb to happiness, or if it was because of what she'd witnessed between her siblings and their partners. Hardly any of the Celtic deities had a lasting love story.

Suddenly, there was the need to touch, to ground her to the here and now. Acting on that instinct, he dropped the tunic sleeve and broke the distance between them by reaching out to touch her cheek. He stared deep into her silver eyes and said with utmost honesty and a baring of his soul, "I chose to have my skin permanently branded for two reasons, my love. The first being that I accept my heritage—I accept my origins and who my parents are. The second being that I choose this life and the woman I have been gifted." He bent his head so they were at eye level and added firmly, "I did this because I choose you, Cal. Always you. The brands along my arm are inconsequential to those you hold around my heart. You hold all of me, inside and out."

His hand curved under her chin now, and he leaned in close to whisper the next words across her lips. "These symbols on my arms merely show others what allegiance I have. But for you, my proud, stubborn woman, they should be yet another brand that ties me to you, another permanent binding that I wear with pride and joy."

On the heels of those words, he closed the distance between them and pressed his lips against hers. Hard.

Cailleach had gone so still, her face so white, that he'd felt an urge to awaken her from whatever thoughts held her captive. But as soon as his lips found hers, she came to life, erupting on a sea of passion that carried them both away in a duel of tongues and teeth, hands and moans.

Cailleach's voice was rasping as she dragged her mouth down his neck, murmuring fiercely, "You are mine, Tritus! Regardless of whether you wear those tattoos or not—You. Are. Mine."

Tritus grunted, his hands curving over her rounded buttocks before sensuously sliding to the front of her thighs. He lifted the long skirts of her dress and ran his hand over the soft skin of her legs, smiling when her breath hitched as he found her center. His heart pounding, his blood surging with lust, he said with a fierceness that tugged at his breast,

"And you are mine, Cal. Never forget it." His finger entered her then, punctuating his message.

The jerk of her hips was instantaneous. Cailleach's body seemed to go boneless in his hands, and the smile that drifted across her face as his fingers worked between her legs eased the emotional tension in his heart, especially when she whispered on a soft sigh, "Then I accept the markings on your body, lover. Now, take me to bed!"

Without another word, and with his heart singing in his chest, Tritus scooped her up in his arms and carried her to their pallet. There, he showed her how much he loved her, with the fire crackling in the background, the smell of fresh pine and warm spices permeating the air, and the vibrant vision of mistletoe and holly shining down on them from above.

MUCH LATER, as they lay entwined together, their passion sated, Tritus broached what was on his mind. "Cal?"

"Hmmm?" she asked, stretching languidly against his side as one of her hands trailed up and down his chest— something she was wont to do after they'd sated their passion.

"This new tradition we are embarking on together is only beginning. In a few nights, I'd like us to visit one of the villages I trade at. I want you to see how your people celebrate Yule. The chieftain has invited us both, and if you are up for it, I hoped you'd want to join in on the festivities. But if it is too much, we can always watch from a distance and return on another day before the solstice ends."

She froze against him, and then her head snapped up to seize his gaze. "To the village? Together?"

He nodded, his face open so she could see his anticipation at the idea. "Yes. You could use glamor so no one knows who you are. The village people know I have a woman; I told them you were a healer of sorts, so your secret is safe. Think on it, Cal; this would be a great opportunity to celebrate the real spirit of Yule, not just with me but with your people as well."

Her face began to close, and his stomach plummeted; she was not open to the idea.

Tritus rushed out, "Please, Cal. This would make me happy. Consider it for that alone."

Her eyes flicked over his features, her own now neutral, careful. "You said...you said that Yule is also a time of fertility. Will we—are you...going to participate?"

He froze. *Did she . . .?* Tritus suddenly snorted. "No, Cal! How could you say that? I am not suggesting we visit the village to celebrate Yule with others! You are the only one I will be sharing a bed with—now and forever." He grabbed her hands and tugged her to him, tilting her face so he could look into her eyes. "You know this, Cal. Deep in your heart, you know this. Stop letting the fear win. Trust in me—trust in us."

Her throat bobbed, and Tritus had the sudden urge to run his hand down her shining, moonlight hair. The strands felt silky soft, yielding to his touch. As if following their lead, Cailleach leaned close, pressing herself into his arms. She released a soft sigh as he silently gave her what she needed, the tight squeeze of his arms pulling her even closer as he whispered against her hair, "I would like us to attend the festivities together, and it will be exciting to freely wander and celebrate without risk of ire or judgment if you are glamored. It will be wonderful, Cal. Trust me."

She said nothing.

Tritus waited.

Eventually, Cailleach pulled away and stared up at him, silver eyes gray with heavy resignation. He didn't know why she looked so reluctant, but that mystery was soon forgotten when she whispered, "Yes, I'll go with you."

CHAPTER 7
TRITUS
3RD CENTURY BC, ANCIENT SCOTLAND

Tritus felt a laugh burst from his chest as he twirled around a large, open fire pit with Cailleach in his arms. The low thump of the drums and the trill of the pipes was lively and festive in the cool night air, the winter weather unable to dampen the spirits of those outside. The snow sparkled in the moonlight, but the woman in his arms rivaled the stars and the moon. Her dress was as white as the glacial ice at the top of the Cairngorms and it, too, sparkled with all the tiny crystals that looked like fireflies threaded throughout the soft gauze of her gown.

The area around the fire pit had been cleared of snow, and the logs that were usually placed beside it had been pushed back to make room for dancing. The villagers had worked hard to make the ground smooth and festive, laying pine needles on the frozen earth, not only to create a fresh, pine scent as people danced, but also to prevent any slips on the ice beneath.

Innumerable blazing torches had been set out in a large semicircle around the huge central fire, casting a soft golden glow that only added to the holiday atmosphere and the delight of the lively revelers. The tempo of the music was fast and festive, a celebration of new life, and Tritus had felt the itch to move in his very blood. He'd caught Cailleach's wide-eyed glance and, without speaking, offered her his hand. As soon as her fingers reached out for his, he clutched them tightly to his chest and tugged her into the mass of merry dancers. She'd come willingly, trustingly, and with her glamor well in place, they danced around the fire pits, one couple among many.

Tritus couldn't believe his luck when, after an hour of watching the villagers from their concealed perch, Cailleach had announced that she would like to join in the festivities. Aware that she hadn't been as excited as he was, he'd turned to face her, incredulous that she wanted to participate on their first night. But she did, and she had come prepared. Because even as he watched, she had waved her hand down her body and her usual periwinkle blue dress had been replaced with the soft, gauzy, snow-white gown she now wore.

His jaw dropped, because Cailleach had not only changed her clothing, but also her hair. Her customary braid had been replaced with soft, flowing locks and a few plaited strands. It curled enticingly around her shoulders and hugged her back in a veritable tide of moonlight. Tritus loved her hair, and seeing Cal in her stunning dress with that mass of silky strands had been a sight to see.

He looked her slowly up and down. The pendant he'd given her was securely fastened around her neck, the cross and stone itself nestled inside the bodice of her gown. His heart had swelled, his lower body, too, and he stood there gasping like a fish for what felt like an eon. Cailleach had giggled, her face losing its seriousness and reverting to that of a young girl, innocent and carefree. "You see, lover, I too can plan a surprise."

The smile that stretched across his face had matched the blooming rush of warmth in his chest. He had reached out and cupped her jaw, his eyes laser-focused on hers. "Thank you," he whispered, the words choking in his throat.

Unable to voice exactly how happy she'd made him, he tugged Cailleach to him and kissed her. The love he felt for her had risen over him like a tidal wave, and he clutched her close, ensuring he could feel every inch of her soft, pliant body against his as he plundered her mouth and sipped against her neck.

When they eventually pulled back, breathless and still yearning, Cailleach put a finger on his lips, her own caught up in a powerful, smug smile. "You can properly thank me later. For now, you promised me a celebration." She stood back and gestured at the villagers, dancing under the night sky around the blazing bonfire. "Lead on, lover. Let us create new, lasting memories as we celebrate the solstice."

With his heart singing and a feeling of profound love flowing through his veins, Tritus had taken her hand in his and led her into the village.

Now, hours later, his throat parched and his legs beginning to feel a delicious burn from all the dancing, he realized Cailleach would also benefit from a break and refreshments. As he twirled her again, he looked outside the circle, trying to locate the barrels of spiced wine and tables of food. He caught sight of them to the left, close to the village roundhouses. That was also when he caught sight of Bryn. She was dressed in a fresh, white tunic standing at the edge of the dancing ring, watching him intently.

The music came to a close then, and as he reached out for Cailleach, tucking her under his arm and steering her toward the refreshments, he caught Bryn's jerk of her head. There was no denying the pinched look to the girl's face or the sharp twist to her lips. He sent her a tentative smile, which she didn't return. Instead, her eyes moved to Cailleach, and there they narrowed.

Why was she looking at Cal in that way? It was a strange response. Tritus tightened his hold on his woman, feeling a surge of protection. Then he sighed at the stupidity of his knee-jerk reaction; Cailleach was all-powerful and could look after herself without his help, and anyway, a young girl like Bryn was no threat. Yet, he couldn't help the instinctual move; Cailleach made him protective, made him want to keep her safe.

Holding Bryn's gaze, he guided Cailleach right up to the young girl, and, with a pleasant smile on his face, he said to Bryn, "Happy Yule to you, Bryn. I'm glad to see you tonight, as I wanted to introduce you to my woman." He turned to face Cailleach, who was now looking at him with a question in her silver eyes. "Cal, this is Bryn. Bryn, this is Cal. I know Cal is as excited and as awed as I am to share in tonight's festivities with you all. Your people have been very kind to invite us."

Bryn tensed when Cal's gaze met her own, and Tritus hid a smile as the hostility on the girl's face turned to awe. He couldn't help wondering what Bryn would really think if she were to see the Winter Goddess as she normally was. The glamor that Cailleach had wrought was effective, removing the ethereal glow that was usually around her form, and it had turned her beauty from extraordinary to lovely. However, on looking at her closely, one couldn't help but pause at the light that shone within, because for all the glamor, Cailleach couldn't hide the sparkle of power in her eyes.

Before entering the village, they'd settled on the name 'Cal.' It was close enough to the truth to be neutral and not cause a slip-up. It was also the root of a few names, including Caitlin or Caillic, which although they wouldn't use them, offered some sort of protection against her real name. Additionally, Tritus wanted their night to be memorable as well as *real*, and he felt using another name altogether would stain the memories they made this eve.

"Cal is from the north," he now said to Bryn in the face of her silence. "I met her on one of my trading trips. I have told her all about you, and she has been very keen to meet you."

Bryn gave Cailleach a cursory glance and an incline of her head, but her eyes did not meet those of the Winter Goddess. It was an odd response, as the young girl was usually engaging.

What was wrong with her? Tritus could see the tense cant to her body, her hands squeezed into fists at her side. Had she come to see him for a reason? A whisper trailed across his skin, a warning. He bent down so they were eye level. "Has something happened, Bryn? Were you looking for me?"

She jerked her head from side to side and forced a smile to her lips, still awkward. "No, no, I just wanted to see if it was really you. Some of the villagers mentioned they'd seen you here. I didn't believe them, as you didn't tell me you were coming back tonight."

There was accusation in her tone, and the swift glance he and Cailleach shared told him that she'd heard it too.

"I'm sorry, Bryn. I wasn't sure what day we'd come down. If I'd known beforehand, I would have told you." Tritus dropped a hand on her shoulder and squeezed warmly, trying to force the young girl to engage. It was as though she'd sought him out for a reason only to shut down on seeing him. He wondered if it was because Cailleach was here.

Tritus realized there was no use forcing the girl, but maybe a distraction was what was needed. He squeezed her shoulder again, forcing her to look up at his face, and asked, "I've told Cal what a great dancer you are. Would you be so kind as to show her?"

Bryn's throat bobbed. "What—here? Now?"

"Of course," Tritus said, sweeping his arm at the nearly-empty dancing area. It appeared most had gone off in search of sustenance. "What better chance than now? I've told her all about your skills."

"But...I need a partner."

Cailleach glanced between them. "Tritus will accompany you, my dear."

He looked at Cal, a question in his eyes. She smiled. "Come, Tritus; you can't very well ask the girl to perform without assistance. You will make a grand partner, and I will enjoy watching you both."

After searching Cal's face for confirmation that she really would be fine on her own, Tritus held his hand out to Bryn and asked with a bright smile, "Shall we?"

Her little hand fell into his, and he guided her over to the dance area, conscious of Cailleach's gaze on his back. He turned to face Bryn, the glow of the fire now traveling over her young, serious face. "Which dance, my lady?" he asked her with a flourishing bow.

Again, she didn't smile back. "Not a lively one."

Tritus nodded, feeling that little telltale flip in his stomach again that something wasn't quite right with this young girl. "All right. How about a dance in reverence to the Goddess of Winter?"

Bryn nodded. "Yes, that would be fitting."

Together, they twirled and moved, a reflection of the Winter Goddess and her power. The cold season and the passing of the animals and the landscape, the fresh breath of snow and the land washed anew.

As Tritus danced, he was conscious of Cailleach's stare. He knew she'd be aware of which dance they'd chosen, and he, with every movement, showed his love for her in the gesture of his hands, his body, and the smile on his lips. His heart felt full and warm when he caught her eyes a few times during the performance, and when he saw the soft sheen to her eyes, he knew she understood his message.

At the end of the dance, he clasped Bryn's hands in his and gave her a formal bow and a warm smile. "Thank you, my lady, for the lovely dance. You are a lively and engaging partner."

For all their efforts, Bryn's face was still tense, the tension visible around her eyes. "Thank you for the dance, Tritus."

"What is it?" he suddenly asked her, hoping this time she would tell him what was on her mind.

Bryn flicked her gaze to Cal and then back to him. "It does not matter anymore."

His hands gripped hers. "Bryn," he said, gravely now, "you can tell me. I will not break your trust."

She hesitated, her mouth opening, then she shut it and shook her head. "I—I...it was nothing; a mistake." And with that, she tugged her hands out of his and rushed off, her long skinny legs kicking up her thin shift as she scampered past Cailleach.

They both turned to watch her go, and when the young girl didn't turn in the direction of the village, but rather out into the cold, dark night, Tritus's stomach turned again.

Bryn wore no shoes and no warm cloak; she'd freeze out there in the snow before long.

He began moving forward to follow her, but Cal was there, her hand on his arm. "Let me go," she murmured.

Tritus looked down into her upturned face and saw the reflection of his concern in her eyes. He hesitated. "Bryn is a prickly little thing. I'm not sure if you'll have any luck getting through to her."

Cailleach shook her head. "That's not true, Tritus. You forget I have other means. It's clear she cannot talk to you, even though she wanted to. Let me go to her. Please."

Tritus assessed Cailleach closely. He couldn't deny her logic. It was obvious Bryn had come to him with something in mind, but maybe Cal was right. Maybe the girl needed a woman's touch to help her share whatever she needed to say. "All right. But, Cal, please go easy on her. I think there is something dreadfully wrong."

Cal nodded. "I think you are right. Don't worry, Tritus, I will get to the bottom of it. Wait here, my love. I will return."

She gathered her skirts in one hand and began to follow the path that Bryn had traveled. Tritus watched her go with a sense of loss that their evening had been interrupted, but the tickling at the base of his neck told him there were other forces at play tonight. And after the way Bryn had spoken to him on his last visit, he had a feeling that Cailleach might just have the touch the young girl needed to share her closely-hoarded secret.

CHAPTER 8
CAILLEACH
3RD CENTURY BC, ANCIENT SCOTLAND

Cailleach released a little of her power, asking the forest and its inhabitants to answer her call. The trees whispered in response, their limbs sighing above, and snow sprinkled around her as a crisp breeze ran through the area. Hearing her call, the creatures of the forest scampered past her in a rustle of leaves and undergrowth as they took off, searching. Before long, Cailleach heard the reply—a sentient call that she knew deep in her bones: the hoot of an owl. A whisper followed through the leaves next: *She's here. Come quickly. She's here.*

Cailleach followed the sound with her third eye, allowing her inner senses to lead her unerringly in the exact direction. The revelry of the festivities behind her soon became muted and lost to the sound of the trees creaking, the forest rustling, and the sighing breeze. It was dark under the trees, but not so dark as to be blinding. The rays of the full moon above were fractured by the heavy boughs of the forest, but the dappled luminance provided enough light to guide her footsteps. Cailleach had no need of the moonlight as her silver eyes could pierce the darkness, but she breathed a sigh of relief that Bryn wasn't shrouded in oppressive shadows.

Since taking on the role of Winter's Mantle, she had become one with the season, one with the forest and her mountain home. She had come close to forming a similar bond with the animals who dwelled there, but it was a tentative connection at best, and Cailleach could not deny that this crown would always belong to her brother, Cernunnos. The Wild God of the Forest was an anomaly, part animal, part mortal, and part deity. Although her sister, Morrígan, and others could claim an association with particular animals, only Cernunnos could claim an allegiance to all of them as he equally belonged in their world and his own.

As Cailleach walked toward Bryn, she mused on how that explained Tritus's gifts. Her lover had a natural gift; he was able to nurture the plants, to coax them to grow and thrive, but also to calm any animals they came across. Time and again over the past year, she'd found him looking after an injured animal. His touch healed the creatures he'd found—or those that found him—and Cailleach felt great satisfaction in the fact that Cernunnos's legacy lived on in this world through his son.

Now, those same creatures urged her on, little paw prints and scampering feet running just ahead of her. She could sense the hurried nature of their movements and knew they were close. When she spied the flash of a white tunic in the distance, her mind called out to the creatures and the forest, *"Thank you. Be at rest again."*

In an instant, the animals were gone, and the breeze died on a soft parting sigh. A few more steps and Cailleach was upon the girl. She could see Bryn, lying in a tight ball on the ground, her small body shivering. With her honed sight, Cailleach could also see that her skin was covered in goose pimples and there were soft puffs of white air hovering in front of the child's face. Cailleach suddenly realized it was freezing. She didn't feel the cold herself, but she instantly understood that if Bryn did not get warm soon, her life would be at risk.

Cailleach was aware that if Bryn saw her, she might turn tail and run again. She would need the child to trust her, and as time wasn't on her side, the only way that could occur was by calling upon her power. Carefully coaxing her magic forth, Cailleach raised her hand. A small ball of blue-white light appeared in the center of her palm. Holding it to her lips, she gently blew on the oscillating substance. It uncurled into a long, thin ribbon before arrowing straight toward the girl.

Cailleach watched as it slid soundlessly into Bryn's ear. She waited a beat, then another, but when the girl didn't move or acknowledge the power, Cailleach released her breath and rose from her crouched position. Unclasping the button at the collar of her cloak, she pulled it from her shoulders, and carefully, slowly, without a whisper of sound, she walked up to the little girl and draped it across her shoulders, mindful not to touch Bryn's skin.

Bryn froze, her head whipping up to stare in shock at Cailleach. "Who? What—? How did you find me?" the little girl stammered, twin rivulets running down her cheeks.

Cailleach gave Bryn a gentle smile and took a seat on a nearby fallen log, arranging the skirts of her white gown around her knees. Hands clasped in her lap, she settled her body and her mind and looked the child fully in the face. "Tritus sent me. He is very worried about you. He wanted me to make sure you were all right." Holding the young girl's gaze, she asked softly, "Are you all right, Bryn?"

At those words, Bryn's eyes welled with tears again, and her lower lip wobbled. "I...I...yes."

"Child," Cailleach intoned softly, reaching out to grasp one of the girl's small hands in hers. Holding it warmly in her own, Cailleach kept her magic tightly in check so the girl did not feel the brunt of her power as she continued, "It is obvious there is something wrong. Tritus talked of you after his last visit to your village." Her eyes shifted, pointedly staring at the girl's upper arms. "Those bruises did not appear there by themselves, Bryn. Tell me what has happened. I am here to help."

Cailleach could feel how tightly strung the child was. Even her body was tense, the muscles rigidly locked. As Bryn struggled to formulate a response, Cailleach sent a tendril of warmth down her own arms and into the child. The goosebumps on Bryn's flesh did not disappear, but Cailleach noticed the fine tremors were gone as the girl finally opened her mouth and replied, "I ran away because I needed to escape. I can no longer stay there."

Cailleach stilled, conscious this admission held a measure of truth. "And why do you need to escape, Bryn?" she asked softly, schooling her emotions to remain soothing and gentle. The child did not need to see her righteous anger. Cailleach was heartbroken that Bryn would feel she had nothing to lose by leaving the village, by venturing into the freezing countryside with no escort and no cloak. If the child really had been running away and hadn't been stopped, she'd soon be dead. There was no doubt about it.

Bryn continued to look down at their clasped hands, and her face crumpled. Her words were thick with emotion as she conceded, "Because I am a reminder. A hurtful reminder. And every time my father sees me, he sees my mother—the woman he cherished and lost. He gets angry that she is no longer here. He—" She stopped suddenly, hiccupping, and Cailleach waited, trying to remain very still, neutral, and non-judgmental, even while her blood boiled with the admission that the child's father was the one who beat her!

Bryn raised her free hand and scrubbed fiercely at her face, trying to erase the tears that showed no signs of stopping.

Cailleach took a breath, still forcing herself to remain calm, and said quietly, "Bryn, you can tell me. I will not hurt you."

The young girl swallowed and then rasped hoarsely, "He is fine during the day. When he's awake, he's out working, hunting and trapping with the other men, but when he's home, he's in his cups...and that's when he sees Mother—and not me." She abruptly hiccupped, and her voice dropped as she added, "And when he realizes I am not her, he—he gets angry, and he . . ."

"He what?" Cailleach pressed, her heart now turning cold, the fine hairs on her neck rising. "You can tell me, sweetheart."

Bryn sniffed, her hand lifting to wipe her face again. She gestured at her arms, to where the bruises were still visible, and kept her eyes downcast as she whispered, "He grabs me and hides me below the floor of our roundhouse. He says it's for my own good and his. That if he can't see me, he can't hurt me."

Cailleach gasped. "He hides you below ground?"

"Yes," the child whispered.

Cailleach struggled to imagine the space. It must be tiny. The roundhouses weren't overly large, and any hole in the ground would be damp and cold, but she supposed it was possible to hide a hole the width of a child under a bed or a table with a rug laid on top. She looked at Bryn's clothing again with new eyes, seeing the dirty tunic as more than just child's play. Struggling now to hide her horror and her anger, she pressed, "And is that all, Bryn? Is anything else happening?"

The child frowned. "Before yesterday, I would have said no. I may be wrong...at least, I hope I'm wrong! But I think that Father—that he—" She stopped and took a breath.

Cailleach waited, silently praying for the child to continue. She allowed another influencing tendril of her power to travel from her body and into Bryn's, using their physical connection to her advantage.

In the next moment, Bryn tightened her grip on Cailleach's hand and said slowly, "I think Father is smuggling children in and out of our village."

This was not the response Cailleach had expected, and unbeknownst to her, with the shock those words carried, the warmth in her hands dissipated in a flash. Bryn gasped and drew back, her face chalk-white, a scream of pain and terror escaping her lips. The piercing sound jolted Cailleach from her blinding, white-hot anger, and with one horrified look at the young girl, she instantly knew what she had done.

The child was inconsolable, cursing and clutching her hand to her chest, tears streaming down her face. Cailleach, her heart bursting with self-recrimination, reached out and placed a hand on Bryn's head. The child instantly slackened, wilting like a flower. Cailleach caught her before she fell to the hard-packed snow, careful to keep her shield in place lest the child be burned again by her power.

With one arm wrapped around Bryn to keep her close, she pulled the cloak from the child's shoulders with her other and laid it upon the frosty ground as best she could. Then, she laid Bryn on top of the cloak, tucking her body in tight, before pulling the corners up and over so the child was fully covered, face and all. Lastly, Cailleach made sure the hand that she'd burned was positioned outside the cloak. With Bryn's warmth and comfort in mind, Cailleach then closed her eyes, drew forth another tendril of power, and touched the cloak. The snow around them dissipated in the blink of an eye. Then, with her eyes still closed, Cailleach internally called out to Tritus. *"Come quick, my love. I need you!"*

It was a half-truth, for Cailleach realized that Bryn also needed Tritus. With his special skills, he could help reverse the wrongs she had done to this child.

"What is it?" came his quick reply.

Cailleach could hear the alarm in his tone, and she sought to set him at ease. *"It's not me, Tritus. It's Bryn. She's hurt, and I need your help. Come quickly."*

"I'll be right there. Maintain a connection so I know where to find you."

Cailleach sent him a gentle caress, brushing a soft hand against their internal bond. She felt Tritus's response and, knowing she'd done everything she could for now, she sat back to wait, watching the child.

The whisper of the trees and the crunch of feet on snow alerted her to his presence sooner than she'd anticipated. Her head whipped up and toward him, a question in her eyes. "How did you get here so fast?"

His long strides ate up the remaining ground between them, and then he was there, wrapping her securely in his arms. She hadn't missed his glance down to the child or his worried green gaze when he saw Bryn's hand. She knew he'd guessed why she called him, yet Tritus didn't say one word about the injury as he replied, "I felt your distress down our bond. I was already on my way."

Cailleach nodded and held him tightly, her cheek pressed against his chest as she listened to the strong beat of his heart. It pounded faster than usual, a testament to the speed at which he'd traveled to get to her so quickly.

After a moment, she pulled away, conscious of the sleeping form at their feet. Her heart was pounding in her own chest now as she said with self-loathing, "I hurt the child. Badly, Tritus. Look at her hand, my love; I have burned it. I hoped that with your healing skills you could reverse the hurt I've caused."

Tritus's face was grave as he turned to the child. Crouching down by her side, he gently reached out and laid a soft finger on Bryn's burnt skin. He sat there, very still, for a long moment.

"Well?" Cailleach asked sharply, suddenly fearing she'd hurt the child so badly that even Tritus couldn't reverse the wound.

Her lover opened his eyes and looked up at her, and she could see his message in the soft smile that crossed his face, even before he said, "It is healed, Cal. A minor burn."

It was true. For now, before her very eyes, the child's hand was once again unmarred, the skin as soft and smooth as it had been before. Cailleach felt her knees weaken, and she dropped back to sit on the log. "Oh, thank the Mother!" she exclaimed, feeling the spark of tears against her eyelids. She closed her eyes, fisting her hands in her lap.

She felt Tritus move, coming to sit beside her. His arms went around her, enclosing her tightly in his fierce, protective embrace. "What happened, Cal? For you to slip like that tells me that whatever Bryn shared was enough to scare you."

Cailleach pulled back to stare at him in shock. "You aren't going to yell and scream and reprimand me for what I've done? I should have known better, Tritus. I should have kept complete control of my power."

He didn't smile; he didn't even blink as he held her gaze fiercely with his, unbending, strong, and true. "I know you, Cal. I know you better than you know yourself. You would never intentionally hurt anyone, not without reason. And Bryn is but a young girl. I know her too. She could not have initiated that response. But given what's happened tonight, and the fact that she ran away—well, it must be to do with what you've found and is most likely the reason the child is still asleep. So, tell me, Cal, what happened? How did she elicit such a response?"

Cailleach swallowed and looked down at Bryn. She wrapped her arms around her herself—and not from the cold. From the chill of horror that came with sharing Bryn's story.

She could feel Tritus waiting patiently as she took a moment before sharing what she'd learned. Eventually, she whispered, "Her father has been punishing her because she reminds him of his dead wife. I don't know how or why Bryn's mother died, but he misses her so much that the demons chase him. She said he drinks himself to oblivion, then beats her, and instead of going further, he...forces her underground for her safety."

Cailleach looked up to face him then, needing his warmth, his love. Holding his vibrant, green gaze, she added, "He places her in the cold ground, Tritus, shutting her in the dark. He hides her, Tritus! He hides her because she reminds him of his lost love!"

She swallowed, fear riding up her throat, threatening to choke her. She couldn't help reaching for his hand, needing to touch him now, to reassure herself that he was still alive. Holding tightly onto his hand, she shared the fear that had crossed her mind after Bryn had told her story—the fear that had driven her to forget her power and burn the child. "Is that what I will become if I lose you? Will I go mad? Insane with loss?"

CHAPTER 9

TRITUS

S hock coursed through Tritus's body.

"What? No, Cal!" He leaned in toward her, his heart pounding in complete denial. "You will never lose me! I am not going anywhere. We are one, and there is no losing either of us. There is only me and you—you and me—forever."

Cailleach's form was rigid, her face frozen in such an expression of horror that Tritus knew he hadn't gotten through to her. She was lost to something: a memory, a vision—he knew not what, just that she was not there with him.

He was overwhelmed with the need to shake her from it and did the only thing he could, the only thing that felt right between them—he reached out and grabbed her. Without hesitating, he banded one of his arms tightly around her back while he used his other to reach out and tip her chin. With her wide eyes tilted up to his, her lips exposed for his taking, he swooped down and passionately kissed her. It was a kiss deeply rooted in his emotions. A kiss that transferred everything he was feeling, everything he held dear, everything that was *them*.

At first, her lips were as frozen as her expression, but then, after a second, they moved just as passionately, just as hungrily. Their lips moved together now, taking, purging, cleansing, reviving—until they were both satiated. As their passion slowed, Tritus brushed his lips over her cheek, her forehead, and then her lips once again before pulling back and looking down at her. His arms were still tight around her back, pressing her close, as he whispered, "I mean it, Cal. No matter what is to come, I'll always be with you."

Cailleach choked, tears welling, but she nodded, her eyes holding his.

Tritus felt a shiver through his very being. Her response bothered him, and a feeling of unease whispered down his spine. "Cal—" He stopped abruptly. No. He'd said enough, and what he'd said was true—no matter what happened, he would always be with her. And if his powerful Winter Goddess knew more than he did as to what was coming in their future, if she'd had a vision or someone had shared one with her, so be it. He would not let it affect their time together now.

So, instead, he said, "Nothing should ever be taken for granted, Cal. We never know how long we'll have, none of us does. All we can bank on is the now, the present moment we live in. I vow to you that for however long we have, however long *I* have, I will make sure that every day we spend together is as if it were the last. I will value every moment with you from now until then. Always." He held her gaze, forcing the belief out of his eyes and into hers.

Her silver irises swirled with power, expanding and receding, but Tritus caught a flicker of understanding in their depths before another sheen of tears limned her eyes.

And even though she didn't respond aloud, she conceded his message with a small nod.

It was enough. Relieved, he pulled back, finally releasing her from his embrace but still keeping hold of her hand. He gestured at Bryn. "Now, what are we to do with this poor girl? She needs help, and fast."

"Yes," Cailleach whispered. Her voice was hoarse, but Tritus could see that she now held firm, her resolve back. "She was running away. She thought to ask you for help, Tritus; but for some reason, she changed her mind. I think it was because she didn't expect to see me with you tonight. But with some gentle coercion, she trusted me enough to share her story...until I hurt her badly, that is." Her face again creased with anguish.

Tritus squeezed Cailleach's hand. "It's all right, Cal. She's healed now," he reminded her firmly. "All you need to do now is ensure she can't remember what happened to her hand. Amend her memory and we'll wake her up so we can figure out the next step."

Cailleach bit her lip but nodded and did as he suggested, placing a gentle hand on Bryn's head. She murmured a few words before stroking the girl's hair. After a moment, she looked up and caught his gaze. "It's done."

He gave her a smile. "Thank you. Now, will you wake Bryn, please? Slowly, mind."

Cailleach reached out to peel back the cloak, exposing the young girl's body. Instead of goose pimples, her lips and skin were flush with warmth. The Winter Goddess's power had kept the child from being affected by the chill and the snow.

Tritus watched as, with gentle fingers, Cailleach reached out and pressed a hand against Bryn's chest, whispering a few words under her breath. The breeze kicked up, and a flurry of snowflakes writhed around the young girl's body. They converged into a peak directly above her before swirling away, carried on a freakish wind, and when the last snowflake was gone, the child stirred, her eyelashes fluttering.

Tritus crouched down beside Cailleach and said in a gentle voice, "Bryn, it's Tritus. You are safe. You are here in the forest with me and my woman."

At his words, Bryn's eyes popped wide open, the brown irises almost black in the shadowed moonlight. "I...fell asleep? I don't remember falling asleep." Her frown of confusion was suddenly wiped from her face, and she bolted upright, the cloak falling from her body. Her head whipped from left to right as she searched the area, peering intently into the shadowed trees. Seemingly satisfied, she turned back to Tritus and Cailleach. "We're alone?"

Tritus nodded. "Yes, it's just us, Bryn. The rest of the village is still celebrating Yule. Don't worry; we have only been here a short time. You will not be missed—not yet, at least."

Her lips pressed together, eyes searching his, before she turned to Cailleach. "I remember telling you about my father," she said slowly. "I just can't remember how I fell asleep...."

Cailleach gave her a gentle smile. "It was not your fault, my dear, but rather the power of the season." The Winter Goddess waved her hands in the air, indicating the tree limbs heavy with snow, the thick buildup of hardening ice on the ground, the fractured moonlight above, and the soft snowflakes still falling around them. It felt ethereal in that moment, and there was certainly a feeling of magic in the air, as if greater things were at play.

"The Winter Solstice is a powerful occasion," she

continued. "I like to think the Mother Goddess and all the deities who celebrate it are out tonight. After what you shared with me, I think they believed you needed time to regroup. It is hard to carry a secret such as you have for so long, Bryn. Harder still to admit that the perpetrator is someone meant to love and cherish you."

Bryn's mouth had hung open at Cailleach's explanation, but now she swallowed, her eyes welling with tears. "I admit it was hard to share, my lady," she whispered. "I do not want to place my father in harm's way, but he...he has become someone else in recent times, someone evil. Not my father. The only reason I sought help is because I know there is— there is—" she stopped abruptly, features tense.

"What?" Cailleach asked softly. "You can tell us."

Bryn released a breath, and her voice was hoarse as she added, "There is another child at our home. Under the ground."

The last three words were barely audible, but Tritus heard them. His eyes shot to Cailleach, seeing the same horror he felt reflected in her silver irises. He swore, his fists clenching and chest tight with the horror of what Bryn shared. "Are you certain, Bryn?" he asked slowly, his voice carefully neutral. He had no wish to scare the girl with the violence now raging in his chest.

She nodded once, her face white. "I am certain. When I heard you were in the village this eve, I returned home to pick up a pack I had prepared. You see, I wanted...I wanted to return with you." The girl ducked her head, now unable to look at him. "And, when I entered our home to get my pack, I heard a whimper. At first, I thought I'd imagined it. I thought it was just my nerves." Bryn swallowed, and the hand she lifted to wipe at the corner of her eye was visibly shaking.

Tritus bit his tongue, tasting a spurt of iron, and just refrained from letting out another curse. Cailleach's form had gone still, and he knew she, too, was holding herself in check. He realized with a sudden understanding that it was a game they now needed to play—a careful game of balance. There was a need to extract this information without upsetting or frightening the child.

Consciously loosing his fists, Tritus forced his voice to contain a soothing warmth as he pressed, "But that noise came again, didn't it Bryn? And you looked?"

Her eyes were huge as she shook her head. "I couldn't look. But I spoke aloud...and she answered."

Rage licked up his spine, but his question remained unemotional. "She?"

Bryn jerked her head. "Yes. At a guess, older than I."

"And did you get anything else?" Tritus pressed.

"Enough," she said quietly. "She told me she had been captured by three men a few hours ago, caught while gathering mistletoe outside her village. All she remembered is being hit on the head hard, then waking inside a sack while being carried on someone's back."

Tritus froze. "Three men?" he questioned, unable to keep the frost from lining his words.

Bryn nodded.

His heart was pounding now, a sick feeling eviscerating all else in his stomach. He *knew.* He knew before she even said her next words that those three men he'd seen a few days ago after leaving this village were the same three men Bryn spoke of now—one of which must have been her father. "And you think the girl was placed there tonight, just a few hours ago?"

"Yes," she whispered. "She said my father placed her in the hole. He muttered something about the solstice celebrations and that he'd return for her before dawn. She also said—" And here, Bryn swallowed, before forcing herself to continue, "She said while she was being carried, she heard the three of them talking about having taken other children."

"For what purpose?" Cailleach asked sharply, her first words since the conversation began.

Bryn's face blanched. Tritus initially thought that was in response to Cailleach's harsh tone, but Bryn's next words crushed that theory. "The Dark Ones."

Ice now traveled down his spine, and with it a hint of fear. Not because he was afraid, but because there was a knowing of who and what the young girl referred to. He looked at Cal, only to find her eyes already on his. An unspoken message passed between them. Acknowledgment that they both felt it—that shadow, which had been hovering over them since the moment they first met. Talorgan. The circumstances that had unraveled thereafter, the druid who had come to visit their mountain every new moon over the past year...he had a hand in this. They could both feel it.

Fate had once again worked to bring them all together, but this time they had a chance to reverse the evil the druid was brewing.

Tritus gave Cal an almost imperceptible nod. It was an acknowledgment that she would lead this discussion. He felt incapable of doing so as the emotions now rioting through his blood could not be hidden from the girl.

While Cailleach took the lead, Tritus turned away from them both, needing to get his body in motion, if just for a moment. He walked around the area, scouting their location for any unusual movement. He used all his senses, concentrating on the internal whisper that was his warning signal, but he found nothing except the animals who hid in the boughs of the trees or under rocks and leaves, all creatures from whom they had nothing to fear.

He returned in time to hear Cailleach ask Bryn, "And what about your brother? Tritus mentioned you had an older brother. Is he safe from your father?"

Bryn nodded, her eyes on her hands, which were clenched tightly together, knuckles white. "Petyr is oblivious of what Father is doing, and I did not want to burden him with another problem. He has dealt with a lot since our mother died—taking on her duties and Father's. Aside from keeping the house in order and putting food on the table, Petyr is left to his own devices. He is much older than I, almost a man, and currently building his own roundhouse. He is only a few short weeks from moving in. I had no wish to burden him with yet more problems before he could escape."

Tritus could understand that. Bryn cared too much for Petyr to force him to choose between her and their father. Most likely, she also didn't wish to expose who and what their father had become. His heart broke for her and what she'd had to deal with, and he kicked himself for not pushing further on his last visit. All of this could have been addressed then. Except, maybe they would not have been aware of the level of depravity that Bryn's father had fallen to. They might not have this chance to rescue the other young girl currently trapped in the roundhouse.

Schooling his tone so his rage was under control, Tritus asked Bryn softly, "Are you willing to explain to me where your roundhouse is? You won't need to come back with me or do anything further. In return, I assure you, we will aid your escape."

The girl looked between them; a shard of hope crossing

her features. "You'll take me in? I had hoped to ask you tonight, Tritus, but when I saw you with your woman"—she gestured at Cailleach—"I didn't think you'd accept a young girl in your home. Please, I won't be any bother. I'll cook and clean and help in whatever duties you need me to. Please say yes!"

Cal and Tritus looked at each other again. Tritus knew the answer at the same time Cailleach did. What Bryn asked was impossible given who and what Cailleach was, not to mention the relationship they shared. They both knew they weren't willing to risk exposure, not yet. It wouldn't be the child's fault, but the risk that always hovered over their heads meant they would be putting Bryn in danger by bringing her home with them.

But she also couldn't stay here—not with her father and the evil that would shortly be exposed. Tritus wouldn't allow it. Yet, as he stared at Cailleach, an image arose of an old couple he'd met three months prior, just before the winter. They lived in another village, two days' trek from here. Both were nearing their sixties, both requiring aid around the house. They were kind and caring, tolerant of the young children in the village, and he knew they'd welcome another person into their home if it meant their daily chores were lessened. And knowing Bryn, she'd be more than kind in return. It would take the young girl a few months to settle in, but he could visit regularly until she felt comfortable.

With this in mind, it was Tritus who answered her request as gently as he could. "I'm afraid you can't come with us, Bryn. Not permanently. We...travel a lot, and it is no life for a young girl such as you. However, I do know of an older couple in another village, who were never blessed with children. I'm positive they would welcome you into their home in return for helping out, and I can vouch for them personally."

Bryn's face pinched, the hope erased from her features as if it had never been. "What? No, I want to come with you! I don't eat much, and traveling doesn't worry me at all. Please, Tritus! You were the first person to look out for me, the first to see that something wasn't right. Apart from Flett, not even my brother, my friends, or the chief understood what was going on, and even the chief didn't have enough power to help me."

She reached out and grabbed his arm, her face urgent. "Please think again, Tritus. I don't trust anyone else. Consider giving me a trial, at least. Can you allow me to live with you for a few weeks?" Bryn hesitated then, looking at Cailleach as she added, "That is, if it's okay with your lady too?"

Cal gave her a gentle smile, and Tritus could see how hard it was for his Winter Goddess to share with Bryn, "I would dearly love to have you with us, Bryn, but the work we do is dangerous. I'm sure it looks and sounds exciting, but trading comes with great risk and many perils. Often, Tritus and I are unsure if we'll see the dawn on some of our excursions. It really is no place for a young child. We would rather that we knew you were safe and cared for, with people who were steady and dependable. Offering you anything less is a crime."

Cailleach had done well sharing the truth without telling Bryn too many lies. She'd made the girl believe that she, too, was a trader, but telling Bryn the truth was out of the question. It was true that Cal's work bringing in the seasons was fraught with difficulties and danger; it was one of the reasons he had to leave her alone to her nighttime work. Tritus didn't have the power or ability to protect himself from the weather she manipulated and being present would only cripple and delay what she must do. But having Bryn present would be even worse. The young girl couldn't very well accompany him on his trading trips, either.

There was also the risk of exposing who and what Cailleach really was. Tonight, she looked like any other woman in the village, albeit to Tritus's mind, she was exquisite beyond compare, both inside and out. But once the glamor was dropped, she would revert to who she truly was—be it the gorgeous, ethereal woman she was born to be, or the haggard, ugly crone she'd been condemned to become. In both guises, Cailleach's power shone through. Power that was overwhelming, dangerous, and magnetizing.

Bryn had no power other than her own intuition and sense of what was right and wrong. She would be unable to withstand who and what Cailleach was, even if they tried to protect her. No, the only way Bryn could remain safe was if she lived with others. And the least he could do was ensure she got there safely.

In response to Bryn's abject disappointment and her panicked features, Tritus said firmly, "I will take you to them myself, Bryn. I promise I will be with you every step of the way, and I'm willing to stay with you for a few days as you settle in. You will not do this alone. I will see to it that you are well looked after. I'm sorry we cannot offer you another choice, but we will make the most of what we have."

He couldn't help a grimace as he added, "At this stage, anything is better than what you have been subjected to. Now, would you please stay here for a moment. Cal and I must discuss how we can help the other girl, and then we'll get you both on your way."

Without giving Bryn a chance to question his actions,

Tritus tugged on Cailleach's hand. They stopped a few feet away, and with a jerk of his head, Tritus suggested that she protect the child from their conversation.

Cailleach nodded. The movement of her hand was almost imperceptible against the folds of her white gown, but in the next moment the breeze blew up again, and this time it was filled with rustling and a slight whistle. Tritus watched Bryn as the breeze flew past them. The Winter Goddess had done well, for the young girl's hair remained about her shoulders unmolested; she was keeping the child warm while still ensuring the privacy of their conversation.

"What is your plan, Tritus?" Cailleach asked him now.

He reached out and captured her hands, unwilling and unable to stop touching her after the horrors they'd heard. She was a balm to his soul, a defense against the evil Bryn had just shared. Taking a deep breath, he said, "We both know that the real evil at play here is Talorgan. I've seen him enough times in my old village to understand the strength of his animosity and the thirst for power that drives him. I've also seen that he is gaining power, Cal; too much power. That means he is gaining traction. His support is coming from somewhere, and the story Bryn just told us is no longer uncommon. I've heard of many misdeeds happening in the past year; horrible deeds that aren't related to the usual quibbles over land or possessions. The sins Bryn has described are something else completely, something rooted in pure evil."

Cailleach didn't disagree with him. "And what do you think we should do? Confront him?"

Tritus shook his head. "No, confronting him would raise all manner of questions. It would also expose us, and I won't do that right now. Selfishly, I want to hold onto what we have for as long as possible." For a moment, he mulled over other options, and an idea came to him. "Maybe we can't approach him right now, but someone else could," he said slowly. "What about Talorgan's elders, The Wise Ones? It is possible I could get a message to Drust, who could then speak to The Wise Ones. Any discipline could be meted out by them, without our interference."

Cailleach nodded. "Yes, that is possible. Drust said he would visit us again after the solstice. He could carry the message back to The Wise Ones. But what of the men currently carrying out such deeds? What of the young girl trapped under the ground? I refuse to leave her there, Tritus." She glanced at Bryn. "Like Bryn, she will be coming with us tonight."

"I agree," Tritus bit out, his rage rekindling at the fact that a father could do such things, not only to other children, but also to his own daughter. "Both girls are getting out of this village tonight—I will personally see to it. But like Talorgan, there is also the question of what we do with Bryn's father and the other two who are helping him."

"Do you have any ideas?" Cailleach said quietly.

He nodded. "Yes. The last time I was here, I met the chief of this village. I know him to be a kind and just man, and I've no doubt he will more than adequately attend to the sins of Bryn's father and the other two men." After thinking on how Braden had questioned Bryn several days ago and witnessing the obvious concern he had for the young girl, Tritus believed justice would be served.

Cailleach didn't disagree. "All right, but you will need to get word to him after the girls have gone. How will you do that?"

Tritus thought on it further. "There is an old man located on the edge of the village. I passed his roundhouse while coming to find you both. I could leave a message with him. He is too old to make the trip down for the solstice, so I'm sure he'll be home this eve."

"Okay, good," Cailleach replied. "I agree with all those courses of action. It also means you will not come under the spotlight." She flicked another glance at Bryn, who was now looking at them with concern. "Where is this old couple and the village you speak of? Is it close to Talorgan's village?"

He shook his head. "In the opposite direction. Two days' walk northeast of here."

"And do you want us both to escort her?" Cailleach asked. She gestured at the winter forest wonderland around them. "You know I can't leave the mountain for long. I came down for Yule, but I need to return tonight. I have been away for four nights as it is."

He reached out and cupped her cheek. "I understand, my love. To be honest, I did not expect you to accompany us; I am aware of your duties. All I ask of you this evening is that you stay here a little longer tonight and watch over Bryn while I retrieve the other child."

"That's it?" Cailleach raised a brow.

He stroked her cheek with the pad of his thumb. "Yes, I do not want you embroiled any further. It pains me that the memories I wanted to create with you tonight will end like this, but I cannot leave these two young girls to find their way alone. I will not rescue them only to have them die on the journey." He looked into her eyes. "I am truly sorry, Cal, to ruin our special evening."

She shook her head, a wry smile on her lips. "You did nothing of the sort, Tritus. And your actions speak of the man you are—the man I love and the man I choose. I support your decisions and the actions to come, but I will not leave you without protection. I will remain here until you return with the other child, and then I will see all three of you off with whatever aid I can give."

Tritus felt as if his heart would burst. Cailleach saw through him to who he was, who he needed to be. He saw now that her barriers had finally lowered, and she'd allowed herself to trust him. It was a gift Tritus had not reckoned on so soon, especially as it was so hard-won. Not once had Cailleach questioned his actions or his decisions; everything she'd said and done was in support—just as she'd entrusted him with nurturing the new seedlings that bravely tried to break through the winter soil. On one hand, Tritus felt as if he'd known her forever, and on the other, he was still exploring this wondrous gift he'd been given, the gift of Cailleach and her love. Again, in that moment, he thanked the Mother Goddess and the All Father for what they'd given him.

"Thank you, my love." The words were a fierce whisper, and he pulled her to him, once more claiming her lips in a passionate kiss—a kiss that breathed of life, a kiss that exemplified their love and who and what they meant to each other.

Aware of Bryn's intent stare, he eventually pulled away. Giving Cal a smile, he said softly, "I'd best be off then."

She smiled in return, her eyes welling up as she reached out a hand to his stubbled chin. Pinching it sharply, she said with a forced grin, "Be quick about it, Tritus, and don't get caught."

Aware that she was feeling a riot of emotions—fear and love for him the most dominant of all—he gave her a cocky grin in return. "The men are in their cups, Cal. Tonight's hunt will be an easy one."

"Mmmm, well, maybe you need an incentive?" She turned to look up at the moon, tracking its rise across the night sky. Turning back to face him, she said in a teasing, throaty voice, "Should you return before the moon peaks, then you'll be granted a special Yule evening with me on your return—one in which I will treasure your body like never before."

At the husky words, Tritus felt his heart kick in his chest. He knew exactly what she was promising. "Game on," he returned sharply, his grin widening. And then, with another quick, hard kiss on her lips and a farewell wave of his hand to Bryn, he swiftly turned on his heel and left his heart behind in pursuit of the young girl trapped underground.

CHAPTER 10

TRITUS

After visiting the old man, Yemen, and sharing everything he'd learned about Bryn's father and the two other men, Tritus now stood on the threshold of a roundhouse, listening intently. There was no denying he was in the right one; he'd spotted Bryn's old cloak hanging on a hook just inside the door. He made a note to grab it as he left, along with her brother's, which hung next to hers.

He could hear the muted sounds of the drums and the laughter and merriment of the villagers as they celebrated Yule around the fire, but all was silent inside the house. However, despite that, he sensed someone else.

Following his intuition, Tritus walked around the small room until he came upon a threadbare rug situated under the lone table in the room. He hesitated beside it, walking back to the row of pallets against the wall, also laid out across threadbare rugs. *No, not here.* His neck was only prickling faintly here. *Over there.*

Tritus returned to the family table. His neck prickled harder this time, insisting. *Here.*

Without hesitating this time, he lifted the table off the

rug, placing it directly beside the entrance to prevent anyone surprising him suddenly, then he dropped to his knees and rolled back the rug. He paused when he exposed a series of small boards, nestled neatly within the earth in a square pattern. Heart kicking in his chest and a sense of urgency driving him forward, he pulled them off one by one, fingernails scrabbling to lift each board, and exposed a deep hole within the ground.

The moonlight streaming in through the small smoke hole above his head was perfectly placed for the sliver of moonlight to pierce the darkness in the ground below. With its pearlescent light, Tritus could see the earthen hole contained a young girl lying in a tight ball on her side. Her eyes were closed, her cheeks gaunt, limbs skinny. Her head was pillowed on her hands, and the tunic she wore was threadbare and smudged with dirt. For a moment, all he could do was stare. A part of him had hoped Bryn's story wasn't true—that such evil did not exist. But the sight before him was impossible to deny.

There was a shout outside, and it pulled Tritus from his shock, stirring him into action. He couldn't linger, he couldn't be found. This girl, and Bryn, must leave the village —and quickly.

He reached down into the hole and gently touched the sleeping girl's arm. She came awake with a start, her eyes wide, mouth opening on an instinctual scream. His hand whipped down to cover her lips before any sound escaped, and Tritus cringed at how firm he had to be; he could feel the skin of her lips tearing at his pressure.

"Shhh!" he whispered urgently. "Don't make a sound. I'm Tritus, and I'm here to help you. The girl who lives here sent me to help you. I'm getting you out of here!"

The young girl's eyes were wide, and she began

thrashing her limbs about. There wasn't any space to do so and, with her wrists and ankles tied, she only ended up jerking awkwardly against the sides of her prison. His heart breaking at the desperate sight, Tritus reached down and hauled her out, pulling him against his chest. With one hand still on her mouth, he repeated what he'd said, slowly and firmly. And then a third time.

After a moment the words filtered through, as did the fact that Tritus did not try to manhandle her any further or push her back into the hole, and the girl suddenly stopped fighting him. Tritus held her gaze with his own and said softly, "I'm sorry, I had to keep you quiet. We cannot alert anyone outside to our presence. If I take my hand away, do you promise to stay calm and not call out?"

She slowly nodded.

Giving her a warm, trusting smile, Tritus released his grip on her mouth, pulling it away very slowly. "Shhh!" he said again, raising his own finger to his lips. "Not a sound or we'll be found. You understand?"

She nodded again, this time her lower lip trembling.

"Good," Tritus said softly. "Very good." He pulled a knife out of his tunic, and she immediately shrank back. Tritus held up a hand, his voice still soft. "It's okay, I'm just going to cut your bonds. All you need to do is stay still. Do you trust me?"

She stared at him, blue eyes wide under the light of the moon, and slowly moved her head in assent.

He gave her another warm smile and slowly reached out to hold her hands in one of his. Then, he carefully positioned the knife just under the rope tied around her wrists, ignoring her reactive flinch. "Just breathe," he whispered, and on her exhalation, he jerked the knife up, cutting the rope around her wrists. Tritus immediately dropped the knife and unraveled the rope before rubbing her wrists to aid circulation. "Better?"

She gave him a nod, eyes new welling. Tritus could see the emotion setting in and knew he had to move quickly before the dam burst. That must wait until she was safe—until they were all safely away from this village.

He indicated her ankles, tucked awkwardly to the side. "Now your ankles," he said, picking up the knife again.

This time she stayed perfectly still. Tritus made the cut and left her to remove the rope as he indicated the hole, the rug, and the table. "Take a moment while I cover this up, and then we'll be on our way."

When she nodded again, Tritus quickly did as he'd said and grabbed a pouch of dried meat and a flask of water along with the two cloaks before returning to her side a moment later. He continued to talk to her, ensuring there were no surprises. She was functioning, but he was well aware of the impending reaction. Time was not on their side.

He crouched down and drew one of the cloaks around her thin frame. "Now, the next move is to escape this roundhouse. Can you walk on your own?"

The young girl's face was tight with fear, but a determined glint came to her eyes as she nodded.

"Good girl, you're doing fine," Tritus soothed. "We are going to get out of here, but in order to do that, I will need your help. All you must do is be as quiet as possible and follow me wherever I go without hesitation. When I say walk, you walk. When I say run, you run. Understand?"

This time, she whispered back, "Yes," and the tone gave him the notion that she was older than she seemed.

"Good," he said again, now coming to his feet and holding out his hand to help her up. "Let's go then."

It didn't take them long to exit the roundhouse and escape back into the forest. Tritus couldn't help thinking that it felt almost too easy, but when he didn't hear any pursuit or warning cries, let alone an interruption to the merry festivities going on behind them, he allowed himself to feel a sense of relief as he urged the young girl toward Cailleach and Bryn.

When they finally arrived, Tritus breathed a sigh of relief that both his woman and Bryn were okay. He took a moment to look up at the moon and felt a wide smile break across his face when he saw it hadn't yet peaked. The pointed glance he sent Cailleach announced his success loud and clear, but with a small, teasing smile on her lips, Cailleach ignored his victory and turned to address his young charge.

"Hello, my dear. I am Tritus's woman, Cal, and this is our friend, Bryn. She told us you were trapped in her father's house. You can trust us. We are going to get you someplace safe."

The young girl at Tritus's side hesitantly approached, her gaze first on Cailleach, then on Bryn. When it alighted on the young girl, she stumbled out, "Thank you. Thank you for telling them of me. I owe you a life debt."

Bryn firmly shook her head. "No, the debt is mine. I am sorry my father had a hand in your capture." For all her bravado, Tritus saw Bryn's throat bobbing at the words, but she pushed on, "What is your name? I am Bryn."

The young girl's face illustrated a similar expression to Bryn's—horror and shock, and a disbelief as to what they'd experienced. "Erin."

A forced smile came to Bryn's face. "Well, Erin, let us be friends. It appears we'll have need of each other to get out of this mess."

Bryn seemed to have gained some sort of backbone while Tritus had been away, and he had no doubt Cailleach had worked on her, building her confidence and her courage. Bryn's journey from here on out would be a tough one, her future colored by the actions of her father and what had happened here tonight—and probably by the many years since her mother's death.

"We cannot linger," he said, turning the girls' attention toward him. "We must be on our way. I am taking Bryn to another village, Erin. I know a couple who would dearly love the help of a young girl to aid them. The village is two days north-east of here. Where can I take you on the way? Which village did you come from?"

Erin's face blanched a sickly white. "I cannot return to my village," she forced out.

Cailleach was watching her closely. "Why not, child?"

"I—my family, they are all...gone."

"Gone?" Cailleach repeated. "They are missing?"

Erin shook her head. "No...dead."

Tritus felt his chest burn at the words. He said into the silence, "I am sorry to hear that, Erin, but I assure you that there will be a place for you. The couple I am delivering Bryn to will see themselves incredibly lucky to have not just one but two young girls to help them. What say you? Would you like to accompany us to the village and find out?"

Bryn immediately stepped forward and clasped Erin's hand in one of hers, giving the girl a gentle smile. "I think that's a wonderful idea. As I will soon have no family either, we shall make our own. Isn't that right, Erin?"

The young girl looked startled, as if certain that she would wake up at any moment.

"Well?" Bryn pushed.

Erin, clearly unable to do anything else, nodded.

But Tritus wondered at Bryn's words. "Even Petyr?" he asked her softly.

Bryn swallowed. "I wish to protect him from the evil that has touched our family. It would be best if he believed I was lost—that I mysteriously disappeared with the fairies on winter solstice." She broke his gaze and looked into the shadowed forest. "If I saw him again, I'm not sure he could withstand the truth of who and what our father has become. I would like to see my brother live a life unblemished by guilt." She looked directly at Tritus then, her eyes pleading. "Please, grant me this one wish."

Tritus felt he had no other option, not when the notion was delivered with such honesty and integrity. It illustrated Bryn's maturity, the level of her inner strength. Right here, right now, she needed his agreement, she needed his trust, and Tritus gave them to her. But even though he nodded his assent, Tritus vowed to ensure that when Petyr was of a suitable age, that Braden pass on to him exactly what had happened to his sister and where she could be found. Bryn and her brother should not suffer for the sins of their father.

A grateful smile crossed her features. "Thank you, Tritus."

Cailleach touched his arm, and he turned to face her. In his mind, he heard her question: *Do you really think the family you have in mind for Bryn will take both of them?*

"Yes, I do. They are a lovely couple."

Her face relaxed at his response, losing its tension. *"Good. I believe they need to remain together. The road to healing is easier shared."*

He patted her hand in agreement and turned back to the girls, who still stood hand in hand. "Well, before we set off, I encourage you to take a moment to eat and drink. We have a long journey ahead of us, most of it to be done by moonlight."

He pulled the pouch of dried meat and the flask of water out of his tunic and passed one item to each of the girls. He observed them as they drank and ate some of the rations, both without a word of protest. When they returned what was left, and he had hidden them once more in the folds of his tunic, he said, "It will just be me, I'm afraid. Cal is going to return home as we have some business she must attend to, but I will personally accompany you to the village."

Bryn looked at Cailleach. "I am sorry we could not spend more time together, but I understand duty. I want to say—" Bryn stopped, swallowing, and Tritus could see tears shimmering in her eyes again.

Cailleach could, too, and she gave the girl a gentle smile. "Yes, Bryn?"

"I want to say thank you, my lady, for your kindness and generosity. Without you, I would have no future."

"Oh, I think not, Bryn. There is steel within you; an unbreakable will. I have no doubt that if we hadn't met tonight, you would have come up with your own plan to help both yourself and this young girl to escape. You should be very proud of yourself, my dear. You chose a path of courage. That is a harder journey to take than one of fear. Please rest assured that you will never lose that quality, my child; it will see you to the end of this life and the next." She came forward and pressed a soft kiss to Bryn's cheek. "May the goddess bless your journey."

Bryn bowed her head as tears spilled down her cheeks at Cailleach's words.

Cal, aware that Bryn needed a moment, turned to Erin. The young girl looked timid and uncertain, but she still murmured a husky "Thank you" and accepted Cailleach's blessing and kiss of farewell. Tritus knew that Cal had also bestowed an aura of protection over them both while doing so and was sincerely thankful for the gesture.

Now, there was just their own farewell to attend to. Tritus turned to his lover, aware they were to be separated yet again. His smile was rueful as he gazed into her swirling silver eyes. Conscious that he must keep this short, he reached out and cupped her cheek in his usual manner, whispering for her ears alone, "I'll see you on my return. Safe travels home, my love."

"And you, my love."

With a last lingering look at his Winter Goddess, Tritus turned to lead the girls through the snow-drenched forest, praying that whatever power Cailleach had released while they were saying their goodbyes was enough to see them safely to the village he had in mind.

CHAPTER 11

TRITUS

Two days later, Tritus bade a final farewell to the old couple and the two young girls now in their care before turning to begin the two-day trek back to Cailleach. There was a bounce to his step, and his heart felt light with a sense of achievement at how everything had turned out. The old couple, Mael and Aidan, had been overjoyed to lay claim to the girls, their faces crinkling into broad smiles and their rheumy eyes lighting up. At first the girls were hesitant, not quite trusting of the couple yet, but they'd innately understood that these people were good, that their intentions weren't cruel or unkind, and in the end, Erin and Bryn had accepted their new place in both the home and the village.

Tritus was relieved that everyone else had been welcoming, apart from a few of the youngsters, whose positions in the hierarchy were suddenly threatened by the presence of the two young girls. Tritus knew the girls would have to find their own place here, and that any help from him or the old couple would only be detrimental to the outcome.

He promised the girls that he'd visit them again soon once the snow had lifted. He knew Bryn believed he'd be back, but Erin was a different story. In order to drive home his promise, he'd left Erin with one of his daggers, asking her to look after it until his return. It was his way of showing that the promise he had made held some standing. Earlier, he found out that Bryn had managed to bring the knife he'd given her, and the mystery of why she'd asked for it was resolved by the story she'd shared.

Even after giving Erin his dagger, Tritus could see she still didn't believe him. She had accepted it with her eyes downcast, refusing to engage with him. Tritus was aware that this would take time. Underneath Erin's prickly exterior was a young woman just waiting for the opportunity to bloom, and he had no doubts the old couple would provide the warmth and security she and Bryn craved; and in return, Mael and Aidan would receive warmth and companionship and much welcome aid in their advanced years. Especially because the girls were adept at running a household, both having lost their mothers at a young age.

Tritus felt as though the burden of securing their wellbeing had been lifted, and he rejoiced in the fact that a horrible situation had been turned into something positive. But he couldn't deny the ache in his body, the *need* to return home to his woman. Without Cailleach, he felt as though he wasn't whole, that the burn in his chest would not relent until he held her in his arms once again.

Over the following two days of travel, his thoughts wandered, moving from the girls they'd rescued to the question he'd asked Cailleach before this winter solstice journey had began. By the time his feet finally touched the mountain where Cailleach had made her home and he started the long trudge upward to their cave near the peak, one thought alone replayed in his mind: *Would Cailleach want children after what they'd just gone through?*

Tritus suspected the evil they'd unearthed would only push her further away from the dream he held. The dangers and risks that a young one could be exposed to was enough to send his own heart racing and to turn his insides to jelly. He felt real fear that a child of their making might be subject to those same dangers...potentially worse. Especially if anyone got wind that their child was the outcome of a union between a mortal and a revered goddess.

Tritus suddenly stopped in his tracks, his leather-bound ankles sinking into the snow. The afternoon sun was weak and watery, its last rays bathing the land in a golden hue of sparkling diamonds. But his gaze wasn't on the breathtaking scenery of the mountain forest around him. His gaze was internal, witnessing a horror that caused his eyes to open wide at the scene playing out in his mind. It was the vision of a child—their child—being hunted and beaten. A scourge of nature who was hated and feared by others— druids, villagers, Cailleach's siblings, even his own people.

The vision made Tritus's blood run cold, and a shiver, bone deep, raced straight to his heart. Cailleach had been right. Bringing a child into this world could very well result in more grief and painful repercussions than they could handle. They'd already unsettled the balance by giving into the feelings they had for one another—even though it was an undeniable yearning, as necessary as the pounding of the heart or the pulsing of the blood in one's veins. Tritus had known that to deny them their union would have meant two lives lived half-empty, forever half-fulfilled. To be together in the face of such odds, in the face of such potential danger, was something worth celebrating, something worth acknowledging. He realized they should rejoice in what they already had and the happiness their union brought. Besides, there was no guarantee a child of their making would enrich what they already held.

The message repeated in his mind, over and over again. *We must be thankful for what we have. Forget the child; we have already pushed the boundaries of acceptance.*

Heart heavy but mind now clear, Tritus forced himself to accept the message and assimilate it with his heart. He blinked, dispelling the image of a dream that he could not have. It withered like a shadow slinking away with the birth of the sun, and he replaced the dream with one of Cailleach, her face filled with undeniable love.

Now, with a renewed sense of purpose and the reminder that he was the luckiest man on this earth, Tritus continued his journey. And as he walked toward the fading sunlight, he understood that the woman he walked toward would always be his one and only lodestar, no matter what life threw at them.

CHAPTER 12

CAILLEACH

3RD CENTURY BC, ANCIENT SCOTLAND

C ailleach did not dally on her trip back home. She felt the drain on her power, not only from sustaining her glamor, but also from the events of the night and the tension and stress it had wrought. She'd been exposed to more than she'd bargained for tonight, more than the promise of a chance to celebrate an innocent, carefree Yule.

The night had begun well. She'd felt the magical spirit in the air, smelled the mistletoe and the pine trees, tasted the spiced wine, and enjoyed the fresh vegetables and delicate meats on offer. Most especially, she'd enjoyed the music and the opportunity to dance with Tritus; it had been a gift to do so. A gift to spend time with him and love him unconditionally in front of others. She had also been given a chance to be one of the villagers, a chance to pretend she did not carry the burden of her role or the power that came with it. It had been truly magical, and the dress she'd chosen was perfect for the occasion.

But the magic of the evening had vanished in the face of the horrors they'd unearthed. Thinking of Bryn's story again, Cailleach's heart raced in time with her feet as she walked toward home. *Those poor girls!* Two innocent little things, bare slips of girls with nothing to them apart from the ragged tunics on their backs. Their stories were heartbreaking and knowing that such horrors were happening was unbearable to fathom.

Her heart had broken at what Erin shared. Broken because Cailleach knew she didn't have the power to stop the three men who had taken her—or any others who might also be doing the same. She knew the story from personal experience, knew that Bryn's father might have once been a good and kind man, but with the loss of someone he loved dearly, he'd turned into someone else, someone driven by such profound grief that he'd become all twisted with the loss. Cailleach's brother, Arawn, was testament to that knowledge.

Her dark brother had fallen in love with a woman. A beautiful woman, but not a confident one; a woman who had no power except for her gentle ways and her ability to coax such deep emotions from her brother. But for all that, Arawn's chosen woman had held more power over him than any other—friend or enemy.

Their union was blessed by their father. The All Father was proud of his dark son, had believed Arawn had changed, ending his trickster ways for the path of love. But what she and her family hadn't reckoned on was how the influence and actions of others could change someone's path, just like the variable ocean tides could erode and transform the coastline into something different than before.

One of their cousins had become jealous of Arawn's rise, jealous of the love he and his woman shared, and jealous of the titles the All Father had bestowed upon him. This cousin had wanted more than he should have, wanted a woman who was not his. The parallels were not lost on Cailleach as she walked onward. There was a sinking feeling of Fate, of the wheel turning and once again coming full circle.

She forced herself to remember the story of Arawn's fall, forced herself to replay the ending in her mind. For lessons for the future were tied into the actions of the past, and maybe she could find a way forward out of this mess? Swallowing hard, she continued walking through the trees, her silver eyes piercing the darkness, not only of the forest in front of her, but also the memories long buried in her mind.

The attack on her dark brother had seemingly come out of nowhere. It wasn't an attack on his person but rather on his heart. Mere days after the coronation of his beloved queen, she had died. The circumstances around her death were still unclear. Some believed her to have been murdered, others that she took her own life, jumping from the tower window to the dangerous, rocky waters at the bottom of the cliff. Regardless, she had gone and never returned.

The death of Arawn's wife had been a blow that reverberated through not only their people on this plane but also those who dwelled Underground, those she was to rule over with her dark king. However, that blow had been nothing compared to the shock and devastation that pierced Arawn. His new persona and the path of fulfillment he had been on was immediately destroyed with the loss of his beloved wife, and Cailleach had witnessed her brother's fall with irrevocable horror.

She'd known his fall was inescapable, known that no one could save him from the loss he had suffered, because just as she'd once witnessed with Dagda and Boann, just as she'd seen the shine of love in their eyes for each other, so too had she witnessed that inconsolable emotion in Arawn's eyes. Even now, she couldn't bear to think of his late queen's name. Indeed, neither could Arawn—he'd commanded that her name never be spoken again, erased from history, erased from his heart.

Cailleach could now fathom that depth of pain. Could understand it, given what she shared with Tritus. And even bringing up an image of Arawn's beloved queen's face was akin to feeling a thousand needles prickle her skin. The loss Arawn had suffered and who he had become was devastating on so many levels. And even now, to this day, his loss drove further horrors as he influenced the actions of others. He was the Dark One, the Dark God who would answer the prayers of those who craved vengeance, those who were driven by evil. He was the Dark God they turned to if their grief required retribution. And here he was, influencing druids and people within the village to embrace their baser natures. Talorgan had clearly changed his allegiance, choosing to worship her brother over the path he'd previously walked. And with the stories the girls had shared, it was obvious there were others on this plane also turning to Arawn for assistance.

Even now, many years later, with a river of dark deeds and loss running between them, she and Arawn were no longer brother and sister, but rather enemies, each to the other.

It had immediately been obvious to Cailleach that Talorgan and her brother were tangled up in the path of the two girls she'd met tonight. The two girls Tritus was now safely ferrying to another village in the hopes of providing them a new and brighter future. Cailleach felt thankful she'd played a part to ensure that future, but also a sense of shock at what she'd been exposed to.

The memories of her brother's loss had ignited a series of thoughts she now couldn't halt. It was like an avalanche, a conglomeration of memories and emotions, a mixture of hopes and fears, and it consumed her every step on the return journey, her mind turning with every implication and possible outcome. In the end, there was only one sharp thought that eclipsed everything else—she was afraid. As soon as the thought entered her mind, Cailleach knew it for the truth. She *was* afraid. Fearful for the future she desired; afraid that someone or something would take not only Tritus away from her—as had been foretold by her father— but also any child they might have.

The revelation shamed her, and it made her angry at the same time, mainly at herself. For she'd witnessed this emotion in her subjects, and in others around her—even in her siblings. It was a crippling emotion, and one that did no one any favors, especially the ones who owned it.

Being afraid was not living. It was an ugly emotion that crippled those who fed its flames, and Cailleach suddenly understood she was doing herself a disservice for feeling it. She was also doing Tritus a disservice, for he did not deserve a fearful woman.

Tritus had proven again and again that he was strong, that he could beat opponents more powerful than himself. His strength came from within, a firm belief in what was right and wrong, an innate understanding of kindness and humility, and he was a source of inspiration and fearlessness in his pursuit of life. Her lover was also unfailing in his quest to make her life better, and he innately understood he was an integral part of that happiness. Isn't that what he'd shown her again in his recent actions?

He'd brought the magic of the season into their home—all for her. Then, he'd arranged for a visit to the village, a chance for them to act just like any other young couple in love—all for her. And of course, there was his unending help in her role as the Goddess of Winter, his solid support and infallible belief that, regardless of her role, she was *good* and deserved happiness—again, all for her.

Those truths speared her mind as she climbed the mountain. They quickened her steps, driving her forward. It had become obvious with this revelation pounding in her head that in return, Tritus deserved her unfailing commitment to their relationship without fear of their future—for however long they had.

Heart hammering against her ribcage, the thoughts came fervently fast, her mind and her heart now singing the same tune—the same desire, the same message. And what rang loud and clear through her mind, free of fear and the future unknown, was that if they were indeed blessed with a child of their union, then that child would be a shining beacon of hope, a gift unparalleled to anything in this world or the next.

A weight she didn't know had existed lifted from Cailleach's mind, and she felt her heart spread its wings and glory in this newfound confidence. She vowed she would not do a disservice to the gift Tritus gave her—the gift of his love. No, she would embrace it fearlessly and now look toward their future with hope.

That vow echoed in her head as Cailleach finally broke through the trees and stepped into the small clearing that accommodated the charred remains of their campfire. And there, a little to the left, was the entrance to their cave. With a sharp movement of her hand, the undergrowth peeled away from the concealed door, and, within moments, she was inside.

The heady scent of fresh pine was heavy in the air, and she blinked at the bright, festive vision of numerous sprigs of mistletoe and holly. The Yule log lay just as Tritus had left it, still faintly smoldering. As she stared it, she decided to reciprocate this gift he'd worked hard to give her, and the few days she had before his return would be sufficient for what she intended.

The vision in her mind hit her hard in the chest, for if her plans were successful, there would not be two people in this cave next year...but three.

CHAPTER 13
CAILLEACH
3RD CENTURY BC, ANCIENT SCOTLAND

"Cal? Where are you?"

At her lover's call, Cailleach lifted her head from the carlin stone and called in his direction, "Here, Tritus."

Her heart was pounding, and she couldn't stop the broad smile stretching across her face.

In the next few moments, Tritus's lean, muscled body emerged from among the trees, his dark hair swinging around his strong jaw. Cailleach couldn't help trailing her eyes down his body and then back up, resting on the tattoos that adorned his right arm. They were symbols of his love and his commitment, and also a symbol of his enslavement to her. Beautiful. He was utterly beautiful inside and out— and he was all hers.

"I hoped I'd find you here," he said in greeting, coming up to her and capturing her lips in a hard kiss. His green eyes drifted over her face. "You look radiant today, Cal—the complete opposite to how I feel." He grimaced and ran a hand down his stubbled cheek. "I think I indulged in too much mead last night."

Cailleach felt her smile stretch even wider as she pushed

herself upright and swung her legs around on the carlin stone to face him. "Yes. So much so that you did not celebrate Imbolc with me."

Tritus's mouth dropped open. "I fell asleep?"

She smirked. "Yes. Clearly this other tradition is not a strong one." Tritus looked guilty at her admission, and she couldn't help reaching out a hand to touch his cheek. "It is all right, my love. I have never before celebrated the point between the winter solstice and the spring equinox, so I was not missing much. Besides, I was also tired."

His face changed then, concern causing his forehead to wrinkle. "You're tired? Is that why you are back at the carlin stone so soon? I thought you were here last night to regenerate your power. Are you...unwell?"

Cailleach didn't miss the sliver of fear that crossed his features. She ducked her head and busied herself with brushing the skirts of her periwinkle dress, trying to remove invisible flecks of dirt and moss as her mind raced with how to answer his question.

How to tell him? She hadn't even had enough time to take it all in. Lying down on the carlin stone had confirmed her suspicion, yet she could scarcely believe it.

"Cal?" This time his voice was clearly worried. He hooked a finger under her chin and tilted her face up to his. "What is it, Cal? What is troubling you? You know you can tell me anything."

His words were perfect; they were a reminder of his unbending strength, his unending love, and his infallible support. All three of which she'd need—that they'd *all* need —for the change now upon them.

Cailleach reached out and grabbed his hand in hers, clasping it tightly. "There is nothing wrong, Tritus. But there *is* something that is causing me to tire easily." Then, still holding on to his hand, she pressed it against her stomach. "I am carrying a gift—a gift of the winter solstice."

For a moment there was confusion in his eyes, but then they widened, and his face split into an enormous, incredulous smile before he threw his head back and let loose a shout of pure, unadulterated happiness and joy.

In return, Cailleach felt laughter bubble up and spill from her own lips. Then, she was pulled tightly into Tritus's arms, and his lips were on hers, urgent, fervent, passionate, conveying everything he felt about the news she'd just shared.

Their breathing was raspy when he eventually pulled away, and with his forehead resting against hers, arms still tightly wrapped around her and his eyes bright with emotion, he whispered in a shaky voice, "You have made me incredibly happy, Cal."

Cailleach swallowed the lump in her throat and returned, "Happy winter solstice, my love."

WHAT DID YOU THINK?

Thank you for reading *Winter's Companion*. If you enjoyed this book or any of the stories included, please can you take the time to leave a star rating and a short, honest review on Amazon, Bookbub, and/or Goodreads? As an indie author, reviews are our lifeblood as they not only give the author (me) valuable feedback, but they also enable our book to become visible to other readers. Therefore, your review is sincerely appreciated.

Additionally, if you'd like to reach out and provide feedback about this book or simply say "hi," please don't hesitate to email me at corina_douglas@live.com as I'd love to hear from you!

DISCOVER THE DAUGHTER OF WINTER SERIES

If these stories intrigued you and you'd like to read more from Corina Douglas, or more of the *Daughter of Winter* series, they are best read in order. Start with the first book of the same name below.

Marked by an ancient prophecy wielded by the gods. Shackled to a dark, enigmatic stranger. And prey to a powerful adversary seeking vengeance. Her life will never be the same again....

Intrigue and danger enter Brydie MacKay's life when Gage walks into her carefully controlled world. He brings news that her grandmother has died, and as her last living relative, Brydie has inherited her estate and must travel to Scotland to accept her legacy and all it entails.

Brydie doesn't want the inheritance, not after the way she was treated, and when a series of actions unfold that illustrate her 'legacy' is not just a physical entity but a turbulent birthright proclaiming she is the descendant of the Celtic winter goddess, Cailleach Bheur, she tries to run.

But Gage won't take no for an answer. He has his own role to fulfill and will do whatever it takes to ensure Brydie returns to Scotland with him—even if that means taking her against her will.

DISCOVER THE MORRIGAN TRILOGY

Badb is the first book in a new dark fantasy romance series based on the myths and legends behind the Irish triple goddess, the Morrígan. This trilogy will focus on each sister in turn and starts with Badb.

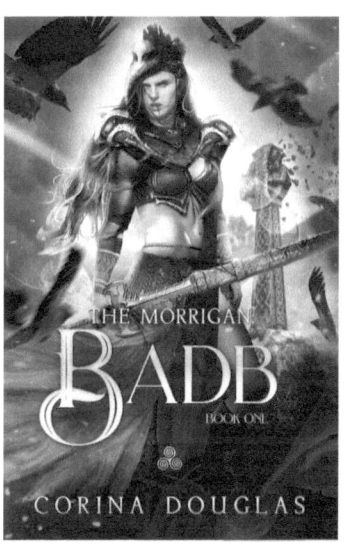

DISCOVER THE CURSED
HEIR SERIES

The Cursed Heir series is a new dark fantasy romance series based on moon mythology and pagan folklore, featuring Celtic deities, selkies, vampires, witches, and shifters. You can begin the series by reading the prequel, *Cold Moon*.

GLOSSARY OF TERMS

All Father (The) — See 'Custodian of Creation.'

Carlin Stone — A prehistoric standing stone associated with the Cailleach. In *Daughter of Winter*, the stone regenerates Cailleach's power, while also acting as a portal to other worlds.

Children of Winter – Children of Cailleach Bheur i.e., those associated with The Oaken Tree.

Custodian of Creation (or the Phoenix) — The Celtic Gods' father—often referred to as 'The All-Father.' His role is to ensure a balance is maintained within this world and others.

Dark Arts (The) – Druidic magic that utilizes the darkness rather than the light. Using it comes with consequences, which are often deadly.

Daughter of Winter – A direct descendant of Cailleach Bheur.

Druid (A) – Children of the Celtic gods, and humans who follow pagan lore and/or wield the natural power of the world around us (thus, even those who are Dormant are still considered druids). Every druidic clan in *Daughter of Winter* is associated with one of the Celtic deities i.e., The Oaken Tree, which is Gage's clan, is associated with the Cailleach.

Gauls – Groups of ancient Celtic people who came from a region of Western Europe, encompassing present-day France, Belgium, the Netherlands, Luxembourg, and parts of Switzerland, Germany, and Northern Italy.

Guardian (A) – The man prophesied to protect the Daughter of Winter. In *Daughter of Winter,* this is Gage, and previously his grandfather before him.

Phoenix (The) — See 'Custodian of Creation.'

Samhain – A day marking the end of the lighter half of the year (summer) and the beginning of the darker half of the year (winter). On this day, the veil between the living and the dead is especially thin, allowing spirits of the dead and those living on other planes to visit our world.

Tuatha Dé Dannan (The) – People of the Goddess Danu. They are a race of supernatural beings who inhabited Ireland before the ancestors of the modern Irish. In *Daughter of Winter* they are referred to as 'the fae.'

The Oaken Tree – Gage's druidic clan.

The Other – An alternative reality where people and all living things are reborn (if not cast to the Underworld for misdeeds).

The Underworld – The Underworld used to be a rich and mystical place of beauty, youth, health, and joy. However, due to events happening between Arawn and his siblings, it turned into a place of sin, death, and depravity. In *Daughter of Winter,* those who turn to the Dark Arts and exercise dark magic are sent to the Underworld on their death, rather than the Other.

Yule – Yule marks the winter solstice, which is the shortest day/longest night of the year, marking the turning point where the sun begins its long journey back to its midsummer peak.

Winter Solstice – The longest night—or when the sun is tilted at its furthest point away from the earth. It was celebrated by the Celts in similar ways to how Christmas is celebrated.

About the Author

Corina Douglas lives in New Zealand with her husband and four kids. If she's not running her indie editing business, *Burning Legacies Publishing,* she can be found exploring the forest, doing that stretchy yoga thing, or with her nose in a good book. She writes dark fantasy romance stories based on Celtic mythology, with a special focus on pagan Scottish, Irish, and Welsh folklore.

Corina loves to hear from her readers. Join her on social media and stay up to date with future works by visiting the sites below. You can also join her monthly newsletter and grab a free short story from her website.

www.corinadouglas.com

amazon.com/author/corina.douglas

tiktok.com/@corina.douglas.author

instagram.com/CDouglas_author

facebook.com/corina.douglas.author

bookbub.com/authors/corina-douglas

pinterest.com/CDouglas_author

www.ingramcontent.com/pod-product-compliance
Lightning Source LLC
Chambersburg PA
CBHW052031240626
47153CB00006B/2037